'Whether writing as Sherrilyn Kenyon or Kinley MacGregor, this author delivers great romantic fantasy!'
New York Times bestselling author Elizabeth Lowell

THE
GUARDIAN

SHERRILYN KENYON

PIATKUS

First published in the US in 2011 by St. Martin's Press, New York
First published in Great Britain in 2011 by Piatkus
This paperback edition published in 2012 by Piatkus

A CIP catalogue record for this book
is available from the British Library.

ISBN 978-0-7499-4255-7

Printed and bound by CPI Group (UK) Ltd, Croydon, CR0 4YY

Papers used by Piatkus are from well-managed forests
and other responsible sources.

MIX
Paper from
responsible sources
FSC® C104740

Piatkus
An imprint of
Little, Brown Book Group
100 Victoria Embankment
London EC4Y 0DY

An Hachette UK Company
www.hachette.co.uk

www.piatkus.co.uk

For L.A. Banks, my birthday twin. Thank you for bringing me light during one of the darkest times in my life. You are, and will always be, in my heart. I miss you, my sister, I always will.

And for my family for being there when I need you. And to Monique who is one of the greatest editors I've ever worked with. And for my entire SMP team who make these books possible. May God bless and keep you all.

"All men while they are awake are in one common world. But each of them, when he is asleep, is in a world of his own."

—Plutarch

PROLOGUE

"Was hell good for you?"

Seth looked up from beneath the strands of his blood-soaked auburn hair, to snarl at the sound of a voice he hadn't heard in centuries.

Noir.

Primal god.

Lord of all things dark and deadly.

Rank bastard.

He would have responded to the stupid question, but his mouth had been bolted shut by the demons who'd been torturing him for the last . . .

Ah hell, who could count that high? And why would anyone want to when every single heartbeat drove home a pain so foul he no longer remembered living without it? Indeed, over the centuries, pain had become its own source of pleasure.

Yeah, I'm even more fucked up than Noir.

With the bolt in place, he hadn't been able to speak since he'd been thrown in here. Not that he would. He'd never give any of them the satisfaction of hearing him beg or cry out. Only one person had ever made him do that and, even after a millennium, his adoptive father's mocking condemnation still echoed in his ears.

Screw them. He wasn't a child now, and he'd die before he ever humiliated himself again by asking for something he knew he'd never receive.

But he would have insulted Noir if he'd been able to. As it was, all he could do was glare his hatred at the ancient being and wish he possessed his full powers so that he could rain down utter misery on all of them.

Almost seven feet in height, Noir made the demons around them tremble in fear. His immaculate black suit and crisp white shirt looked out of place in the cold dark room—a room with walls that were splattered and stained with Seth's blood.

Noir reached up and patted him on the cheek like he was a dutiful puppy. "Mmm. I have to say hell doesn't appear to agree with you. I've seen you look at least a *little* better than this sorry state."

"Fuck you," Seth said, but his words were indistinguishable. The bolt kept him from moving his mouth or tongue. All it did was shoot an excruciating jolt of pain through him.

Like he needed that.

Noir arched his black brow. "Thank you? I can't imagine why you'd be thanking me for this misery. You are a sick bastard, aren't you?"

Seth ground his teeth. The playful light in Noir's

black eyes told him that the pig only said it to piss him off.

It worked. Not that Noir had to make the effort. The mere fact that . . . Seth couldn't think of an insult bad enough. That Noir lived was enough to grate his last nerve.

Noir glanced around at the others. "Leave us."

Could that tone be any more commanding?

Oh yeah, wait. We were talking about Noir. Of course it could.

And the ancient god didn't have to say it twice. The demons immediately vanished, terrified that Noir's wrath would deliver to them the same "hospitality" he'd shown Seth. After all, Seth had once been Noir's most beloved pet—one he'd lavished with gifts in between the abuse.

The dark god had never been able to stand the demons who served him.

Hell, I'd run, too, if I could.

Seth envied them that freedom as his naked body hung lankly from the ceiling, with his hands shackled over his head. He'd been in this position for so long that his wrist bones protruded through the open cuts the manacles had worn through his flesh.

He was sure it had to hurt, but that pain blended in nicely with all the others so that he couldn't tell where one ache began and another throb ended. Who knew torture could have benefits?

Once they were alone, Noir returned to stand in

front of him with a snarl that was as impressive as it was cold. "I have a proposition for you. Are you interested?"

Not even a little. He'd had his fill of bargains. No one could ever be trusted to hold up their end of them. Let Noir go roast his nuts in a fiery hellhole somewhere.

The gods knew, in this place, Noir wouldn't have far to go to find one.

Seth looked away.

Noir tsked. "You know you have no choice except to obey me, slave. I *own* you."

And that ate on him even more than the flesh-devouring vermin the demons had salted his wounds with. *Damn you all.* His own family had sold him to Noir when he'd been nothing more than a child. It was something no one ever allowed him to forget.

As if he could.

Noir buried his hand in Seth's hair and yanked his head back. That action caused the bolt to dig deeper into his throat and tongue.

The sudden pain of it made his eyes water in protest as his old wounds were reopened and blood poured into his mouth.

Maybe this time I'll drown from it. But he knew the sad truth. He was immortal. Death would never save him from this misery, any more than it had spared him from the rest of his violent past.

His only way out was Noir's ever missing mercy.

Noir tightened his fist against Seth's skull, wrenching his hair even more. "I have need of your *special* services."

I have need of your rank heart in my fist.

The bastard smiled as if he could hear that thought. "If you fail me this time, I can assure you that your next stint here will make this one seem like paradise. Do you understand?"

Seth refused to respond.

Noir snatched a handful of hair out as he released him. Pain seared his scalp, causing the vermin in his body to bite even more ferociously as they scrambled toward the fresh blood.

Seth's breathing turned ragged as he locked his jaw even tighter to keep from groaning out in utter relentless agony. He squeezed his eyes shut and fought the wave of unconsciousness that threatened to take him under. They only made it worse on him when he passed out.

Don't do it, asshole. Focus . . .

Damn you, stay awake!

He gripped his restraints as his vision swam.

Noir gave him an acidic smile that didn't reach his eyes. "You will do me proud and get what I require, or . . ."

He didn't finish the threat. He didn't have to.

They both were more than aware that Seth would do anything to keep from returning to this sorry state of existence. In spite of all his bravado, he knew the bitter truth.

He'd been broken by their cruelty.

And he would never be the same.

There was nothing left inside him except a hatred so profound, so deep, he could taste it. That bitter hatred mixed with the steel of the bolt, and blood—it was all he'd had for nourishment these centuries past.

Noir's smile turned genuine. "I knew you'd come around eventually." He snapped his fingers.

The manacles on Seth's hands broke free. He fell from the ceiling to land on his legs. But centuries of abuse and nonuse kept them from supporting his weight.

He crumpled to the ground where he lay so weak, he couldn't even lift his head. No part of his body worked anymore. It'd been too long since he last used his muscles.

Noir kicked him in the stomach hard enough to turn him over, onto his back. Curling his lip, he raked Seth with a sneer. "You're disgusting, you pathetic dog. Get cleaned up." Then he vanished into the darkness.

Seth lay on the floor, his mouth still bolted closed. Blinking hard, he stared at his blood on the walls around him. The shadows there seemed to make the bloodstains dance. And in the flickering, he saw the outline of his naked, ravaged body.

All this because he'd once made a bargain with the only person he'd ever called friend.

I will never again be so stupid.

Because no one had helped him. Not once. Not

in all this time. Not a single entity had come to offer him any kind of compassion or solace . . . not even an apology.

A sip of water . . .

It, too, was a lesson he would remember.

Whatever Noir asked of him, he would do. Without question. Without mercy. Anything to keep from returning here and being hurt anymore.

Just one minute of peace . . . please. Was that really too much to ask?

His resolve set, he braced himself for the new onslaught of pain and slowly pushed himself up on trembling limbs as he felt his god powers finally returning. With every heartbeat he grew stronger. Still, they wouldn't go to full strength.

Ever.

Noir had never allowed that. Either he or Azura would drain Seth whenever his powers became too strong.

But he had enough that he could finally clothe himself and stand upright, even if it was on unsteady feet. And when the demons returned, he gave them the payback they deserved.

They begged him for clemency. But he had none left. Not after they'd ruthlessly violated every part of him to the point he couldn't remember a time when his body hadn't throbbed from their torture. Minute by minute, for countless centuries, they had brutally stolen any lingering shred of humanity he might have once possessed.

Nothing would ever take that away and he would never, ever again trust another soul. No matter what. May the gods help whoever Noir wanted him to go after.

For he would take no pity on them whatsoever.

CHAPTER 1

Hell had many connotations, each one as unique as the individual who defined it. To one person, the idea of being trapped for eternity in a Michael Bolton video was the epitome of horror. To another, it was being stuck in an elevator with someone talking too loud on a cell phone, and not being able to gut that person for their rudeness.

To Lydia Tsakali, hell was the darkness surrounding her that echoed with the screams of the damned being tortured. It wasn't just their loud misery or their pleas for mercy to the ones who didn't care that made it so bad, it was the memories those screams evoked. The haunting terror of something she never wanted to think about again. Long buried, those flashbacks of that one night in her life, and the raw emotions they exposed, still had the ability to bring her to her knees.

Don't think about it.

How could she not? That night had been the last time she'd had a family who loved her. Then, like now, she'd only been able to see the oppressive black that had made her eyes ache. The darkness had pressed so hard against her that she'd feared herself blind as well as mute. And when she'd finally breached the dark to see light, all she'd found was blood and terror . . .

You're not a pup anymore.

No, she was a jackal full grown. More than that, she was a well-trained warrior with over a thousand years of hard combat training behind her. There wasn't a single soul in Azmodea who could harm her.

You forgot about Noir.

All right. There was one.

What about Azura?

Okay, two . . . But that was all right. She'd had much worse odds more times than she could count.

Yeah, but they didn't have the powers of a primary god.

Mind? Are you trying to turn me coward?

I'm trying to talk sense into you before it's too late. We haven't lived this long by being eat up with stupid—not with all the people out to kill us. And for what? Solin? He'll slaughter you when he finds out you did this.

What kind of idiot are you?

Apparently one with a limitless supply of stupid. If it'd been anyone other than Solin trapped here, she'd have never done this.

But she loved him too much to leave him to this

end. He'd taken her in when no one else would. Had trained her and stood by her. Taught her how to survive and how to fight. Without him, she'd be dead.

Even he would call you stupid for this.

And he would, too.

Kindness is a rotten fruit that poisons anyone who partakes of it. Throw it in the face of your enemies and let it ruin them instead.

How many times had he said that to her?

Yet, in spite of the hatred he'd carried in his heart and had voiced repeatedly, he'd raised her like a beloved daughter. Never once had he been stingy with his love, patience, or kindness.

Not with her.

Others . . . they saw a side of him that he very rarely turned in her direction. Thank the gods.

The personality is defined by its inconsistencies, not its consistencies. Another favorite Solin quote. *It's what makes us unique and who we are.* The sound of his voice in her head was enough to make her smile in spite of the danger she faced.

I've got to find him.

He would come for her if she needed it.

Yeah, right.

But she knew the truth in her heart that denied what her head tried to tell her. Solin would be there for her always. To her, he *was* a hero.

Something moved to her left. Lydia froze as her hyper hearing picked up on the slight sound. The surge of adrenaline kicked her other senses into high gear. Her nostrils widened as a new scent hit her. Male. Demon.

Close.

Don't breathe . . . Don't breathe . . .

Not because she didn't want it to detect her. But because the stench would be sickening for a human. To a half-breed Were-Hunter it was beyond painful. She clamped her fingers down on her nose to block the odor from getting in.

Still, she could smell it. *Don't gag . . .*

What? Did demons bathe in shit? She hated to be so obscene, but really . . . What was it about demons that made so many of them nauseating?

Out of nowhere, he appeared directly in front of her. A smile curved his bulbous lips. "My, my . . . what have we here? Didn't realize I'd ordered delivery. How nice of you—"

To die for me. She finished his sentence in her head as she grabbed him by the throat, and cut his words off.

But when she moved to stab him, he evaporated from her grasp into a smelly purple fog.

Crap.

Lydia turned a small circle in the blackness, trying to get her bearings and locate him before he told anyone she was here. She could no longer smell or hear him.

Definitely not good. At least not for her.

A piercing shriek drowned out the cries of the

others. She clamped her hands over her ears. *Just what I need. Bleeding eardrums.*

The shriek grew louder.

It was getting closer.

Something hard struck her back, knocking her down.

Even though the mere thought of it killed her, she dropped her hands from her ears and pulled her other dagger out. *Here, demon, demon . . . come get some.*

The sound of slithering moved to her right. She ran for it, lashing out in a hope of striking whatever foe was there.

Instead of drawing their blood, she drew her own the minute she slammed into a closed iron door that had blended in perfectly with the darkness.

Sonofa . . . She hissed at the pain exploding through her skull. Blood poured from her nose.

She kicked at the offending door.

To her surprise, it slammed open, rattling on its hinges. Light flooded into her tiny space, temporarily blinding her. She blinked until her eyes adjusted, then frowned at the sight of some luminescent tubing that provided the light from the slick ceiling above her. How weird. It vaguely reminded her of a glowstick, but this fluid was thicker and a vivid and eerie blue.

Now she could see the dank walls that appeared to bleed and breathe. She curled her lip in distaste. What was that?

Bet it's what smells.

Nah, only demon toe funk could be this abhor-rent. And speaking of demons, hers seemed to have vanished completely.

Where are you, you bastard?

Her luck, going for friends.

But that wasn't her main concern. Where was Solin? She'd tried repeatedly to use her telepathy to contact him, but whatever was holding him had somehow blocked that ability. She couldn't even reach him through a dream state. Which, given both of their powers, shouldn't have been a problem.

She hated this feeling of being completely alone. It reminded her of those weeks in her childhood when she'd had no one. The time she'd staggered through the blistering desert looking for water . . .

We're always alone. You can be in a crowded room and still feel the bite of loneliness. Person-ally, I find that it bites deepest whenever others are around. Another thing Solin forever harped on.

He was ever the pessimist.

She turned a corner and froze.

The smelly demon was back.

And as she'd feared, it'd gone for friends . . .

A *lot* of friends. Maybe two or three dozen. And the moment they saw her, their demonic eyes lit up and radiated color even brighter than the glowing tubes. They might as well have drool dripping from their chins.

Run!

She wasn't a coward, but only a fool would face that number without backup. And she wasn't a fool. After throwing her right dagger at the tallest one, she turned and ran in the opposite direction as fast as she could. She hoped that dagger had made contact and brought down at least one of them. But she wasn't going to wait around and find out.

Rule one in pursuit: Never look back.

Instead, she put her head down and kept going as fast as she could. She would have turned into her jackal form, but was afraid she might need her opposable thumbs for another invisible door.

She skidded around a corner, into a new hallway. Here the light wasn't quite as bright, but it was enough to let her see where the walls and doors were.

Unfortunately, it didn't let her see the floor. Or the thing that tripped her.

For a moment, she flew through the air until she landed face down on the ground. Putrid water splashed against her skin as pain throbbed in her knee, stomach, and cheek.

She pushed herself up and wiped away at the foul water and blood. Even though it hurt, she forced herself to start running again.

Pull out.

She could flee this realm for the time being, and then return again to search later. At least that was the thought until she heard something familiar from behind the door to her left.

"Fuck you and your little dog, too."

Solin.

She'd know that acerbic tone and deep Greek accent anywhere. Smiling in spite of her pain, she opened the door, ready for battle.

What she wasn't ready for was the giant . . . whatever it was that was trying to eat him. A mass of dark green skin with red markings, the demon turned toward her.

And this one did salivate as its yellow eyes pinned her with a salacious stare that gave her dancing heebie-jeebies. *Not on your best day, buster!*

"Lydia?" Solin asked incredulously. He was beaten so badly that but for his voice, she'd have never been able to identify him. "Child, what are you doing? Get the hell out of here while you can."

"Not without you." Since she couldn't speak with a voice, she sent her thoughts to him.

"I taught you better than that. Survival Rule Number One."

Save your own ass above all others. She knew it well. But someone following that rule wouldn't tell a rescuer to flee before freeing them.

Classic Solin.

Raising her dagger, she rushed at the demon. He moved a lot faster than something his size should be able to. With an impressive twist, he dodged her attack completely and caught her from behind.

She tried to break out of his hold. It was like being drowned in sticky Jell-o. Smelly three-month-old Jell-o.

He laughed at her useless attempts. If that wasn't bad enough, he licked her cheek. "What a tasty little morsel you are."

She cringed. *For the sake of the gods, haven't any of you heard of breath mints?* Pardon the pun, but Altoids could make a mint down here.

She jerked her head back, slamming it into his nose, and at least this time he satisfied her with a deep groan.

"You'll be sorry for that." He lifted her off her feet and threw her down on the floor.

Ignoring the pain that said she'd probably broken something, Lydia flipped herself back to her feet.

"Don't do this, Dee. Don't."

She ignored Solin as she and the demon circled each other slowly.

Right when she went in for another attack, the demon vaporized, just like the other one had done. All he left was his stench. *That* she'd have gladly done without.

She turned to look for him, but before she could do more than draw breath, he appeared behind her and kicked her into the wall.

More agony tore through her body, dulling her sight.

The demon seized her. "It's over for you, kitten." He tightened his grip, squeezing the last of the breath from her lungs.

Her ears started buzzing.

Just as she was sure he'd kill her, she heard a

loud shout resonate off the walls. "Release her, demon. Now!"

Definitely not Solin. That deep, gravelly male
voice was unique and filled with an unfathomable
rage that came from someplace dark inside him.
His accent was unlike anything she'd heard before.
Lyrically sweet and beautiful, yet at the same time
harsh and commanding.

The demon let go and shrank back in terror. That
reaction only made her panic more. If something as
scary as he was afraid of the newcomer, what
chance did she have?

But she wasn't a coward. If she was going to die,
it would be fighting to the last breath.

And she'd take as much of him with her as she
could.

Coughing, she turned around, putting her back
to the wall to confront this new creature. She wiped
the sweat from her eyes and focused them on the
door where the stranger stood.

Her jaw went slack as her gaze focused on the
massive form that was bathed in that eerie blue light.

Holy mother of all electronics . . .

I'm so dead.

CHAPTER 2

Lydia couldn't move. She couldn't breathe as she stared at the . . .

Demon?

There was no other way to describe him. It was the only thing he could possibly be . . .

Other than a god. And neither Azura nor Noir would ever allow a god in their domain, unless it was their sister, Braith. Gods as a rule didn't share territory easily. Not even with their family.

No one in their right mind would share territory with a creature this feral.

Dark, deadly, and scary as hell, he was enveloped by an aura of supreme power—one that made the air between them crackle with its preternatural strength and intensity. His was a presence that would make Darth Vader run screaming for his mama. It even raised the hair along her arms and nape. Never had she seen the like and she'd seen some seriously terrifying things in her thousand-plus years of living. He didn't just enter the room.

He dominated it.

No. He *owned* it.

Her breathing ragged, she took a moment to study her enemy, hoping to find a weakness of some sort.

Yeah, right . . . It was like trying to find a way to harness a hurricane. And while he was calm right now, she had the distinct impression that he could explode into violence with no more provocation than her arching her brow in a way he didn't like.

His straight dark auburn hair was severely pulled back from his face, exposing a widow's peak on his forehead, and held in a small ponytail at the crown of his head. That hair wasn't one single shade of red, but rather the individual strands were every-thing from blond to mahogany, to chestnut, to black. Somehow they came together to give the impression of hair the color of dried blood.

Well over six feet in height, he was the most in-timidating wet-your-pants-'cause-he's-going-to-suck-out-my-soul-and-eat-it thing she'd ever seen. And when you took into account the fact that she could surf everyone's nightmares, that said it all.

His entire face was painted white with sharp, angular red and black lines drawn over it in a way that reminded her of a fierce Kabuki warrior. Then again, given that he was a demon, that might not be paint. It could very well be his skin. The red lines were drawn in such a way as to give the impression of a permanent, sinister sneer and frown. His eyes were ringed by black that went down the side of his nose to form a sharp point right at the tip. Likewise, the black went up from the corner of his eye to his hairline. The dark color only emphasized how pale, cold, and merciless those steel blue eyes were.

Soulless. There was nothing in them except the promise of a brutal death and a pain so profound that those eyes alone would traumatize anyone with an ounce of self-preservation.

Given his massive size, he would have been intimidating on his worst day. Couple that with the burgundy-and-gold spiked armor caked in blood, and the real snarl on his face, and he would send the devil himself to the nearest corner to cower.

Help me . . .

Lydia wanted to take a step back from him, but the wall was right there, stopping her. She had no retreat. The only way out was through *him.*

Yeah, that ain't gonna happen. Not even a Mack truck would be able to move him. It would be like trying to run down Godzilla. She let her breath out slowly, waiting for him to attack.

"Don't you dare hurt her!" Solin growled from where he was chained down on the table. "I swear to the gods, I'll gut you from asshole to appetite if you so much as breathe on her."

That succeeded in making one of the demon's finely arched brows shoot up into a mocking expression. "We've already ascertained that there's nothing you can do, except stain my armor with your blood." He turned that brutal steel gaze back to her. "Who and what are you?"

Dead would be the most obvious answer. *Just let it be quick.* She didn't want to linger in misery. Not for anything.

And everything about the demon said he would enjoy watching her suffer.

He started forward as if to attack her. "Answer me, damn you!"

Who would have thought he could get any scarier?

She'd rather face Freddy Krueger thirty minutes after she'd swallowed three sleeping pills than confront this overwhelming mountain of demon power.

Lydia gripped her dagger hard in her hand and pressed herself against the wall, trying to teleport out.

She couldn't.

I'm trapped. Something blocked her powers and held her here like an insect trapped inside a science jar.

The demon was almost on her. "Speak, woman," he growled low. "Now!"

"She can't."

Solin's words brought him to an abrupt stop. He narrowed his gaze on Solin's bleeding body. "Explain."

"She's mute."

The demon twisted his lips into a mocking smirk. "You lie."

"I have no need to lie. She's never been able to say a single word, so you can't torture her for anything useful. Not unless you can read minds or sign language."

Seth paused to consider the veracity of Solin's words. Was he lying?

Why would he?

Why not? It was what people did. Many times for no reason whatsoever, and any time they thought they were under assault and wanted to protect their own worthless asses. If he knew nothing else about humanity and the gods, he knew that one simple fact.

No one could be trusted. Ever.

Still, he was curious about her presence. Why would anyone in their right mind come to this forsaken hell realm?

There was only one reasonable explanation he could think of . . .

"What is she to you, dream god?"

Solin refused to look at her. Instead, he glared at Seth with a strength of spirit that would garner respect if Seth was capable of giving such to another. "Nothing. Just a Dream-Hunter sent in to rescue me."

This time he knew Solin lied. And he was through bleeding and suffering because of the bastard's steadfast refusal to give him what he needed to free them both. Rage ripped through him as he turned and went to finally kill the imbecile once and for all.

Little did Solin know, this would be a mercy killing.

As he raised his sword to remove Solin's head, the frightened little mouse launched herself at him with everything she had. The weight of her small body slammed into his with more force than he would have thought her capable of. Grabbing his wrist, she actually tried to disarm him. When that failed, she stabbed him in the arm so deep, she buried the dagger's blade in all the way to the hilt.

Seth would have mocked her for the assault had he not been so stunned. No one had had the balls to openly attack him when he was unfettered since before his confinement.

What the hell?

She punched his throat—something that would have worked on anyone else. But too many centuries of being tortured had numbed him to physical pain.

Curling his lip, he raised his arm to backhand her.

"Don't you dare!" Solin strained so hard against his chains that every muscle in his body bulged.

Seth frowned at the dream god's violent reaction. Solin hadn't fought like that in weeks. If sheer strength of will could sever chains, Solin would have easily broken free.

He'd been right with his assessment. The woman meant something to Solin . . .

No, he realized as he saw the murderous rage in Solin's eyes while the god cursed Seth's being and parentage. She meant *everything* to him.

This is priceless.

Seth grabbed her hands, spun her around in his arms, and pinned her against his body so that she faced Solin. Furious, she fought him like a lioness protecting her pride.

Interesting . . .

Solin broke off into a string of more profanity as he tried even harder to reach them.

Very interesting.

He was willing to die to protect her.

I finally found the key. She was the tool to break Solin once and for all. The gods had finally taken mercy on him and thrown him a bone. A slow smile curved his lips.

Until she slammed her head into his jaw with enough impact that it flashed him back to his centuries of torture. It took everything he had not to break her in half. In that one moment, all he could taste was her blood. It was all he wanted.

Kill her and Solin is useless. He'll never talk then.

That knowledge was the only thing that saved her life. But she wouldn't be breathing much longer if she kept this up. In fact, his control slipped even more as she sank her teeth into his hand and bit him until he bled.

Flashing them out of the interrogation hole, he took her to his room. There, he flung her away from him.

She twirled about twice before she caught herself. Her black hair settled down around her shoulders into a silken mantle as she fell into a crouch like some deadly predator about to go for his throat.

He glared at her. "Don't."

Lydia froze at that one word that promised her an excruciating death if she disobeyed. Still, she remained in position, ready to attack if he took even one single step toward her.

His cold gaze held hers prisoner as he reached to his arm and jerked her dagger free of the wound she'd given him. She'd been able to drive it between the armor plates and knew from the blood on her own hands that she'd succeeded in wounding the beast.

But other than the bloody dagger he dropped to the floor, he showed no sign of it. He didn't even grimace from the pain. If anything, he seemed to enjoy it.

I am so screwed.

Who was he?

What was he?

He wiped the blood on his hand across his armored breastplate as if it were nothing. It left an ominous, bright red smear that didn't quite blend in with the burgundy. "You can't kill me, Greek. All you can do is piss me off. I suggest, if you want to keep breathing, you don't do that."

Forget screwed. This went so far beyond that it wasn't even measurable. This was screwed on steroids.

What am I going to do?

Die, no doubt. But not without one hell of a fight.

Seth saw the sanity return to her eyes. Feline topaz eyes that literally glowed with her intrepid spirit. He'd never seen anything like them. And they were what had told him Solin was a liar. The Greek Dream-Hunters, those who protected sleepers from nightmares and other predators of the unconscious, all had vivid blue eyes.

Never had he seen eyes akin to hers.

"Can you speak?" He wanted to know if Solin had lied about that as well.

She shook her head slowly.

At least she could understand him. That was something. Not much, but something.

She started moving her hands in a graceful dance. It was beautiful to watch. And it took him a minute to realize it was her language.

"I don't understand you."

This time she flicked her nails at him. That gesture of obscenity, he got. "Back at you."

Now she moved her hands rapidly and with obvious anger. No doubt she was cursing him as much as Solin had.

Damn, she was beautiful. Not in a classic, perfect way, like a goddess or demon. Her eyes were too large for her oval face. So much so, they almost overwhelmed it. And her nails were ragged as if she chewed on them from a nervous habit.

But her lips . . .

Plump, full, and bright pink, they were perfection. The merest thought of them, stirred his body into total rebellion. It made him ache to possess the very thing he should be killing.

No wonder Solin was so protective of her. If she was his woman, he'd kill anyone who came near her, too. How could you not? It was a primal instinct to protect the things that mattered to you.

Not in your case.

True. He was an animal who cared for nothing except himself. It was all he knew. He didn't live life. He endured it. Noir had driven that point home and nothing would ever dislodge it again. His entire existence was basic survival. There was no higher functioning in his mind. None. He did what he was told.

He had no other choice.

And right now, he had a god to break.

"You will stay here," he told the woman. Then he returned to question Solin for what would hopefully be the last time.

Lydia stopped moving as she found herself alone. Where was the demon?

More to the point, where was she?

Like the rest of the realm she'd been in, the room was dark, with the only light coming from that eerie blue tubing on the ceiling that strangely reminded her of blood. A damp chill clung to the air, making the place even more depressing.

The strangest part though, was the absence of a door. Not a single trace of one. Nor a window either. She walked around the room, double checking. Sure enough. The only way in or out was teleportation. Something she still couldn't do.

Damn it!

Trapped, she saw a large canopied bed in the far corner. Fur blankets were draped over it, but it didn't appear to be slept in. In fact, it had a layer of dust over it. The walls were the same damp stone that made up the hallways she'd been down.

There was a fireplace, but no fire to chase away the deep chill in the room that cut all the way to her bones. Next to that was a large, extremely neat, Baroque wood desk. A laptop, of all weird things, rested on top of it. That was the only personal item in the room.

Curious, she walked over to it, intending to turn it on. But the instant she touched it, the top slammed down, barely missing her fingers.

What the devil?

She tried to open it, but it refused. It was as if the thing was alive and knew she wasn't supposed to use it. Yeah . . .

But at least she wasn't being tortured.

Yet.

What am I going to do?

Pick up her dagger, which she did, and wait. She grimaced at the amount of blood on it. It looked like she'd hit an artery. And he hadn't even reacted to her stab. Obviously, he was an immortal. One who liked to be in pain.

I am so dead.

What else would he do with her, other than kill her?

The obvious answer to that terrified her even more than the thought of dying. *I won't be raped.* She might not be able to kill him, but she could geld him and that she would definitely do if he laid a hand on her.

With that thought foremost in her mind, she went to the corner and sat on the floor with her back against the wall. Now she was ready for him and she would renew their battle whenever he returned.

"Where's Lydia?"

Seth paused at Solin's belligerent tone. So that was the woman's name.

Lydia. It was pretty . . . like a song. But he wasn't a poet.

He was death, and she was nothing but a pawn to get what he needed. Narrowing his gaze, he went to the table that held Solin in place by chains. All too well, he knew how much it hurt to be pinned that way.

How humiliating. There was no worse feeling

than to be at the mercy of someone else and to not be able to fight back or even protect yourself. To lay there with no clue as to when the next round of torture would begin.

To have no dignity.

No hope of escape . . .

Deep inside, a part of him felt sorry for Solin.

Don't you dare! his mind snarled at him. It was that very thing that had gotten him punished to begin with. And if he didn't get what he needed, he would be there again.

No one ever came for you. He must never forget that. No one had ever tried to help him. He'd never had a single ounce of compassion from anyone.

Not even his own mother. The memory of her brutality was as fresh today as it'd been when he was child, cursing her for intentionally leaving him to die.

Unprotected.

Alone.

But Lydia had come for Solin. She'd risked her life trying to help him. Jealousy plowed through his heart. What about Solin was so special and deserving that he warranted such concern and loyalty? Such personal sacrifice?

How dare you proclaim that pathetic backwash as my divine offspring! How dare you name him after me, you bitch! You both sicken me. Get it out of my sight before I gut you both. Those had been the last words his father had said to him. It was what everyone since had seen him as. Nothing but worthless garbage to be used and discarded.

Walked over.

And that set fire to his temper.

He closed the distance between them and grabbed Solin by the hair. His nostrils flaring, he forced Solin to meet his gaze. "Tell me what I want to know or I'll kill her."

Solin looked down at the blood on Seth's armor. "How do I know you haven't already?"

Seth sneered at the question. It was his own blood staining his armor, not Lydia's. Blood brutally taken from him because he had yet to break the Greek.

Only Solin had the ability to end Seth's suffering and the stubborn bastard wouldn't. Damn him for it.

So he tormented the Greek in turn—not nearly as badly as Noir had him, but enough to make Seth feel better. "What would be the fun in that? It's more torturous for you to know that I have her at my disposal. I can do anything I want with her and there's nothing you can do to stop me. Nothing."

Solin exploded into a string of profanity so foul, it was a wonder his mouth didn't spontaneously combust.

Seth tightened his hand in Solin's hair. "If you want her safe, tell me where the key is."

"I don't know."

"Bullshit! I know for a fact that you're the only one who has access to it."

Solin shook his head in denial.

Seth wanted to crush his skull. Noir was grow-ing more impatient by the heartbeat. If Solin didn't break soon, Noir would return him to his hole and bolt his mouth shut again.

This time, it would be permanent and he'd never be granted another reprieve from it.

May the gods help Solin then. Noir would never take the pity on him that Seth had. As badly as the idiot thought he was suffering now, it was a walk in paradise compared to what was coming for him.

He knew from personal experience that the worst place to be was between Noir and whatever it was Noir wanted.

C'mon, you stupid bastard. Give me what I need to save us all. "One word from you and I'll let you both go."

"Fuck you."

"Not the word I wanted." Growling, Seth re-leased him. This was the same as it'd been for two weeks now. And he was through with being Noir's scapegoat. With being blamed and punished for Solin's obstinacy. Given what they were doing to him, he might as well be pinned to the table beside Solin.

But no more.

"Fine. I'll go question Lydia. Let's see what she knows."

Solin let out a scream so loud and pain-filled that it had to come from the deepest part of his soul. "Don't you hurt her. Don't you dare! I'll get you whatever it is you want if you'll release her."

For once he believed him. The emotion in Solin's voice and eyes was too real to be faked, and that scream . . .

It was one born of desperate love. Seth had absolutely no concept of that word. But he'd seen mothers who had died protecting their young. Of men who sacrificed themselves for friends, family, and women.

Did Lydia really mean *that* much to Solin?

"Would you give me your life for hers?"

Solin didn't hesitate with his answer. "Yes."

Fascinating. What could make a god want to die to keep another safe? "Do you think she'd do the same for you?"

"She came for me."

Those words stung him. Solin was right. She'd risked everything to try and rescue the dream god. "You love her?"

Solin didn't answer. Rather he did the one thing he'd never done throughout any of his torture.

He begged. "Please, please don't hurt her. I swear if you keep her safe, I will bring the key to you and put it in your hands."

Relief coursed through him as he finally heard the words that would save his ass and spare him more degradation.

Provided Solin wasn't lying to him. Did Lydia really mean so much?

Trust was not in his nature. Whenever he'd made that mistake, the repercussions had been shoved down his throat and stomped into his stomach. The only thing he had faith in was other people's willingness to lie and screw him over.

But in this, he had no choice. He had to have that damn key. Sooner rather than later.

He glared at Solin. "You have three days to return. If I don't have the key then, I'll send you her remains." Stepping back, Seth snapped his fingers.

The chains melted away.

Solin lay there, panting and weak. Just like he'd done when Noir had finally freed him. A part of him was remorseful for his part in it. He hated to see someone else in pain. But better it be Solin than him. At least he hadn't bolted Solin's mouth shut. He rubbed the back of his hand under his chin as a phantom pain reminded him of how much that had hurt. Nor had he violated the private parts of Solin's body. The stupid bastard thought he knew what torture was. He had no idea how gentle Seth had been compared to the others who called this hell home.

Solin should be down on his knees in gratitude.

Seth held his hand out and returned Solin's clothes to him. "Three days, Olympian. Do not fail me." Then he used his powers to send Solin back to the mortal realm he'd stolen him from.

How he wished he could go with him. But Noir had taken his ability to leave the moment he first brought him here. He could only pull others out of the human realm or return them.

Never himself.

But right now, that didn't matter.

Seth let out a relieved breath at the thought of handing the key of Olympus to Noir. It would make his overlord happy. Or at least as happy as the miserable son of a bitch could be.

Maybe then he'd be forgiven and allowed to remain without chains.

And with luck, Solin would be back in a few hours.

In the meantime, he wanted to understand what about the woman was so special that a god like Solin would give his life for her.

Was Solin out of his mind for putting her safety above his own? People lied and they betrayed. Especially where love was involved. It was only a tool the strong used against the weak.

He knew that better than anyone.

I love you. He sneered at the thought. Cheap, meaningless words bandied about by selfish asses incapable of understanding the meaning of it.

Lydia was just like all the others. She would turn on Solin.

And he would do the god a favor.

He would prove it.

CHAPTER 3

When he returned to his room, Seth expected to find the woman alert and crouched, ready to tear into him again. Instead, she sat in the corner with her arms crossed over her knees and her head lying atop her forearms. The soft, gentle snore let him know that she was sound asleep.

How could that be?

He hadn't been able to do more than nap since he'd been freed. And even those came in very short spurts. Spurts where he jerked awake at the slightest sound or merest stirring in the air. Real or imagined.

Yet here she was in the middle of enemy territory, and . . .

She slept.

Deeply.

You're such a fool.

Most of all, she was a curiosity wrapped by enigma and contradiction. Why? Why would she risk her life and body for someone else? Why would she come here?

Really?

Before he even realized what he was doing, he'd closed the distance between them and knelt on the floor by her side. His armor creaked ever so slightly from his movement. Her long black hair spilled around her shoulders and legs, forming a shining weblike mantle. In that position, she looked even more frail and tiny than she had before . . . Like a little dark rose on his floor. And she smelled like beauty. Most demons had an odor to them, but not her.

She smelled like the summer sunshine he hadn't seen since he was a boy . . . back in the days when he'd believed in beauty and decency. When he'd looked forward to a future he'd stupidly believed would be bright.

Back before his innocence had been so violently torn from him, and then thrown in his face.

Hesitant, but too curious to stop, he touched a lock of her hair that dangled by her side. The softness of that one fat curl startled him. It was like touching a rose petal. At least this was what he remembered them feeling like.

Slowly, he lifted it to his nose so that he could breathe in the pleasant, sweet smell that seemed to be a part of her. Oh yeah . . . It made him think of a home he'd never known or had.

He closed his eyes to savor the scent as it ran through his blood like fire. Against his will, his thoughts turned to what she might look like naked. How she'd feel beneath him as he tasted her tanned skin and took her.

No, better yet, on top of him. Yeah, that was the image he coveted. With this soft hair tickling his skin while she rode him like no one ever had before. Slow and tender. With gentle kisses that didn't draw blood.

Like he meant something to her.

Don't be stupid. Since when did you become an old woman? Sex was sex. It was a meaningless animalistic act that the body needed from time to time. Only an absolute imbecile would drag emotion into it.

And since when was sex ever tender? Especially for something as disgusting as he was? Hell, he was lucky any female would lower herself to screw him.

Lydia would never do so.

That thought stung deep. But it was true. The first thing he'd done after his strength came back was find a demon lover to sate what he'd missed most—the only pleasure Noir hadn't taken from him. He'd needed release in the worst sort of way. But the she-demon's pale gray skin had been cold and dry, her touch rough and demanding as she'd clawed and bit him until he bled. She'd even knocked loose some of his teeth. And her hair had been rough and brittle. Nothing like the warm softness of his little flower.

Open your eyes, sšn.

As if she heard his innermost wish, she let out a low sigh and rubbed her cheek against her folded arms. She blinked once, then jerked as she realized he was right beside her. She immediately scooted away from him with panic in her topaz eyes. To his dismay, her actions caused her hair to fall out of his grasp. Her entire body tensed for battle, as if she expected him to break into violence for no reason whatsoever.

"I . . ." he caught himself before he promised not to hurt her. He refused to give her that power.

Better to be feared. Always.

So instead, he moved to confront her.

Lydia pushed herself up after he rose only to realize it didn't really matter. He still towered over her and made her feel as if she'd fit into his pocket. May the gods help her if he did turn violent. It wouldn't be much of a fight on her part. She'd already done her best and stabbed him, and he'd pinned her so fast and easily that it still staggered her. But she would fight. So long as she breathed, she wouldn't give in without one.

That being said, he made no moves toward her at all.

She stared at the demon, wishing she had some way to question him. If only she had her powers. Then she could send out her thoughts.

As it was . . .

Her best action remained staring her hatred in his general direction.

She tried signing to him again. But all that did was cause him to frown. Something made twice as sinister by the black and red lines on his white face.

"Is that how you speak?" he asked her.

She nodded.

He cursed under his breath.

Using Charade movements instead of sign language, she tried to tell him that if he could return some of her powers, she'd be able to talk to him.

His frown deepened. "What? The ceiling? What about it?"

She let out a frustrated breath and tried to think of another way to illustrate her powers. She waved her arms around like smoke.

He grimaced in distaste. "This is annoying."

The demon had no idea.

She stopped as she tried to think of something else to try. There had to be a way she could write . . .

Before she could blink, he manifested in front of her. The sheer size of him, and shock at his sudden appearance in her face, made her gasp. At a distance, he'd been fierce. Up close like this, she could literally feel his powers. They were like an electrical current in the air that made the hair on the back of her neck rise.

He absolutely dwarfed her and it wasn't due to the armor bulking him up. He *was* this large.

Those blue eyes scorched her with a coldness so frigid, it was a wonder she didn't have frostbite.

In the next heartbeat, he wrapped one well-muscled arm around her and pulled her into his arms. His eyes glittered an instant before he lowered his lips to hers.

For the merest nanosecond, she was stunned by the warm softness of his lips. The gentleness of his embrace as he swept his tongue against hers in the sweetest kiss she'd ever known.

Until she remembered he was a demon who'd been torturing Solin. Her fury igniting, she bit his lip with everything she had.

He pulled back with a curse.

"You bastard!" Lydia froze, wide-eyed, as those words flew out of her mouth instead of the empty breath she normally spoke. Shocked, she clamped her hands over her lips and throat.

Had that really been *her*? Was that what her voice would sound like? It was alien and foreign, and . . .

Unbelievable.

The demon's eyes turned deadly as he wiped the blood away from his lips with the back of his hand. "You're lucky I don't kill you for that."

But that wasn't her greatest concern. What had he done to her? How could he have given her a voice when no one else had been able to do it?

No one.

Not even Solin.

With a sinister snarl curling his upper lip, he licked the area where she'd bitten him. "You can speak now."

"How?" The sound of her own voice made her jump.

He rubbed his thumb over his bottom lip, then

grimaced at the pad that was coated red from his still-bleeding wound. It matched the red lines bisecting his face. "I have all kinds of powers. That's just one of them."

"Is that why you kissed me?"

His gaze turned even more glacial. "Not at all. I had yet to have my lip busted open today so I thought I'd better see to it. Thank you so much for being kind enough to oblige me."

His sarcastic humor caught her off guard. For a moment, she didn't see him as a terrifying demon. He almost seemed . . .

Human.

Disturbed by that thought, she looked around nervously. "What other powers do you have?"

Her question brought the scary right back to him—with interest. When he spoke, he growled out his words like the demon he appeared to be. "Pray you *never* find out."

Fine. If he wanted to play that game . . .

"Why did you bring me here?"

His gaze drifted in the direction of the bed.

Heat scorched her cheeks. "You can forget it. Unless you're into necrophilia, it ain't ever gonna happen."

"Necrophilia?"

She steeled herself for the probability of his attack. "I'd kill myself before I let you touch me."

Seth went completely still at those words as

they struck him harder than a blow and took him straight into the past. *You rotten piece of filth, you're beneath me.* She didn't say that, but her tone and indignation implied it. Suddenly, he was a young man again, being laughed at for his ineptitude.

Rebuffed.

Humiliated.

Not good enough even to keep.

He felt now, just as he'd done then. Raw and sore from a truth he couldn't help. He hadn't asked to be born, and he damn sure hadn't asked to be immortal. He'd tried to be decent. Once. And what had it gotten him?

Tortured for centuries.

His anger ignited and it took everything he had not to strike her and knock her from that gilded pedestal where she looked down her patrician nose at him.

But the one truth he knew better than anyone— the truth that had been spoon-fed to him until he'd gagged on it—was that words were far more painful than physical strikes. They were always what lingered long after the cuts healed and the bruises faded.

Verbal blows cut to the soul and ate at the heart for eternity.

"Don't flatter yourself, woman." He raked a sneer over her body. "I'd rather masturbate with flea-infested sandpaper than touch you."

Lydia was momentarily stunned by his crude and vivid insult. No one had ever said anything like that to her before. "Then why am I here?" Nothing else made sense.

He answered her question with one of his own. "Why did you come for Solin?"

Why did he think? "Because he was in trouble and he needed someone to help him."

"You would risk your life for him?"

She scoffed at his ridiculous question. "I think that answer is obvious. I'm here, aren't I?"

That seemed to confuse him all the more. "But why?"

"Why what?"

His scowl deepened even more. "Why would you risk your life to protect his?"

She realized that he honestly had no concept of what she was talking about. It was as if they were speaking entirely different languages again. "Is there no one you protect?"

Proud, he straightened his stance. "Myself."

"And . . ."

Vivid emotions played across his features. Surprise, thoughtfulness, shock, and finally he just looked even more confused. "No one. Sentient creatures are treacherous at best, cruel at worst. None are worth a drop of my blood or sweat."

Well. That was that, then.

He was a demon, through and through. No

soul. No ability to value or love anyone except himself. Why would she expect anything else here? "Then that tells me all I need to know about you, doesn't it?"

He arched a thick painted black brow. "What does it tell you?"

"That you're a bastard."

He didn't smile, but she could tell that insult bitterly amused him. "Aren't we all?"

"No." She lowered her voice into an adamant tone. "No, we're not. Not by a longshot."

He curled his lips into a sinister sneer that had probably given countless people nightmares or strokes. "Then you're a fool. Solin has already left you. He didn't even look back for you when I freed him."

Yeah, right. She knew better. "You're lying to me."

He held his hands up to form a mist. There in the middle of it, she saw the room Solin had been in. A room that was now completely empty. "You see? He's gone and yet you remain, even though he knows I'll most likely torture and kill you for being here."

The demon was lying about her . . . She refused to finish that thought in case he was in her head. Solin would never do such a thing. She knew that for a fact. "Then he had a good reason for leaving me."

"Yes, he traded your freedom for his."

She shook her head in denial. "I don't believe

you. Not a single word and not for a single nanosecond." And she didn't, even though her animal instincts said he was telling her the truth. She had faith in Solin.

She would always have faith in him.

Seth was amazed by her steadfastness to someone he was sure didn't deserve it. The only thing he held that much belief in was the willingness of others to hurt or sacrifice him for their own whims, personal gains, and pleasures.

How could anyone her age be so stupid and blind?

Suddenly, he heard Noir calling for him. But for her presence, he'd wince. He knew what his overlord wanted and he knew how the bastard would react when he disappointed him with his report.

Again.

This was going to leave a mark . . .

But he had no choice. To make Noir wait would only worsen his punishment.

Sighing in resignation, he manifested food for the woman on top of his desk. There was no point in making her starve when he didn't know how long he'd be gone this time.

His gut tightened into a knot that choked him. Not from fear, but dread.

"I'll return."

Lydia started to ask where he was going, but he left too quickly.

Grateful for his absence, she tried again to find

some way out of here. There were no windows. No closet. Just this one room and nothing else. How weird . . .

"What do I do when I have to go to the bathroom?"

Not that she had to right now, but . . .

A loud swoosh behind her made her jump sideways. She turned around to see a door in the wall. Her heart pounding, she ran to it, hoping it led to a hallway.

What was there actually startled her more. It was a huge, gleaming bathroom with a marble steam shower and a claw-foot tub. The bright decadence seemed out of place with the austerity of the bedroom. Obviously this was where the vain bastard spoiled himself.

She rocked the door back and forth as she considered its appearance. Was that how things worked here? You asked and . . . "I want to leave."

Nothing happened.

C'mon. Don't do this to me. You know you want to let me out of here. She tried again. "Where do I leave? What do I do when I have to leave?" Maybe the key was in the phrasing.

But again she was disappointed when no door appeared.

You didn't really think it would be that easy, did you?

A jackal could hope.

Speaking of which, she tried to turn into one. But

even that innate ability was taken from her. She was as good as human.

How horrible. Not that being human was bad, but she didn't like the feeling of vulnerability. She liked having her powers. All she had left right now were her heightened senses.

At least you have something.

Oh, goodie. Lucky me! Maybe tomorrow I'll win Shirley Jackson's Lottery.

Yeah, that would be her luck.

"But I do have a voice now." She couldn't resist saying that out loud. It was so strange to be able to speak after a lifetime of silence.

The last time she'd spoken . . .

She flinched at the horror that had cost her her voice. Her mother had stolen it from her to keep her safe. In the end, she wished her mother had let her scream and die with the rest of them.

It would have been a far kinder fate. Especially if the demon did to her what he'd done to Solin.

Wanting distraction from the past that hurt too much to even contemplate, and the future that wasn't looking any better, she returned to the bedroom, where the warm pleasant scent of food beckoned her to the desk.

She pulled back the ornate silver lid to find a strange assortment. Fried bananas? Ironically, she loved them. Could he have picked that out of her brain? That thought actually scared her. She didn't like the idea of anyone reading her thoughts.

The other dishes made a little more sense—pastries and some kind of fried meat pie. There was also an abundance of fresh fruit and wine. Enough to probably feed her for days.

It all looked scrumptious, which begged one question. "Is it poisoned?"

With a demon, there was no telling. Though to be honest, if he wanted her dead, he certainly didn't have to resort to that. He could most likely kill her with his thoughts. And definitely with his hands.

Surely the food was safe.

Taking the empty plate, she filled it, then sat down to eat in the lair of her enemy.

"Well?"

Seth despised that one word with a furious passion. It ranked right up there with eye-gouging, gutting, and castration.

He wasn't afraid of Noir. Merely, he knew what the bastard was going to do to him when he answered, and he dreaded the coming pain.

Just don't geld me . . . Sex was the only source of remote pleasure he could have here. Sadly, he'd hate to lose it.

"I'm close, my lord."

Noir hissed like a snake that was gearing up to strike. "Close? Is that not what you told me two days ago?"

No, I told you to leave me alone to question him,

*King Moron, and you sent me on so many effing
errands that I haven't had more than an hour to
question him in over forty-eight hours.*

Seth ground his teeth to keep from saying those
words that would have him castrated. He forced
himself to keep his gaze trained on the floor at
Noir's feet. If he looked up, Noir might pluck his
eyes out. But what he really wanted to do was beat
the shit out of him.

If only he could. Without his powers, he wouldn't
get in a single punch before Noir would have him
pinned. And because he'd tried that enough times,
he knew exactly the punishment for *that* particular
stupidity.

"I have finally found a way to break him. I will
have it for you very soon."

Instead of placating Noir, it sent him off into a
homicidal rage. "Tell me truthfully, does it hurt to
be that stupid? I just have to know. Really? I would
think by now you'd have learned what I do to fail-
ures."

Seth braced himself as pain exploded throughout his entire being and his armor vanished. As
soon as he was naked, Noir blasted him through
the stone wall behind him. He landed in a painful
heap on the floor where he tried to catch his
breath, but it was impossible to breathe through
the throbbing agony. Noir rapidly closed the distance between them and pulled him up by his throat,
choking him in an iron grip. There was no missing

the evil gleam in Noir's eyes that said this wasn't about punishment.

It was all about pleasure.

Yeah, it's going to be a really long night.

CHAPTER 4

Lydia walked a circle in the bedroom that she'd memorized every detail of, right down to the design of the cracks in the floor. She'd eaten and then started pacing for what had to be hours and hours . . .

If not a whole day.

Frustration made a bitter lump in her throat. How could she—

The air stirred behind her.

She turned, ready to fight.

The demon was finally back. But something was wrong. The jackal in her could sense it even though he stood there as proud and fierce as he'd been before.

Tense and nervous, she waited for him to do or say something.

Like her, he didn't budge as they sized each other up. The weight of that frigid, frightening steel gaze sent a shiver over her . . .

What was he going to do?

Seth held his breath as he silently debated what

action to take. It was stupid to be here while wounded. He knew that.

His room had always been the one place in hell he could retreat to that was safe from everyone except Azura and Noir—there was no way to keep them out.

But with her here . . .

What are you bitching about? You'll be abused regardless. At least she didn't have her powers. There was only so much pain she could give him.

With the others . . .

It would be limitless, especially after his payback.

I have no place else to go.

He would have rather locked her up before he passed out, but Noir had drained him completely after he'd finally grown tired of beating him. Seth was so weak now. So sick. It was a wonder he'd made it back here at all.

Don't fall, damn you, you worthless piece of shit. Don't you dare *show a weakness.* He was steadfast in spirit. But his body refused to cooperate. Against his will, his legs gave out and he hit the floor so hard, he was surprised he didn't break the stone. He tried to stay conscious. To crawl toward his bed.

His body wouldn't even give him that much. It was too tired and too sore.

Against everything he tried, the darkness took him under.

Lydia stepped back as she watched him lying on the floor in a giant metal armor heap. Was it a trick?

Why would it be? What could he gain by falling down in front of her?

Still . . . demons in Azmodea were treacherous. Evil. One never knew what viciousness they were capable of. Not until it was too late and they were on you.

Ever cautious and curious, she crept forward, ready to bolt if he grabbed her.

He didn't.

It wasn't until she knelt down that she saw the blood seeping into his like-colored hair, as well as on his armor and face. In several places, the blood ran from underneath the steel plates and dripped onto the stone floor.

He'd been beaten. Viciously. No, savagely. The blows had smeared the white paint and the red and black lines on his face, showing her that it was makeup after all and not his skin tone.

What do I do?

There was no one to call for help. And in the back of her mind was the fear that if he died, she'd die too. No one knew where she was. Probably not even Solin.

Crap.

Just how badly was he injured? The answer was obvious—bad enough that something as lethally ferocious as he, wasn't conscious. Given what she'd seen of him, that seemed to be an impossibility.

Yet here he lay as still as a dead man. And there was already a pool of blood forming underneath him.

She reached for the buckles on his armor and began removing the heavy pieces. And they were heavy—like lifting lead planks. How could he walk around in them and not fall over? No wonder he was so massively huge. He'd have to be to support it all.

Beneath the armor he wore a black, thinly quilted suit that must be padding to keep the metal from bruising his skin. Carefully, she peeled it back to examine his wounds.

As she exposed his neck, she made an unexpected discovery. There was a curious tattoo of a beautiful, multicolored swallow. The tail of it started at the hollow of his throat and swooped down along his collarbone with its wings spanning from just over his shoulder to right above his nipple. A nipple that had a vicious scar running through it as if someone had pierced it, then ripped the piercing out. She cringed at the very thought and compulsively reached for her own breast.

Gah, that had to hurt.

Trying not to think about it, she continued to study the tattoo. For the most part the swallow was blue, but the wings were also red, yellow, green, and white. The bird's tail was split, and in between the two streaming tail feathers was what appeared to be a broken, dark red heart.

How very strange. That whimsical bird didn't match his evil persona at all. It was something an optimist or dreamer might want.

Not the right hand of evil itself.

But she didn't have time to contemplate that now. As she kept going, she uncovered a well-muscled, tawny body whose absolute perfection was marred again and again by countless scars, cuts, and bruises. Bruises that lay over other bruises, and scars and injuries that bisected each other. There were also numerous bite marks where the biter had left a dental impression so clear a dentist would envy it. And by those, she could tell at least three different beings had attacked him.

Her stomach tightened at the physical manifestation of a lifetime of utter misery. Good grief, how many times would someone have to be beaten to carry this amount of damage?

Honestly, she couldn't choose between them as to which one would have caused him the most pain. Although the one under his chin did look particularly nasty.

Even worse than the vicious, jagged scars were the deep fresh gashes and welts left by a barbed whip. That must be what had caused him to collapse. She sucked her breath in sharply. Someone had torn him up good and by the looks of it, they'd enjoyed it. She saw the defensive wounds on his forearms and biceps where he'd tried to keep the lashes from hitting other parts of his body and had failed.

Obviously the demon wasn't at the top of the food chain here. Which begged the question of who would have done this to him.

Noir? Azura?

And why?

What had he done to make them want to hurt him so viciously?

With no answers, she stripped him down to the long black shorts he wore beneath his armor and padding. They reminded her of bicycle shorts and they hugged his lean hips and muscular thighs.

Lydia tried to keep her gaze from the bulge there that told her his muscles weren't the only part of him that was huge. The gods had definitely been kind to him in that area.

Stop it.

But it was so difficult not to stare. He had the kind of body that a woman didn't see every day. The kind that you wanted to drape yourself over and just feel the warm hardness of it against your own skin. And while he was most likely evil to his core, there was no denying the fact that he was exquisitely formed.

No, he was so lickably delicious that she could almost understand why he'd been bitten into. But the other marks . . .

Those she didn't understand at all.

She returned her attention to his head, where

blood seeped from a nasty gash just above his left ear. He was still unconscious.

And bleeding all over. She couldn't even begin to catalogue the list of injuries.

Her gaze dropped to his arm where she'd stabbed him. He had so many wounds there, she wasn't sure which one was hers. That thought nauseated her. No wonder he hadn't reacted to it. She'd most likely stabbed him in a bruise.

Or another wound.

And though she didn't exactly like or trust anyone, she didn't want to hurt them either. Not even him. It pained her that she'd added to his damage and she hated herself for that weakness.

She shouldn't care about his pain in the least. He'd certainly taken no mercy on Solin. So why then did she ache to see him so ravaged?

Because I'm not a soulless demon like him. She found no joy or humanity in abuse or meanness.

Her stomach churning in sympathy, she went to the bathroom to run a basin of warm water so that she could clean and bandage his injuries.

The bandages she had to tear out of his bedsheets.

It took some time, but she very carefully cleaned and wrapped each wound. Once she was finished with his body, she dumped the water, cleaned the basin, and then ran more so that she could tend to his face and head.

As she washed the harsh makeup from his features, she slowly uncovered the truth of her "demon."

He was beautiful. Absolutely stunning.

There was no other word for it. He would have been as pretty as a woman but for the rugged cut of his masculine jaw and the sharpness of his cheekbones, both of which were dusted by a day's growth of auburn whiskers. No wonder he wore the makeup. It would be hard to terrify the demons of this place looking like he did, even as tall and ripped as he was.

Not to mention, she was pretty sure he used it to conceal the bruises on his forehead, cheeks, and jaw.

Before she realized what she was doing, she ran her finger over his soft lips, remembering how good they'd tasted until . . . She winced as she saw the mark where she'd bitten him, too.

Obviously, the last thing he'd needed was more pain. And she'd stupidly thought he was joking when he said that he hadn't had his lip busted open today.

"I'm so sorry," she whispered, wondering if he'd ever had a moment of happiness in his entire life. By the condition of his body, she'd say no.

How long had he lived in this hell realm?

One minute would be too long.

Her throat tight, she washed the blood from his hair. Hair that drew up into perfectly tight auburn spiral curls the minute she wet it.

So it wasn't straight after all. Those curls were incredibly soft and boyishly charming, like you would see on a collectible doll. Who would have thought?

Now that she had him bare and clean, the only thing scary about him was how flawlessly handsome he was. How inviting. It was almost impossible not to stare at him.

He's still the one who tortured Solin . . . the one who would have killed him had you not stopped him.

True. His looks didn't change the cruelty of *his* actions. No matter what, he was her enemy. And he would always remain so.

If you were smart, you'd stab him through the heart and kill him while you can.

Her dinner knife was only a few feet away.

And what if I did? He'd told her that he couldn't be killed. She had no reason to assume he'd been lying. His beating and scars, and the fact that he still breathed, told her he'd been honest about that.

Plus, even if she did kill him, she'd continue to be trapped here. That wouldn't change. Without him, she had no way to leave and no way to communicate with anyone.

He was her only hope for eventual release.

If only she could get a message to someone on the outside. But the more she tried, the more trapped she felt. *What am I going to do?*

She'd never felt more lost.

An eerie chill went down her spine as she saw her future and it wasn't pretty.

For now, it was better to tolerate the demon she knew than the others who waited outside this room.

Seth came awake slowly to find himself lying facedown on the hard stone floor. He stared at his gloomy bedroom wall, dreading the moment when the pain would kick in and he'd ache anew. But as he waited for it, he realized that his head was on a soft pillow and the weight on his body wasn't his armor.

Someone had covered him with his blankets?

What the hell?

Frowning, he started to move only to hear a warm, sweet voice chirp at him.

"Careful! You'll reopen your back."

From the shadows, he saw an angel appear. Yeah, one with sharp teeth, he reminded himself. But the current throbbing in his lips wasn't from her nip, it was from Noir's vicious backhands.

His head swam as the pain found him and kicked his teeth in. Yeah, this was what he was used to. Utter fucking misery. For a moment, he feared he'd pass out again.

"Here."

She picked his head up from the pillow with the gentlest touch he'd ever known and helped him drink water from the goblet he'd left with her dinner.

He swallowed carefully, his throat burning from internal injuries, until she pulled the cup away. Then he scowled at her. He'd ask her why she was helping him, but the answer was obvious and undeniable. He was the only way she could get out of here and she knew it.

There was no emotion behind any of her actions. They were solely self-serving.

Like everyone else's.

But at least she hadn't taken advantage of his condition to hurt him more. That, in and of itself, was a novelty.

Even stranger was the fact that she'd bothered to tend him at all. His scowl deepened as he focused on the bandage she'd wrapped around his hand and knotted over his knuckles. "I told you, I couldn't die."

"Yeah, but you're not exactly a speed healer, either. I had to do something. You were bleeding all over the floor and the smell of blood was nauseating me."

Seth ignored that as he pushed himself up so that he could stand on unsteady feet. Dizzy from the blood loss and pain, he felt so weak . . .

Suddenly, Lydia was beside him. She pulled his arm around her shoulders and wrapped one slender arm around his waist to steady him. The warm scent of her filled his head, making his heartbeat race. Better still was the soft curves of her body against his. Curves that made his mouth water and his cock so hard, he could probably use it as a hammer.

"C'mon, let's get you to bed before you fall down again."

Those words brought images to his mind of him

deep inside her while she arched against him. Of her lips teasing every inch of his body until he was made drunk by it.

Oh yeah, he could already feel her there.

Warm. Wet.

Supple . . .

Don't be stupid. It wasn't an invitation, and she most certainly didn't give a shit about him.

But it was nice to have someone who pretended to care. If only for a minute.

How pathetic am I that something so fake and trivial means so much?

And he was pathetic. Craving a woman who'd rather gut him than bed him.

Don't let this soften you. There would be hell to pay if he allowed anyone to weaken him.

And that would be different from normal, how?

Disgusted with himself, he moved away from her. "I don't need your help."

She held her hands up in surrender. "Fine. Bleed wherever you want to."

Seth crept to the bed and sat down before he passed out again. He brushed a hand through his hair, then froze as he felt those detested curls he never wore in front of anyone.

Shit.

That was followed by a fear so foul, it nauseated him more than his wounds. He brushed his hand against the whiskers on his cheek. "Did you wash—"

"Yes."

He winced as he realized she was looking at the real him. The part he never wanted anyone to see. "Why?" He had to struggle to keep the venom out of his voice.

"You had a nasty head injury and a bad bruise on your left cheek. I wanted to make sure no bones were broken."

So what if they had been? "Would it have mattered?"

She let out a tired breath before she answered. "No, Captain Bad-Ass, it wouldn't. Sorry I tried to help."

He didn't respond as he ran his hand underneath his chin where that repulsive bolt scar marred his skin . . . he could still feel it piercing his mouth and tongue.

It bothered him that she knew what he looked like. No good had ever come from anyone seeing his real features, especially not here. In Azmodea, it was always better to be feared than desired. A very harsh lesson he'd learned the moment Noir had brought him here and drained his powers, leaving him an unguarded victim for all the others until he'd regained enough strength to fight back. It was another reason there was no way into his room except by teleportation.

No one would ever victimize him again.

Except for the two who owned him. There was no way to protect himself from Noir or Azura's particular brand of brutality.

His stomach churned with the thought of that and the fact that he felt like he was naked in front of her. That made his anger rise even higher.

"Don't do it again. Ever."

Lydia rolled her eyes at that overstated growl as his armor and makeup reappeared to cover him. *Whatever makes you feel better, babe . . .*

An instant later, the remains of her food were gone and replaced by more.

She gave him an arch stare. "I take it you're hungry."

He shook his head. "You probably are. How long was I out?"

"I don't know. You don't have a clock"—She gestured to the wall—"or window so that I can check time. Offhand, I'd say a day, maybe."

Still, he didn't move. He merely sat there like an angry gargoyle, plotting revenge on some poor pigeon.

Ignoring his foul mood, she went to the food, hating the fact that she was starving. She'd been living on the fruit, but that hadn't been enough to really satisfy her. She was craving protein in the worst sort of way. "You want some?"

"No."

"Maggot!"

Lydia jumped at the fierce shout that reverberated off the walls around them.

Seth's features tightened into a mask of murder.

The hatred in his gaze seared her. Without a word, he flashed out of the room and left her again.

Seth manifested in Noir's dismal office that was as dark as Seth's heart and mood. "You summoned me, my lord?"

"Well?"

He never wanted to hear the damn cursed word again. And he was confused as to why Noir was using it. "I don't understand."

Noir backhanded him so hard his head snapped back and his neck made a loud popping sound. For a full minute he saw stars as Noir wrapped his hand in Seth's hair and yanked him closer, so that he could snarl in his bleeding ear. "Then I shall speak slowly and use small words so that even a pathetic idiot like you can follow." Noir jerked his head with every syllable to punctuate it even more. "What. Is. Your. Progress? Do you have my key?"

Seth ground his teeth. There was no way to win this. If he told Noir the truth, he'd beat him again.

Please give me my powers for one second, you sorry bastard. That was all he would need to make Noir feel his wrath.

Damn you, Father. Damn you straight to hell! I hope Sesmu is squeezing the blood out of you right now and making you drown in it. More than that, he hoped his father was roasting in the ovens of the Underworld.

But none of that changed his slavery. None of it changed this moment.

Or what was about to be done to him.

And he hated most what he was forced to do. Subjugate himself. "I'm doing my best for you, my lord."

Noir caught him by his throat and squeezed so hard that he wheezed. "You better tell me why you have no more news than that."

Seth coughed as Noir's grip tightened even more. "I—I couldn't."

"Why?"

Even though he knew what it would get him, Seth met Noir's gaze and let him see the full weight of his hatred. "I was left unconscious from your punishment."

"That's what you get for being weak, you pathetic dog. If you were a man you'd have been able to take it."

Only weak because you steal my powers . . .

He grabbed Noir's wrist and tried to drag it from his throat.

"Do you dare challenge me, slave?"

Seth didn't answer with the truth. He knew better. But he wanted to. Desperately. "I live only to serve you."

Noir backhanded him again. "You'd best remember that."

How could he ever forget? It burned inside him like a bitter furnace.

"Yes, my lord." He focused his gaze on the far wall to make sure he didn't look the bastard in the eye and incur a worse wrath.

Noir slapped him. "Are you paying attention?"

It took every ounce of will he possessed not to strike out at his overlord. *Don't do it. Don't.* It wouldn't be worth the cost.

Still, he wanted to fight back so badly, he could taste it.

"Yes, my lord."

Noir shoved Seth away from him. "Your time is growing finite, dog. As is my patience. You either give me what I need, or I'll return you to your pit and let the demons there have you for eternity."

Then why are you wasting my time by making me appear here when I could be pursuing it? That question burned in his throat. *Effing idiot.*

"I understand, my lord."

"I don't think you do, slave. But you're about to."

CHAPTER 5

Solin shook in uncontrollable fear and rage. Yes, he was in excruciating pain, but that didn't matter to him as he entered the home of his enemies.

Olympus.

The hall of the Oneroi, to be precise. He hadn't been here in so long, he'd all but forgotten what it looked like. Nothing shy of major desperation had him here now.

Only for Lydia would he do this. And for her, he would do absolutely anything. No questions asked. All she had to do was call and he would come to her, no matter the consequences.

His heart pounding, he entered the chambers that he was banned from.

Madoc, the eldest leader of the Oneroi, looked up with a fierce frown that quickly melted into a mask of total disbelief. Like every full-blooded Dream-Hunter in existence, Madoc held an exceptional beauty that made it hard for humans to look at him in the flesh. His short hair was jet-black and his blue eyes practically glowed.

He rose to his feet. Resting his fists on the conference table, he leaned forward in an obvious sign of aggression. As if that would ever intimate him. "Solin?" His tone was low and hushed, as if Madoc thought he might be hallucinating.

Solin kept his face stoic. There was no need to alienate Madoc quite yet. "Yes, hell froze over." It would have had to for him to be here asking Madoc for any kind of favor.

Madoc arched a condescending brow. "Why are you here?"

Because the gods knew that while they'd formed a truce years ago in Greece, they had never been friends. Neither of them trusted the other.

They'd fought each other too many centuries for that.

Solin stood on the opposite side of the table and duplicated Madoc's stance. "We have a problem."

That only amused him. Madoc snorted a rude denial. "We?"

Solin was about to knock the smug look right off Madoc's features. But he didn't need his fists to do it. His words would be much more effective for once. "Remember the key to Olympus?" All of them had come after Solin for it.

For centuries.

They had tried everything to find and destroy it while Solin had protected it with every ounce of his strength.

That key held the only thing that could kill the

Olympian gods and destroy their entire existence. The blood of the three races that Zeus, Apollo, and the Fates had wrongfully condemned and punished.

Blood that was mixed with that of an Atlantean goddess who had cursed them when they killed her only son and then trapped her in the Atlantean hell realm. The goddess of absolute destruction, Apollymi, had promised them the day of retribution when the beast of the past would come and confront them all for their numerous transgressions.

"Unless you send Apollo to me, and that bitch Artemis, it will bring forth my justice and avenge my innocent son whom Apollo butchered like an animal . . .

"A combination of all you have sought so desperately to destroy, it will survive against all odds. And its blood mixture will be your poison.

"And on that day when it comes for you, my laughter will ring in the Hall of Zeus, and every Greek god will feel my wrath as they die in utter agony.

"He sah te, akram justia!"

All hail the queen's justice.

For over eleven thousand years, it had been the horror story used to frighten all of them. And it was the real reason why the Fates refused to allow the Were-Hunters to choose their own mates. Why they wouldn't allow a Were-Hunter to mate with any but their chosen one . . .

But destiny refused to be denied forever.

And even the best-laid plans eventually led the architect straight to hell.

He sah te, akram justia . . .

Madoc's entire face turned as white as his shirt the minute he realized what was coming next. "You mean the key you swore to us you'd destroyed? What of it?"

"I'm sure it won't come as a surprise to you now to learn that I lied. The key wasn't destroyed."

Madoc cursed. "What happened to it?"

A new pain tore through Solin as his fear overwhelmed his fury. If he told the truth, they would kill Lydia.

If he didn't, Seth would kill her.

The sword of Damocles hung directly over him now. But the one truth he knew for a fact was that he couldn't negotiate or bargain with Seth. He'd been trying for that and the bastard was steadfast on destroying them.

Don't betray me again, Madoc. Above all, the Greeks were his family. Madoc could be rational at times, and like Solin, he'd been captured and tortured by Noir himself.

In the end, no argument trumped the one bitter truth that Solin kept coming back to.

The gods he'd fought against for centuries were his only hope for saving Lydia's life.

His only hope.

Solin took a deep breath and braced himself for Madoc's answer. "I want you to swear by the River

Styx that you won't destroy the key when I tell you how to find it. That you will stand with me, brother, to protect it."

Madoc laughed bitterly. "You know I can't do that."

"You have no choice in this."

Madoc scoffed at him. "I—"

"If you don't swear," he snarled, cutting him off, "all of you will die. And I do mean *all* of you. There won't be a single Greek god left."

A tic started in Madoc's jaw. "I won't be held hostage by you, and you know how Zeus is when confronted."

Solin shrugged with a nonchalance he definitely didn't feel. "Then you will die painfully . . . just like D'Alerian and M'Ordant." They, along with Madoc, had been the ruling council for the Oneroi for centuries.

Until Noir had turned the evil Oneroi against their brethren. He'd almost succeeded in destroying every one of the Dream-Hunters.

Almost.

And they were still recovering from his attack. Madoc was one of the few prisoners Noir had taken who'd survived. He, Delphine, who had been instrumental in saving them, and Zeth, one of the evil Oneroi Noir had turned, were now the leaders. And while Delphine led them, in this, he knew Madoc was his best hope.

As for D'Alerian, he'd been the Dream-Hunter

Noir had tortured and killed to find out that Solin had been the one who hid the key in the world of man. Bloody bastard for not keeping his mouth shut. And in the end what had it gotten him?

A slow and painful death.

Madoc pushed himself upright and crossed his arms over his chest. Annoyed, he let out one feral breath. "Fine. I swear on the River Styx that I won't destroy the key. Now where is it?"

Solin swallowed as another wave of pain ripped through him. He blamed himself for this. He should have known what would happen. But it was too late now to focus on what should have and could have been done.

They had to fight and fight hard.

"It's currently in the hands of Noir's guardian."

CHAPTER 6

Lydia paused as the demon reappeared in the room with her. Even though he stood as proud and fierce as he always did, she saw the shame and self-loathing in his icy blue eyes before he blinked and averted his gaze, then slowly limped to his desk.

As he sat down in the ornately carved chair, she started to ask him if he was all right, but didn't want to wound his pride any worse than it already appeared to be. There was no need to ask that when she could already tell he was embarrassed and upset.

And it was painfully obvious that he wasn't all right. He was hurting and she didn't mean the physical pain of his injuries. An air of hopeless despair, and utter grief and sadness clung to him. She'd never seen anything like it. Not even in nightmares.

Without a word, he carefully wiped at the fresh blood trickling from the corner of his nose and swollen mouth. There was more blood from his ear, running down his neck in a bright red stripe that matched his makeup. The fact that he ignored it completely told her just how often this happened to him. He no longer reacted to it.

For some reason she couldn't name, that image of him sitting there, looking so lost and yet fierce, touched a part of her heart and made her ache for him as if it were her own pain.

He wore a mask of tough, unshakable power and yet . . .

She didn't see the demon's painted-on face right now. She only saw the man who hid himself behind it. And even though they were enemies, she wanted to soothe that side of him.

Maybe, just maybe, if she could reach it, he might help her and Solin. The gods knew he had no reason to side with Noir. Not when the bastard abused him so.

There was a flesh and blood man inside his soul. One in eternal pain. And having been wounded and orphaned in a world that was suspicious of and angry at her kind, and hateful beyond belief, she understood the need to draw inward and hide. The proclivity to strike out and hurt them before they hurt her.

It was a survivor's instinct. A fighter's way.

But for Solin and his love, she wouldn't have been any better or kinder than the demon was. There was no telling what she would have become ultimately.

One person could make such a difference in someone's life. Either good or bad. With their actions and words, a single individual had the power to save or destroy another.

She'd been so lucky. Solin had appeared when she needed him and taken away her pain. He'd taught her to laugh again and to love, even when her past told her to keep her heart closed.

But the demon . . .

He didn't have a Solin to hold him and tell him that everything would be all right. That he would kill anyone who harmed him, and protect him no matter the threat. A Solin who promised him that in time the pain of the past would fade to a dull ache and that he would learn to love and laugh again.

Solin had been her greatest gift.

Instead, too many had attacked this demon and tried to destroy him, and they had failed.

Perhaps it was time someone tried another tactic besides violence. One he might not be able to defend against.

She crossed halfway to where he sat, afraid to get too close lest he put his defenses in place and repel her. "What's your name?"

Licking at the cut on his lip, he furrowed his brow as he finally turned his attention to her. "Excuse me?"

So the beast had manners after all. It was refreshing to see them.

"Your name. What is it?"

Seth sat in silence as he pondered how to answer

what should be a simple thing. No one other than Azura's servant, Jaden, had used his given name since he'd left the human realm.

To his face—whenever he wasn't pinned down and unable to strike back—the demons called him Guardian or Master. Noir and Azura only called him by insults or Slave, so much so that he wasn't even sure if they knew his name.

Bastard was probably the most common or least offensive epitaph he bore.

Still . . .

Why would she want to know his name when no one else ever had? Not even Jaden had asked. He'd merely plucked it out of Seth's head, without his permission, the first time they met.

Honestly, he wasn't sure if he wanted to hear it on her lips. A part of him was even afraid of that small intimacy and what it might do to him. No good could come of her calling him by name.

None.

"Why do you want to know it?"

Lydia sighed wearily. "You are ever suspicious of everything. Are you really that afraid of me? What in the name of Olympus could I, as small as I am, do to you?"

She could weaken him, and here, in this hell where he was forced to live, that could get him hurt a lot worse. To care about anything or anyone . . .

Those were the most lethal of weapons. It was exactly why he was holding her.

To weaken and control Solin.

I will never be such a fool. Not for anyone or anything.

He'd come into this world alone and alone he would forever remain.

"I'm not afraid of you, woman," he sneered. "I fear nothing." How could he? His entire life was nightmare after nightmare. If he feared something, it was used against him.

So any fear he might have once held had been purged centuries ago.

Now . . .

He was empty at best and furious at worst. Those were the only two emotions he had. The only two he was capable of understanding anymore.

Her topaz eyes filled with sadness, she shook her head. "Exchanging names is what people do when they meet."

"Yes, but I'm not a . . ." he stopped just short of saying "person." They had long ago stripped that last bit of dignity out of him. He didn't know what he was anymore. Not really. But she didn't need to know that either.

"You're not what?" she asked after a minute.

"Human."

Lydia sensed that that wasn't what he'd started to say. "But you do have a name, don't you?"

He nodded. "You may call me Master."

Fire burned bright in her eyes as she curled her lip derisively. "I call no man Master. Ever. And that includes you, for the record, buster. So get over your-self. Gah! I can't believe the nerve of you."

Those words angered him. "Are you mocking me?"

Lydia seethed at his ridiculous question. "Aren't *you* mocking *me*?"

He actually managed to appear stunned by that. Several other emotions she couldn't identify flick-ered over his features as more blood trickled from his nose. Absently, he wiped it away before he spoke again. "How so?"

She closed the distance between them, wanting to strangle him for it. Was he really that dense? "Tell-ing me to call you Master? What kind of bullshit is that? No one owns me and they damn sure don't control me."

Her anger didn't seem to faze him at all. Of course, he lived and served Noir who, she'd been told, lived in a state of constant PMS. He was prob-ably immune to any form of heated words.

"Fine then," he said in a calmer tone. "Call me Guardian."

She made a deep sound of disgust. Like that was any better? Good grief. Was that really the only choice she had? Master or Guardian?

She shook her head at him. "Your mother named you Guardian? Really? She must not have thought much of you for that." She'd meant it as a joking barb, but he went ramrod stiff as pain flared deep

in his eyes—something that told her she'd uninten-
tionally struck a nerve.

Crap . . .

"I'm sorry, Guardian. I didn't mean anything by
that." She reached out to touch him.

He shot to his feet and stepped back so fast, he
almost tripped over his chair. "Don't touch me."
Those snarled, angry words came out like rapid
gunfire.

She balled her hand into a fist as she saw a huge,
fresh, ugly bruise on his cheek through the white
makeup. It reminded her of all the others marring
his flesh—the bite marks she'd seen on his chest,
thighs, and neck. And it was then she fully understood his secret.

His true pain.

"Has anyone ever given you a touch that didn't
cause you pain?"

Seth didn't move as her question slapped him
hard in the face. But the most painful of all was the
harsh truth. Once, a long time ago, he'd lived like a
normal person. He'd had people he thought loved
him. A family who said he was a part of them.

But that had been a cruel lie. He'd have been far
better off without knowing their fake kindness. All
that had done was show him what he was missing.
Show him what other people took for granted.

Show him what he was unworthy of having.

It doesn't deserve to breathe the same air as I,

never mind share my name! How dare you name such a wretch after me. If you think by whelping it you would endear yourself to me, think again.

With his father's words ringing in his ears, Seth started away from her.

But she stepped in front of him, cutting off his retreat. Before he realized her intent, she laid a gentle hand on his cheek that still burned from Noir's fist. The tenderness of it shocked him.

Closing his eyes, he savored the warmth of her touch, and tried to imagine a life where such a thing wasn't a rarity. But the truth wouldn't let him have even that much comfort. It shouted angrily in his head, reminding him of who and what he was.

Who could ever love a mongrel like you?

You're disgusting. Pathetic.

Worthless.

Get out of my sight, wretch, before I vomit. Even when he pleased Azura or a she-demon, they threw him out of bed the minute they were finished with him. He was only a tool to pacify a bodily urge.

Nothing more.

He mattered to no one and no one mattered to him.

Seth opened his eyes to see her staring up at him with kindness burning bright in her topaz gaze.

That lie slammed into his stomach with the force of Noir putting him through a wall. She didn't give a single shit about him and he knew it.

Solin was the one she loved. He was the one she'd come here to save.

A woman like her would never risk her life to save something like him.

Rage tore through him as he realized her ruse. He knew what she was trying to do and he hated her for it.

He snatched her hand away from his face. "What kind of fool do you take me for?"

She actually managed to look shocked. "I don't understand."

Yeah, right. She knew and she was trying to play him. To weaken him. "I'm nothing to you, but an enemy to get past. Don't insult either of us by pretending otherwise."

Lydia winced as his grip tightened on her wrist and he dragged her toward his bed. Panic swelled inside her as she feared his intent.

She started to fight him, until she realized he wasn't going to attack her. Rather he manifested a chain that ran from the bedpost to her ankle.

His eyes glittered like ice as he released her and then returned to his desk.

"You're just going to leave me chained here?"

"Yes." He opened his laptop.

"Really?"

He refused to look at her. "Is that not what I said?" He started typing something.

She was flabbergasted by his overreaction to a

simple question. "Are you honestly that afraid of a touch?"

Turning his head, he glared at her over his shoulder. "I told you, I fear *nothing*."

But she knew better. He wouldn't give her his name. He wouldn't let her see his real face or offer him comfort of any sort . . .

"You can lie to yourself all you want to, Guardian. *I* know the truth about you."

A deep scowl lined his brow. "What truth?"

"You fear people. Why else would you live like this?"

He slammed his hands down on his desk with enough force that it made her jump, and it lifted the laptop a good inch before it clamored down and landed sideways on the desk.

"I don't fear people," he said between his clenched teeth. "I fucking *hate* them." She could taste the venom he spat out with that one word. "Do you understand? They lie. They steal. They cheat and deceive. There is absolutely nothing about them that I can stand . . . And if you don't leave me alone, I'm going to take your voice away again."

A part of her was tempted to test him on that, but the saner part of herself won out.

He wasn't one to bluff.

Fine. Whatever. Let him stew in his misery. It didn't really concern her anyway.

Not like I have to deal with you much longer. Sooner or later, Solin would free her. She knew it.

With nothing else to do, she sat on the bed and watched as he worked on whatever it was he had on his laptop. She tilted her head as minutes dragged by and he hit the keys so hard, she was rather surprised it didn't lock up or break.

It was woefully obvious that he had no idea what he was doing, and he became more agitated by the second. Boy, did she understand that. As the old saying went, a TV can insult your intelligence, but nothing rubs it in like a computer.

And for some reason she couldn't name, she felt a smug satisfaction over it.

Good. I hope you stew in frustration until you're pruny from it.

That'd teach him to be nicer to her.

Seth tried to focus on his research, but all he really noticed was the faint sound of Lydia's breathing. Every time she made the smallest move, his body reacted to it against his wishes.

Why had she touched him? Between that and his kiss when he'd given her her voice, he'd screwed himself. Now he couldn't help wondering what it would be like to have sex with a woman and not a demon.

Were all non-demonic women like Lydia? Did they smell that good? Feel so soft?

Don't look at her.

He heard his inner sanity and yet he couldn't resist glancing over his shoulder to catch her staring at his back from where she sat cross-legged on his bed. With her elbows braced on her knees, she rested her chin on her folded hands. He had no idea why he found that adorable, but he did.

"What are you doing?" he asked her.

"Trying to read through your big head."

"Why?"

She gave him a droll look. "Oh, I don't know. Maybe because I'm bored out of my friggin' mind and there's really nothing else to do since I'm not sleepy. What do you do for entertainment? Other than surf online porn, that is."

"Porn?" She used a lot of words he didn't have a definition for.

"You know? Pornography? Naked women showing off their happy places to lonely men who can't get dates? Or, in your case, guys who live under rocks and never get to see a normal woman's happy place."

He was both appalled and intrigued by what she described. Did women really do such a thing? And you could actually see it?

Of course, during his brief time in the human realm, people had been very open sexually. Obviously, they still were.

"I'm not surfing porn." He didn't realize he could do that, but now that she brought it up . . .

Where would he go to find it? He hadn't had the computer long. Only a little more than a week. He wouldn't have even known they existed but for one of the slug demons who'd mentioned it while he'd been questioning Solin.

Once he got back to his room, he'd manifested one and it'd taken him awhile to figure out how to use his powers to make it connect to the human world.

The rest of it, though . . .

Some special kind of sadistic demon must have invented this damn thing.

But Lydia seemed to know how to work it. "Do you . . ."

Don't ask. Don't do it.

She arched a brow at him. "What?"

He hesitated. He'd stopped asking others for help a long time ago. Either he was ignored, or humiliated over it. It was a no-win situation for him.

And he'd been kicked in his teeth and insulted enough for one day. "Never mind."

A knowing light sparkled in her eyes. His cock jerked at that playful expression.

"You want me to help you, don't you?"

Yes. But he'd never admit that. "I can figure it out on my own."

She tsked at him. "It doesn't make you weak to ask for help when you need it. Rather, it's a strong man who knows and acknowledges his limitations."

And it was a fool who exposed himself to ridicule. "Do you mind? I need to concentrate." He turned away from her.

Lydia wanted desperately to tell him where to

shove that laptop. But the almost boyish shyness about him kept her from being hostile.

He'd started to reach out to her and then something had made him pull back.

Something? *Hell, girl, you've seen his body.* It wasn't an intangible thing that reeled him in. It was years of abuse that had taught him to stay inside himself.

There came a point in everyone's life when they'd been slapped too many times for reaching out. After a few concussions, they stopped doing it. She understood that better than most.

"Guardian?"

A tic started in his jaw as he turned toward her with a scowl so fearsomely evil, she wondered if it was one he'd practiced in a mirror to scare the other demons of this place.

Good thing she didn't scare easily.

Instead, she smiled at him. "Computers are extremely annoying and hard to operate if you're not used to them. Sometimes even if you are. If you'll let me go, I don't mind helping you do whatever it is you're trying to do." She jiggled the chain expectantly.

Seth didn't move for a full minute as he debated with himself. It was safer for his sanity when she stayed away from him.

Who are you fooling? She might as well be on top of you, the way you react to every breath she takes, even when it's across the room.

And he needed to get this done. His time was running fast through an hourglass he couldn't stop or break. Noir wouldn't give him any kind of extension and he knew it.

Steeling himself, he nodded.

Lydia finally breathed again as her chain vanished instantly. Whoa . . . those were some scary powers he had and she still didn't know the full extent of them.

Trying not to think about it, she got up and went to his desk.

He moved out of his seat and offered it to her.

Cracking her knuckles, she sat down, then hesitated as she reached for the laptop. "This thing isn't going to eat my fingers is it?"

"Pardon?"

"I tried to use it earlier and it slammed shut on me. It almost took a couple of my phalanges with it."

Something twitched at the side of his mouth that might have become a smile had he allowed it. "No, it won't hurt you."

Still a little skeptical, she carefully pulled it over to her. But he was right. It wasn't hungry anymore and she was able to type in safety.

She looked up, and saw another new lumpy bruise on his temple that wasn't visible until you got close to him. Her stomach clenched. Knowing he would never talk to her about it, she focused on what they were doing. "Okay, what do you want to know?"

He took a step away from her. "I need to learn more about the key to Olympus."

Okay. She had no idea why and had never heard the term before. But then there were a lot of things she didn't know about her native culture. Solin had raised her in other parts of Europe. For reasons he wouldn't name, he kept her away from her heritage. While he'd schooled her on the gods and her Were-Hunter branch, he'd always been insistent that she never try to contact them.

And since she hadn't interacted with others of her kind after her family had died . . .

She was pretty ignorant of anything other than the major facts.

"Did you Google it?" she asked him.

He frowned. "Google?"

"Yeah, Google. You know, *the* search engine."

He sniffed and jerked his head as if he'd had a pain shoot through his nose. Then he placed the heel of his hand over his left eye and held it there. "What's a search engine?"

"Are you okay?" Even though he didn't complain, she had a sneaking suspicion that he was really hurting right now.

"It'll go away in a minute." He lowered his hand and blinked his eye open.

Lydia gasped as she saw that the entire white of his eye was now completely red. Blood red. "Oh my God. Does that hurt?"

Seth had no answer to her question. Every part

of him currently hurt. Especially his inflamed cock that kept begging him to take her regardless of her protests.

But he wasn't that much of an animal. Having been raped on several occasions, he wasn't about to do that to anyone else. For that matter, he couldn't even remember the last time he'd had sex that hadn't raped either his body or his soul.

As she'd noted earlier, after age thirteen, he'd never known a touch that wasn't angry or bruising.

Not until her . . .

She reached up to touch him.

For an instant, he was frozen by the desperate need he had to feel her skin on his.

Don't. All it will do is remind you of things you can never have.

She belonged to Solin. Not him.

He quickly moved away.

But she didn't take the hint. Instead, she pursued him across the room.

What the hell? Every time he moved, she was there, trying to touch his injured eye. He didn't even want to know how stupid he must look while he dodged her.

"Stop!" he finally snarled.

She pulled back as if he'd slapped her and that made him feel like a total ass. "I just wanted to help you."

"Help me do what?" Die of unsated lust? That was his biggest threat in the room at present.

She shook her head. "Your eye is completely red. It's like it's filled with blood."

That explained the haze over his vision, but the pain he felt was from his eye socket where Noir had punched the shit out of him after Seth had given in to the incessant need to question Noir's parentage. "I must have broken a blood vessel. It happens."

Lydia felt sick about the nonchalant way he spoke of something so horrible. Broken blood vessels didn't just happen. Anymore than his bruises had just appeared on his face. She took a step toward him.

He took one back.

Fine. He wasn't going to allow her near him again. And to think, she'd actually been afraid of him forcing himself on her. Yeah . . .

"You still haven't told me what a search engine is." He licked, then sucked at his busted lip right before he ran his hand across it.

How could something so ferocious look so vulnerable and uncertain? These small glimpses of the real him were actually sweet. And even worse, they were charming her a lot more than she was charming him.

"You really don't know what it is? I mean, I realize you live in . . ." she glanced around the dreary room. "Or rather under a rock, but you do have a computer."

"I haven't had it long and I didn't figure out how to make it connect to the human world until about an hour before you arrived. And you know how little time I've had to work it since then."

That explained a lot. And yet . . . "You had one before this, right?"

He shook his head. "I'd never heard of one until a demon told me about them. He said it would help me learn things quicker. But I honestly don't see how. Books are much faster to navigate. I figured out how to open up one of those the instant I touched it. It took two days just to find the on switch for that damn thing."

His words stunned her. Had he honestly made a joke? She laughed, hoping it didn't offend him.

Seth froze at the sweetest sound he'd ever heard. A true and sincere laugh. And it wasn't at his expense.

No one had laughed like that around him in . . .

He had no idea. Had he ever heard laughter that wasn't mocking or cruel? If he did, he had no memory of it. Nor had he seen anyone's eyes light up like hers did.

She was so beautiful that it took his breath away. Worse, it drew him toward her when he knew he should be running for the door.

His lips twitched as if they wanted to smile, but that, too, was something he had no memory of. Surely he'd smiled as a child? Hadn't he?

Why couldn't he remember?

She pressed her lips together and sobered. "Sorry."

Her apology confused him even more than her

laughter had. It, too, was something he couldn't remember hearing from anyone. Ever. "For what?"

"I don't know. You looked upset. I wasn't laughing at you, I swear."

"I know."

Lydia felt suddenly very awkward. Even though he had an extremely expressive face, she had a hard time reading it. And he never reacted the way she thought he would. Things that should make him happy made him angry and things she thought would offend him, didn't.

She offered him a smile. "If it makes you feel better, you're not alone with that thought. Computers make fools of us all. But I have to say that I'm highly impressed."

"By what?"

"You got it up and running when you'd never seen one before? That's impressive. I have to call the Geek Squad every time I buy a new one and I've had one for years."

Again with the dancing, indecipherable emotions on his face. Finally, he settled on a stricken look that she didn't understand the source of. "Did you just compliment me?"

She widened her eyes as she debated how to answer. Was he offended that she'd complimented him? It was how he acted. But that made no sense whatsoever.

"Um . . . yes."

This time there was no mistaking the fury in those accusatory blue eyes. "You mock me."

"How?" She was completely baffled by his behavior and attack. "By saying I think you're intelligent?"

His breathing turned ragged as fury darkened his gaze. "I'm well aware of my flaws. *All* of them. The last thing I need or want is *you* patronizing me for it."

What had they done to him that he couldn't even take a well-meant compliment? It broke her heart that she'd hurt him with an innocent comment that she'd intended to make him feel good. "I wasn't patronizing you. I promise. It was my honest opinion."

Still, the angry doubt lingered in his eyes.

"I'm sorry," she said again, then returned to his desk. "I really wasn't trying to offend or anger you."

Seth hated himself for stealing her happiness. Had she really meant that as she'd said? Was it possible she thought him intelligent?

Why would she? No one else ever had. He knew he was slow to learn. He'd always been stubborn that way. It was why it'd taken him so long to understand that machine. Why he still couldn't get it to work.

It was why Noir beat on him all the time. He could never learn to counsel his tongue or keep his eyes down. Never learn when to shut up and not speak. Only an absolute idiot would keep confronting someone he knew was going to hurt him.

Subdued and wary, he joined her at the desk and watched as she opened things he couldn't read or understand. "What are you doing now?"

"Well, I was looking for your bookmarks."

"But it's not a book."

She looked up at him with an irritated twitch in her eye. "You know, if I made that comment to you, especially in *that* tone of voice, you'd get all testy with me and stalk off." In a tiff, she turned back in her chair. "I'm well aware of the fact that it's not a book. Jeez!"

Seth took a minute to think about that. She was right. He'd been rude to her without meaning to. "I'm only trying to understand."

She was still pissed, but at least she explained it to him. "You bookmark favorite pages so that you can go back to them if you want."

"Like bookmarking a book."

She nodded. "Hence the term. But you don't have any."

"I know. I told you I had trouble setting it up and turning it on."

Lydia frowned at him. "Did you follow the instructions?" Not that it ever really helped her, but still . . .

"I couldn't."

"You didn't have a manual?"

"No. I didn't understand the language it was written in."

Her jaw went slack. He was illiterate? "But you

speak English flawlessly." Granted it was with a thick accent she'd never heard before, but she'd met natural-born speakers who were less fluent.

Some days even her.

"Yes. I can understand spoken languages easily. I just can't read them."

Good grief, he was even more intelligent than she'd guessed. How he could have gotten as far with a computer as he had without a manual or while he was unable to read the language was beyond her. "Did one of the demons help you?"

He shook his head.

"Did you ask one of them for help?"

"No. No one here really talks to me."

Surrounded by many, yet always alone. In that moment, he reminded her so much of Solin that it choked her. "Is that why you gave me a voice?"

His features turned to stone as that familiar anger sparked in his chilling gaze. "I don't need anyone to talk to me. Ever."

She had to force herself not to roll her eyes. At this point, she didn't think she'd ever get past his defenses when he was so determined to misread her every comment and intention. "It doesn't make you weak, you know? Everyone needs someone to confide in."

"I don't."

But she knew better. Even Solin, who didn't like people as a rule, did occasionally talk to them. He'd even learned to become friends with Arik, another Dream-Hunter he'd helped out a few years back.

However, those kind of changes only happened when the person who had the issues decided to move forward. The Guardian was nowhere near that level.

And who could blame him?

It was a wonder he was even sane. The fact that he had any form of compassion was nothing short of a miracle.

Sighing, she went back to the computer.

"What are you doing?" the Guardian asked.

"I'm typing in google.com so that we can get to the site that will allow us to search for your term."

He actually moved closer to her so that he could see better. "How do you know how to do all of this?"

"I spend ungodly amounts of time surfing."

He glanced at her. "You keep saying that word. What does it mean?" His enthusiastic curiosity reminded her of a little kid.

"We're surfing the Web right now. It's a term people use whenever they're online."

"Ah. So where do they surf to?"

She smiled at him. "Anywhere they want to go."

Surprise widened his eyes. "Anywhere?"

"Yeah. Name me something you'd like to see."

He fell silent for a few seconds as he pondered it, giving her time to realize that his eye was even redder than it'd been before.

Did it really not hurt?

He blinked twice, then met her gaze. "Can we see sunlight on it?"

"Sure." She did an image search.

The moment the photos displayed on the screen, his jaw went slack. Dropping to his knees, he reached for the laptop and reverently touched the first image of the sun shining through a set of clouds. "Does it still look like that?" He spoke as if he were whispering a prayer.

That sense of wonder in his voice and on his face brought tears to her eyes as she realized something else about him. "How long has it been since you last saw daylight?"

He refused to take his gaze off the images. "I don't know. A long time." His awed expression made her want to cry for him. She couldn't imagine being banned from daylight and the rest of the world.

"Can you show me more?"

"Sure." She leaned forward to take his hand.

He hissed as if she'd burned him, and jerked it out of her grasp.

"I was only going to show you how to navigate the browser. Don't you want to learn how to do this without me?"

Seth hesitated. No. He didn't want think of a time when she wouldn't be here to do this for him.

But he couldn't keep her and he knew it.

"Okay." He slowly held his hand out for her.

Lydia would have laughed had it not been so tragic that he was so reluctant for her touch. She brushed her hand over his bruised, swollen knuckles and laid his hand on the touchpad. The cuts there scraped her palm as she showed him how to use the pointer and click to get to what he wanted to see. There were vicious scars on his wrist that looked like someone had tried to cut off his hand.

What had they done to him?

She could feel every one of his tendons and muscles moving. More than that, she could smell the masculine scent of his skin and hair. Those two things combined were enough to make her salivate.

Even worse was the sudden desire she had to tease his earlobe with her tongue.

He'd probably hit the ceiling like a rocket if she tried. That thought made her laugh.

Until he grimaced at her. "What did I do wrong?"

"I wasn't laughing at you. It was just a silly thought I had that had nothing to do with the laptop."

"Oh."

Leaning back in the hard chair, she watched him explore every photo in great detail.

Her gaze went to the bruises on his face and the vicious dark blue handprint on his throat. Injuries that reminded her of where and how they'd met.

A part of her wanted to strike him over what he'd done to Solin. It'd been so cruel.

Worse, he would have killed Solin had she not been there to stop him. How could she have forgotten that?

Don't let him fool you. He's evil to the core of his being.

And yet, she'd seen more to him than just a soulless killer. Besides, she knew plenty of people who thought Solin was the epitome of darkness. Those who had tried their best to kill him. In turn, he'd killed others.

Things were never black-and-white. But rather varying shades of gray.

"Why did you torture Solin?"

He paused as a muscle began to thump a steady rhythm in his jaw. "Noir told me to."

"Do you do everything Noir tells you to do?"

He turned that cold gaze to her with a fury that terrified her. "I'm not weak," he growled between clenched teeth.

The horrendous scars all over his body testified to that. Those wounds would have killed anyone else. Or at least left them hiding in a hole somewhere. "I didn't say you were."

"You implied it."

Maybe. But . . . "I'm just trying to understand your role here. What does a Guardian do?"

The shame she'd seen earlier was again mirrored in his eyes. "I enforce Noir's laws."

"How so?"

"What do you think? I punish the ones who break them." He was arguing in circles and refusing to answer her question. She couldn't tell if it was deliberate or so ingrained in him that he couldn't help it.

"How do you decide what punishment to give them?"

"I don't."

Now she got it completely. "You do what Noir says."

He nodded slowly and it was obvious how much he hated what he was forced to do. It bled from every molecule of his body.

But that only confused her more. "As powerful as you are, why don't you leave this place?"

He clenched his teeth before he answered. "I can't leave any more than you can."

"You're a prisoner, too?"

"I'm his slave," he hissed with enough venom to bring down an elephant on PCP.

Oh. That changed things a lot. She didn't know how Noir kept him here, but it must be strong stuff. No wonder he was so miserable.

No wonder he'd wanted to see sunlight.

Lydia swallowed hard as pain for him moved deep inside her heart. He didn't deserve this.

No one did.

"If you return my powers to me, I can free you."

He curled his lip at her. "I know better. I fell for that lie once. I won't do it again."

"Fell for what lie?"

Seth moved away from her as he tried not to remember the last time someone had promised to free him. He'd upheld his part of the bargain, and . . .

No one would ever help him. No one. It was the one lesson he'd learned most while pinned in hell.

And it was a mistake he would never be so stupid as to repeat.

Not ever.

He was here to stay. Nothing could be done about that and all fighting did was get him hurt more. Every time he'd attempted to run, Noir had brought him back and made him regret it.

I'm through being stupid.

And that meant finding what Noir required before the bastard summoned him again. "I need information on the key. Show me how to search."

She sighed heavily. "Yes, Master." Her voice was strange and staccato as she said that. "Whatever it is you require." She narrowed her gaze on him, then returned to her regular voice. "You could say please once in a while, you know? It won't hurt you. Kindness never does."

He scoffed at that bullshit. "You're a naive fool if you believe that. Kindness destroys the one who gives it, every time."

"I'm not a demon."

"You don't have to be. Trust me."

Lydia hesitated in her typing as she caught the odd note in his voice. It gave her a sudden insight into him. "Has no one ever been kind to you?"

Seth didn't speak as he remembered the handful of years after he'd been saved from the desert. He'd been happy there for a time. His foster family had been kind.

Or so he thought.

But in the end, all that had done was make their betrayal even more cruel than his mother's and father's. At least to his memory his parents had never pretended to care for him. He'd always known where he stood with them.

It was the lies that had hurt the most.

No, it was the belief that his adoptive family had cared. That he'd meant something to them when he hadn't. How else could they have turned on him the way they had when all he'd ever done was love and cherish them? He'd always done his chores without being asked and without complaint. Not a day had gone by when he hadn't told them how grateful he was to have them in his life.

And for what purpose?

He had loved them and they had only used him for free labor. And in the end, they'd sold him like he was nothing but an unwanted piece of furniture.

Seth swallowed hard against the bitterness that was his constant companion. "Kindness is a lie and I don't want anything to do with it."

Her features indecipherable, she didn't speak as she ran his search. When she started clicking on things, he couldn't make them out.

"I don't understand what that is."

She read over the results for him. "Olympus is also a brand of camera. All of these hits have to do with it and not the mountain in Greece. What exactly are you after?"

"I don't know. Noir said it was something that

belonged to Solin. Something he can use to access Olympus and kill Zeus."

Lydia widened her eyes in shock. "You would make Noir even more powerful than he already is? Why?"

"Because when I tried to weaken him, it didn't go so well for me."

"What do you mean?"

Seth flinched as he saw Noir's face all those years ago when he'd discovered what Seth had done. It was not a moment he ever wanted repeated. "Nothing."

Lydia yearned to kick him for his blind stupidity where Noir was concerned. "Don't you understand what Noir will do if he regains his full powers?"

He cut a glare at her that seared her to her seat. "What I understand is what he'll do to me if I don't get him what he wants." He ran his hand under his chin where that ugly scar lay. "I have to have that key."

"And you don't care who you hurt to get it?"

"Why should I?"

She couldn't believe the honest sincerity behind that one question. "Because it's wrong. You don't hurt people."

"They hurt me."

"No. They don't. People are decent and—"

"Wretch!" A female screech echoed through his room, cutting Lydia's words off. "Here. Now!"

"Azura," he whispered. "I have to go."

He vanished instantly.

Lydia sighed in disgust. She couldn't believe she was trapped here. With him. But at least she wasn't being beaten.

Yet.

However, as she sat there, listening to a silence that was deafening, she had a bad feeling *that* wasn't going to last much longer.

Something horrible was coming for her.

She knew it.

CHAPTER 7

Lydia tapped her fingers against the Guardian's desk in total boredom, waiting for him to return.

You still have the laptop, you know.

Yes, yes, she did . . .

And with it, she could e-mail Solin! Why hadn't she thought of that earlier?

'Cause I'm an idiot. And honestly, she didn't want to get caught doing something that would get her hurt.

But . . .

He wasn't here right now.

Her heart pounding, she went to her gmail account and prayed she had enough time to finish before the Guardian returned.

Her fingers flew over the keys.

Solin,

I'm still here in Azmodea. I know you didn't abandon me by choice, but I need a way home. My powers are gone. I can't get them back by myself. I don't know how long the Guardian intends to keep me. For now, I'm safe and unharmed. Please tell me what you're planning.

Whatever you do, do not give him the key, whatever it is. I'm not worth it.

Love you always,

Dee.

He was the only one who'd ever called her that and it was her way of letting him know that e-mail was really coming from her. She hit the send button and held her breath until she was sure it'd gone through.

With any luck, he'd check his mail soon and get back to her.

Even though it hadn't been said explicitly, she had a really good idea that the Guardian was holding her until Solin handed that key over.

And to save her life and free her, Solin would. Without hesitation.

Please don't. Her life wasn't worth what would happen to the world should Noir tap the power of Zeus. Under no circumstances could that be allowed.

She reloaded her e-mail, hoping for a response.

For over an hour, she did that to no avail . . . until she felt the Guardian's return. There was no way to miss the change in the air whenever he was near. His powers were tangible.

As was that fierce presence.

But he didn't come into the bedroom. Rather he was in the shower.

At least she assumed he was the one running the water in there.

After logging out of her e-mail, she went to check for sure. 'Cause if it wasn't him, she was going to give someone a lot to regret.

She crept slowly toward the closed door, ready to bolt if it was another demon in there. Not sure if she should do this, she shouldered it open, then froze.

The Guardian's armor lay in a heap on the floor outside of the shower. A shower she hadn't realized earlier had a glass door.

Now she saw it.

And she saw him.

All of him.

The hot water slid over a magnificent body that rippled with chiseled muscles and sinewy grace. Oh yeah, baby. He'd make a fortune with a Web cam.

Holy cow . . . Not even the bruises and scars detracted from the absolute beauty of him.

Oh my word. I want a piece of that. Never in her life had she wanted to bite a heinie so badly.

Her throat went dry as a wave of desire burned through her blood like lava. Unaware of her presence, he scrubbed at himself with such vigor that she was surprised he didn't remove skin with it.

He turned slightly to get more soap, then froze as he caught sight of her.

Time hung still as they stared at each other

through the glass and steam. Her eyes widened the instant his cock began to swell.

"Sorry!" she shouted before she jumped back through the door and slammed it shut.

Oh good grief! She was mortified at being caught . . .

Seth still didn't move. He couldn't get the sight of Lydia standing there out of his mind. Why had she watched him?

How long had she watched him?

Did it matter?

Sighing, he returned to bathing. It stunned him that he could get hard again, given what Azura had just put him through. But all he had to do was think of Lydia and his body reacted against his will.

Damn treacherous beast.

He turned the water off and summoned his loose black pants and a loose, long-sleeved black shirt. He'd never liked showing off any part of his body. Not after what had been done to him.

Grabbing a towel off the bar, he considered putting his makeup back on, but why bother? She'd already seen his real face and hair.

And hopefully both Noir and Azura were through with him for at least a day.

I just want a some peace. If only it was possible.

He rubbed the towel against his wet hair as he opened the door to find Lydia, still red-faced, sitting in his chair. "Did you need something?"

She shook her head, refusing to look at him.

It was just as well. "Is there anything I can get you?"

"Besides my powers?" The sass in her tone caught him off guard.

She was ever persistent. Not that he blamed her. "Yes, besides your powers."

"I'm good. Really, really good."

But he wasn't. He wanted to walk over to her and brush his hand through her dark hair to feel its softness again. More than that, he wanted to bury his face in the hollow of her throat and inhale her scent until he was dizzy with pleasure.

He'd also want to kiss her again if her kisses weren't as violent and painful as everyone else's. Between Azura's mouth and Noir's fist, his lips were always burning and aching. And when it came to a she-demon . . .

Yeah. At least Lydia's bite hadn't left a scar.

It made him wonder if she bit Solin like that whenever she kissed him.

And for some reason, the thought of her with the dream god made his blood boil. He had no idea why. She was Solin's, after all.

But he didn't like it. Not one bit.

Lydia swallowed as she felt him draw near her. Every molecule of her body perked up, aching for her to reach out and rub herself against that long, hard body.

She glanced up, hoping his war paint would settle

her desire, and remind her of who and what he was. But when she met those light blue eyes set into an unbelievably handsome face that was framed with thick, unruly spiral curls, she melted even more. Until then, she hadn't realized how young he was in appearance. He didn't look any older than his mid-twenties. Actually, if not for his whiskers and the sprinkling of hairs on his chest, and the cut definition of his muscles, he'd probably look even younger.

And how much more handsome would he be without the bruises and cuts on his cheeks and lips? Without his jaw swollen and the broken blood vessels in his eye?

Her heart aching for his pain, she dropped her gaze to the swallow's tail and wing tip that peeked out from beneath his shirt. "Does that have any special meaning?"

In response to her question, he began clawing at it as if he wanted to scrape it off. "No."

"Then why did you—"

"I don't want to talk about it."

He moved the towel to cover the tattoo, and it was then she saw the additional bite marks on the other side of his neck and along the underside of his jaw. Two of them were over what appeared to be really bad hickeys. She also realized his lips were more swollen than before, and the upper one was bleeding again. And when he brushed his hand through his thick hair, there were bleeding finger-nail marks on the back of his neck.

"Are you all right?"

He nodded, but didn't speak as he paused by her side. That familiar scowl returned to his beautiful features. "What is that noise?"

She listened carefully, but didn't hear anything out of the ordinary. "What noise?"

He pulled the laptop closer so that he could bend over and place his ear near it.

She laughed as she realized what he'd heard. "You mean the song?" She'd turned it low when she came back after the shower fiasco.

A light that could almost be called joy shone in his eyes. "You have music?"

"Yeah. I downloaded some while you were gone." She turned it up for him.

He didn't smile with his lips, but his eyes did. She'd never seen him look like that. Like a poor kid at Christmas who'd received everything on his list. "I've never heard anything like this."

"It's OneRepublic. 'Come Home,' from their album *Dreaming Out Loud.*"

"I swear I only understand about half of what you say."

She smiled at him. "I get that from a lot of people." She watched as he closed his eyes and listened to the lyrics of one of her favorite songs. He was so close now that her hand itched to touch those dark red curls and feel them wrap around her fingers.

But she knew he wouldn't approve. Nor would he let her.

Frowning while he explored her playlist, she couldn't get past the harsh bruise on his cheek and the sight of his abused lips. Against all sanity, she wanted to get him away from this place. To show him that the world wasn't what he thought it to be.

That he could be happy.

She was desperate to teach him to smile and to laugh. To give him real sunlight. Not some flat picture whose only warmth came from the electrical charge of a power cord.

Most of all, she wanted to protect him—like that made any sense given the size of him compared to her. He was so powerful and strong, and yet vulnerable in a way she'd never dreamed possible.

He actually jumped in startled alarm when the next song, Sevendust's "Never," started playing.

"Sorry about that. I should have warned you. That one's a little heavy." She reached to turn it down, but he stopped her.

"I like it."

She barely understood his words. Her attention was focused on how good his rough hand felt against her skin. And how much she'd like to feel his touch somewhere else on her body.

Seth recognized the lust in her gaze as she stared at his lips. He ached to taste her again.

But he was in enough pain for one day. The last thing he wanted right now was to have his back clawed again. Or his lips ripped open.

If only he could convince his body of that. It

still wanted a piece of her even if it meant being ravaged.

I am such a sick bastard.

Suddenly, she opened her mouth and yawned. Then she yawned again. "Goodness. I'm so sorry. I didn't sleep well last night."

"I understand." He moved away from her. "You may take the bed. I won't bother you in it."

"What about you?"

What about him? A thousand years of torture had ruined his ability to close his eyes for any length of time. "I don't sleep much."

"Why not?"

Because he didn't like being weak. Sleep left him open to attacks from creatures other than Noir and Azura. Cowards who would only come out when they thought they were safe. He despised them most of all.

She waited expectantly for his reply.

Instead, he conjured her a warm nightgown and held it out to her. "Here, woman."

Lydia was touched by his gift. Mostly because she knew how rare it was for him to do this. "Thank you. And by the way . . . my name is Lydia. Not woman."

He nodded and stepped away from her. "Sleep in peace, Lydia."

She felt a knot in her stomach at the sound of her name on his lips. With his accent, it sounded more like Lah-deeah. And all she wanted to do was rise up on her toes and kiss him.

If only she could.

Taking the white cotton gown, she went to the bathroom to change.

When she came out again, he'd dusted off his bed and turned the covers down for her. For a man who didn't believe in any sort of kindness, he certainly was showing a lot to her.

But that just made it all the more special. Such things didn't come naturally for him. He had to make an effort to think of them.

As she walked past his desk and went to the bed, he glanced askance at her, but made no comment. He was still playing her music while he looked at more pictures of sunlight.

Her poor demon. Soon she would be gone from here, back home. And he would be . . .

She choked back a sob at the thought of them torturing him. "Good night, Guardian."

"Good night," he said without looking at her.

She slid beneath the covers and tucked her arm underneath the pillow so that she could watch him. As promised, he didn't disturb her at all. He was too consumed by his small window that showed him a world he couldn't visit.

Blinking, she wanted to stay awake for a little while longer, but she'd been through too much for that. All too soon, she was adrift in her other realm.

Seth knew the moment Lydia was asleep. Her breathing leveled out and her body went completely limp.

Only then did he dare look at her. One hand dangled over the side of the bed while her black hair spread out over her and the pillow. But the cutest part was her toe that peeped out from beneath his furs.

I hope Solin knows what he has in you.

Obviously, he did. Why else would he have fought so desperately to save her?

A part of him wished that Solin would fail. If he didn't return with the key, Seth could keep her.

But for how long? Sooner or later, Noir or Azura would find her here and when they did . . .

He couldn't even think about what they'd do to her for being here, and to him for concealing her presence from them.

No, Lydia would have to go home. And his life would go on as it ever had. He winced as he accidentally brushed his tongue over his damaged bottom lip.

Nothing ever changed. He'd had his one shot at freedom and look what had happened.

Still . . .

Heartsick, he got up and went to the bed so that he could stare down at her angelic features. Before he could stop himself, he leaned over and placed his cheek against hers. The softness of her flesh made him hard and aching for something he knew he could never have. He inhaled her exquisite scent, treasuring it above all.

"My name is Seth," he whispered in her ear,

knowing she couldn't hear him. Even so, he wanted her to know.

He'd kill to hear her say it.

Just once.

Breathing her in, he placed a kiss to her cheek, then pulled back.

He finally understood why Solin was willing to die for her. It now made total sense now. Beauty and spirit like hers should be cherished and protected. And he hoped that nothing ever tarnished their loyalty to each other. That would be the greatest tragedy of all.

I won't spoil her for you, Solin. No one deserved to know that pain.

Seth returned to his desk and turned the music off. He didn't want to see or hear anything else he couldn't have. There was no need in torturing himself when he had so many others willing to do it for him.

Solin looked around at the faces of the men and women who'd once been his bitterest enemies. Now they were joined together to fight a common enemy, again.

They'd done it one time before, when his brother Arik had been under attack. But that was years ago and now the consequences were even higher.

His clutched his hand around his iPhone, grateful Lydia had written to him. But there was no way he would leave her there.

Not with that animal.

However, getting into Azmodea was proving extremely tricky. They had an emergency call in to the Hellchaser overlord, Thorn. If anyone could sneak them in under Noir's nose, it was the entity who shared that realm with him.

While Thorn wasn't the most reliable or kindest of creatures, he did hate Noir as much as they did.

Solin had no doubt that Thorn would help and back them.

Hang on, baby. The cavalry's coming.

And his first order of business was to pin the Guardian's testicles to Noir's forehead.

CHAPTER 8

Lydia woke up with the strangest sensation. Never in her life had she not dreamt. But not a single dream had come to her last night. When the Guardian had said he'd stripped her powers, he wasn't kidding.

He didn't even know she had that one.

Did he?

Stretching, she rolled over to find him at his desk where he'd been when she fell asleep. Still dressed in his loose black clothes, he'd pulled his chair around so that he faced the bed and his back was to the wall. But he wasn't paying her any attention.

Instead, he held an old-fashioned leather-bound book in his lap with one large, graceful, masculine hand. He leaned back in the chair with his arm propped on the desk and his undamaged cheek resting on his fist. His insanely long legs were stretched out before him, and crossed at the ankles. She smiled at the unexpected sight of his well-shaped bare feet.

They were so cute and she'd never thought that about feet before. Normally, they grossed her out.

How strange that the sight of them succeeded in making him seem like any man, anywhere.

Well, not *any* man. Men this handsome were few and far between. Men this good-looking and ripped were even rarer. And finding one with his body, hair, and eyes was like finding a unicorn. In fact, she'd never seen a man with red hair who wasn't freckled or pale-skinned—not that there was anything wrong with that. It was just what you expected whenever you met a natural redhead, male or female. But there wasn't a single freckle anywhere on his body and even though he hadn't seen daylight in who knew how long, his skin was tanned and tawny.

Gah, even bruised and scarred, he made her mouth water.

How could that pose be so incredibly sexy? So lickably luscious?

With the one hand he had on the book, he turned the page without looking up.

She smiled at the sight of all those unruly auburn curls. Shirley Temple had nothing on him. And yet they still managed to be unbelievably masculine. More than that, she really, really wanted to play with them.

And as she studied his features, she noted that the bruise around his blood-filled eye had turned an ugly shade of dark purple. He had another new bruise on his ear that had been bleeding the night before. The handprint was also more pronounced today, as were the swollen, fresh bite marks on his neck.

She wanted to weep at the sight of them. Yet there he sat, so used to them that he didn't even comment on the pain they had to be causing him.

I'm so sorry I stabbed you. He was so not what she'd thought him to be when they first met. How could she have misjudged him so?

But then it wasn't entirely her fault. In spite of the legion of beatings and insults he'd endured, he carried himself as fiercely and confidently as any warrior or king. He exuded so much power and authority that no one would ever suspect he was Noir's punching bag and, from what she'd seen last night, most likely Azura's bootie call boy-toy.

But then maybe that was his shield. His way of not letting other people know his shame.

It kept them at arm's length, and in this hellacious place, it probably kept others from hurting him, too. That thought made her want to wrap her arms around him and hold him close.

If only he'd let her.

Clearing her throat, she finally spoke. "Did you not sleep at all?"

He shook his head, but didn't elaborate. "Are you hungry?"

"Not yet. I need to be awake for a few before I eat." Sitting up, she frowned at the closed laptop. "You stopped researching?"

"There was nothing to be found and I got tired of trying to decipher a writing form that makes no sense to me."

But he'd been so happy when she'd gone to bed . . . at least she thought it was happy, looking at all the pictures and listening to her music. Now he was back to that solemnity that seemed to be hardwired into his DNA.

She slid off the bed and went to see what he was reading, but she couldn't understand *his* alphabet. It definitely wasn't Egyptian, but it kind of looked like it. "What is that?"

"Bilgames."

Whoa . . . that was a new one on her. "What people spoke Bilgames?"

He frowned. "I don't understand."

Well, at least she wasn't the only one in the room lost. "What kind of language is Bilgames? Where does it come from?"

"It's not a language. It's the name of the story." Then his features relaxed as if a thought had occurred to him. "I think your people know it as Gilgamesh."

"Oh . . ." Now she knew how he'd felt last night when she kept using computer jargon. She had half the puzzle. But the other half was even more intriguing. "What language is it written in?"

"Akkadian."

Holy snikes. She was floored by his disclosure. She didn't know much about history, but she was extremely old and that predated her living knowledge . . . In fact, she'd barely heard of it, it was so old. "And you can read that?"

His eyes snapped fire at her. "I'm not *that* stupid, nor am I illiterate."

"Obviously not. No one who can read something that complicated in an alphabet that is basically scribbled nonsensical lines could ever be called stupid."

That seemed to soothe him. "It's not that hard."

"For *you*. If you're as lost looking at my alphabet as I am with this one . . . it says a lot." She continued to study it, but it was like trying to read Braille. "So are you Akkadian?"

"Egyptian."

"Really? You don't look Egyptian."

He arched his brow at that comment. "Been there a lot have you?"

"Well . . . no. But I've seen pictures. They're usually dark-skinned and certainly not redheaded."

"Shows what you know. We traded extensively with many nations and had people who came to live in Upper Egypt from all over the known kingdoms."

"You're feisty in the morning, aren't you?" she teased. But it did explain why his skin tone was so dark, given his blue eyes and red hair. "So you can read hieroglyphics then?"

"Of course."

"I bet you're a hoot in a museum. Have you ever

walked past a mummy, looked down, and said, hey Uncle Imhotep, how you doing?"

He didn't show even a glimmer of amusement. "A museum?"

That was what he fixated on? "Never mind. What other creepy old languages do you read?"

"Greek and Sumerian."

"What about Latin?"

He frowned. "What's Latin?"

Her stomach lurched. Did he predate Rome? That was probably the most terrifying thought imaginable. Because if he did, he'd been locked away here for more than three thousand years. "You know Rome, right?"

"No. I was never allowed to roam. It's forbidden."

"Not roam around. The Roman Empire. You know, Nero, Octavian, Caesar, other people with funky names . . ." Names she should have paid more attention to in school. "That giant fearsome empire that conquered the world and subjugated everyone, even Egypt."

"I've never heard of this place you describe."

Yeah, he was older than dirt. She'd ask him what year he was born, but that would be worthless. His calendar, if they even had had one then, wouldn't be the same as hers.

And he'd been under Noir's fist all that time.

Damn.

She frowned as another random thought hit her . . . did they have books then?

Surely not. But then . . . She studied the brittle pages and the worn leather binding.

"So how did you get a book written in a language that old?"

His mood turned dark as an air of profound sadness engulfed him. "Noir used to give them to me whenever I pleased him."

Desperately, she wanted him to elaborate on what pleasing Noir entailed, but her animal senses told her not to pursue it. Whatever it meant, it was obvious it caused him a tremendous amount of pain to think about.

Noir must have bound the original scrolls into books. That would make sense.

"Is this the only one you have?"

He shook his head. "I managed to save five of them."

"What do you mean?"

"Noir also destroyed them whenever I made him angry, which has always been a lot. I hid as many as I could, but he eventually found all but the five."

"That bloody wanker bastard." The profanity flew out of her mouth before she could stop it. But honestly, it infuriated her that he would destroy something so priceless. And take from her demon the only thing that had most likely ever given him any kind of pleasure in this hellhole of an existence.

Seth was stunned by her outburst. The fact that she was angered over what had been done to him . . .

No one had ever cared before.

She's faking. Don't be stupid.

But it didn't feel like that. It felt . . . real.

She cleared her throat as her face flamed bright red. "I'm so sorry."

That confused him even more than her outburst. Anger he always understood. But her incessant need to say that one word all the time . . . "You apologize a lot and for things you haven't done. Why?"

"I'm not apologizing because I did something. It's a conveyance of emotion that means I hurt *for* you or with you."

He still didn't get it. "Why would you ever hurt for me when I'm nothing to you?"

"Because that's what people do. They sympathize with others and try to help them."

If he were capable of it, he'd laugh at the absurdity. "Obviously you haven't met the same people I have. I've never known anyone like you describe."

"I'm not talking about demons. I'm talking about humans."

"And they are even worse. You expect cruelty from demons. They're open with their treachery and make no attempt to conceal it. Humans . . . they lure you in, and just when you make the mistake of believing in them, in trusting the lies they spew with conviction, they stomp all over you."

Lydia's head spun at the heated emotion in his voice. What had been done to him? "No one ever helped you? Really?"

"No."

"Not once? Ever?"

"If they did, I paid for it eventually with my flesh, bone, and my blood. So no, I don't count that as help. It's even crueler than doing nothing. Trust me."

She would give him that. But man . . .

In that moment, she was even more grateful for Solin. Without him, this would have most likely been her fate. "I wish I could make it better for you."

"Make what better?"

"Your life. Your memories. My past isn't perfect and I've had people who have hurt me. Bad at times. But not like you describe. Not to the point that they poisoned my very soul. For that, I'm sorriest of all."

Nothing would ever ease the pain of his past, she realized. He was as broken as anyone she'd ever met. And who could blame him? Noir's cruelty would make anyone insane.

Seth swallowed at the sincerity he saw in her eyes. A part of him was desperate to trust her. If only he could. But a lifetime of betrayal stood between them.

They'd only just met. And she was his prisoner. Like him, she would say or do anything to escape.

Even sell her soul. So what would a few well-placed lies and some tender looks mean if it achieved her goal? How could he ever trust someone in her position?

Only a fool would do it. And he was anything but.

She reached out and touched the edge of his book. "So is this what you do for entertainment?"

"It is."

She bit her lip as she thought it over, then a wicked light gleamed in her topaz gaze. "Haven't you ever wanted to bust loose and do something wild and different?"

"Like what?"

"I don't know. What's outside this room?"

Hell. Misery. Blood-soaked walls. Statues that would come alive and try to eat your eyes. Demons who would attack for no reason. Not to mention two assholes known as Azura and Noir.

Maybe he should tell her that, but in the end he went with a more vague answer. "Nothing worth seeing."

"Really?"

"Really. Azmodea is vast with several realms in it, but none of them are worth the danger it takes to explore them. May your gods take mercy on you if you get caught by some of the roaming demons who do nothing but scout victims. And even worse than that, some of the other realms are ruled by beings who make Azura and Noir look like pacificists in comparison. If they should ever lay hands on you . . . it's not pretty."

Lydia nodded. By his tone and the way he unconsciously rubbed at his thigh as if reliving some pain, she could tell he had firsthand experience with that.

"So you just sit here in this room and read, then?"

"When they allow me to, yes."

She couldn't imagine a more boring way to live, especially since he only had five books to keep him company. "No offense, that's kind of pathetic, don't you think?"

His eyes turned brittle as he went ramrod stiff. "I don't care for that word."

Given his tone and the I-want-to-rip-out-your-spine vibes he was bashing her in the head with, that was an understatement and then some. She definitely wanted to know which word he objected to so she didn't say it again. "Kind?"

"Pathetic," he spat it out with enough venom to adequately get his point across.

"All right then. I'll take it out of my vocabulary."

Closing the book, he set it aside. He stood up and hesitated as if he was still struggling to get his temper under control. When he spoke again, there was an undercurrent of residual anger. "I put some clothes for you in the bathroom."

"Thank you."

That seemed to embarrass him, but at least it knocked the last remnants of anger out of him. "If you need anything else, let me know."

"Okay."

She went to the bathroom, where she learned that he'd left her a whole wardrobe. Silk dresses, silk and cotton blouses, along with jeans and shoes.

When she got to the underwear, she couldn't suppress a laugh at his choice. Red thongs. Why didn't that surprise her?

Because he was a man after all. Even though he refused to touch her, this was the kind of underwear a guy would buy a woman he wanted to see wearing it. There was no other reason for it to have even been invented. And she was sure the original designer of it must have been a direct descendant of the Marquis de Sade.

Gah, it's like wearing a perpetual wedgie.

And the bras . . .

They matched, but offered her no support whatsoever. Yep, the headlights would be on and shining, and she'd jiggle like Jell-O every time she moved. Still, she was amazed he'd thought of them. And by the looks of it, he'd given it a lot of thought, too.

She went to the shower and turned it on, then noticed that the clothes weren't the only additions he'd made. There was now a variety of shampoos, conditioners, and other toiletries for her.

So her demon could be extremely thoughtful and giving. Who would have ever thought?

Shaking her head, she removed her gown and stepped inside.

*   *   *

Seth's heart pounded at the sound of the shower running. She'd be in there naked . . .

He didn't know why he wanted to see her like that, but he did. In the worst sort of way. More than that, he ached to shower with her.

Why?

Sex was good, but the pleasure never lasted long and it was usually tainted with biting, vicious hair-pulling, and clawing, sometimes even stabbing and gouging. After a quick momentary release and a glimmer of perfect pleasure, the old pains set in, and he was told to leave.

Needless to say, he'd never really craved it all that much—at least not when he had access to it. During his confinement, it'd been yet another thing his mind and body had tortured him with.

But with Lydia, it was never far from his thoughts. At times it seemed to be all he could think about.

No, *she* was all he could think about. It was why he didn't ask her many questions. He didn't want to know her any better. What he already knew of her would haunt him for the rest of his immortality.

He needed no more pain in his life.

Trying to distract himself, he went to the bed to straighten it up. But the moment he touched his pillow, a whiff of her sent a stabbing pain straight to his groin, and it made him instantly hard for her.

What he wouldn't give to have her precious scent on his skin. To have her rub her body across his and tease him with her dark hair.

His breathing ragged, he closed his eyes and imagined himself deep inside her, while her breath tickled his skin.

Was she a biter like Azura, or would she claw at him like a demon? At this point, he didn't care. He'd be willing to be flayed for a week if he could only taste her.

He pressed his hand against his groin and gently rubbed it, wishing it was her he felt there. Just the mere thought of it being Lydia was almost enough to make him come.

Stop it. Now. The last thing he needed was to leave evidence of his desire for her to see.

It would shame him to the bitter core.

His hand trembling, he smoothed her pillow down, then dressed himself in his armor and paint before he returned to reading.

The moment he finally succeeded in putting her out of his thoughts was the one when she opened the door.

He glanced up, then dropped his book straight to the floor.

CHAPTER 9

Seth stared at Lydia in a state of complete and utter shock as the sight of her sent fire burning through every part of his body. And that heat concentrated itself right in his groin. *Why did I give her that one? Why did she have to choose it?*

A low-cut, rust-colored dress, it hugged her curves in a way that should be illegal. More than that, the color heightened the gold in her eyes, making them all the more vibrant.

As if she needed that.

His cock swelled against the metal plates to the point it caused him pain. Vicious, biting pain. But not even that was enough to distract him from the deep V that showed the swell of her breasts. Breasts with nipples that were tight and jutting through the silken material. He could see every outline of them. His throat went dry even as his mouth salivated for a taste.

He rose to his feet.

Lydia hesitated as she felt the weight of his icy

stare on every part of her. The way he looked at her . . .

It was terrifying.

"Did I do something wrong?"

When he didn't answer right away, she really started to panic.

Finally, after an extremely long minute, he blinked. "No, not at all." He picked his book up and returned it to the desk. "I . . . um . . . I saw those on the computer last night. I wasn't sure if they were right or not."

"I don't know how you did it, but they all fit perfectly." As if they'd been tailored to her body. "Thank you."

Still, she hated that his makeup was back in place and his hair straightened out again with that small ponytail holding his bangs back out of his eyes.

She missed the kinder looking Guardian. The fearsome one was . . .

Well, scary as all get out. And as hard as it was to decipher his emotions without the makeup, it was ten times harder with those red and black lines that kept his face in a perpetual snarl.

With his mercurial mood swings, she didn't like being without those facial clues.

Completely stoic, he stepped away from the desk so that she could see he had a tray waiting for her. One with banana pancakes, muffins, eggs, bacon, and juice. Her stomach rumbled at the abundance.

"I hope all of this means you're planning to join me."

He shook his head.

Lydia sat down and reached for the empty plate. "Don't you ever eat?"

"Sometimes." There was a peculiar note in his voice that made her wary.

"You do consume food for nourishment, right?"

His eyes flashed angrily. "I don't eat babies or drink blood if that's what you're implying."

She held her hands up in surrender. "It didn't even cross my mind. Why are you so defensive about everything?"

That familiar tic started in his jaw. "I get tired of being accused of things that I'm not. Of doing things I haven't done."

She could understand that. No one liked being misjudged, though it might help if he looked a little less terrifying. "I'm not accusing you of anything. I was only curious about you. You don't eat. You don't sleep. How do you live?"

When he spoke, his voice was completely flat and empty. "I don't die."

His answer confused her. "Huh?"

He looked away as he paced the same path she'd worn out the first night she'd been here. "It's not that I live so much as it is I can't die. So it doesn't matter if I eat or sleep. My body will continue functioning without either."

"Were you born immortal?"

"Apparently. I certainly wouldn't have chosen this existence otherwise."

Yeah, she could believe that. Who would want to live here? Even for immortality. It wasn't worth it.

She, too, was immortal. A gift from her father. It was something she hadn't realized until she'd lived long after most Were-Hunters died.

And, like the Guardian, she'd never physically aged past her midtwenties. "When did you find out you were immortal?"

"When I was seven."

She poured syrup over her pancakes and savored the delectable scent. "What happened? Did you get sick or have an accident?"

The anguish in his eyes broke her heart. "I have to attend my duties. I shall return when I can. If you need me, just call and I will hear you."

Lydia sighed as he vanished. He was such a mystery to her. And his kindness belied the cruelty she knew he was capable of. She pulled the laptop over to her and turned it on to see if Solin had responded.

She smiled the moment she saw his e-mail in her inbox. He'd written to her in the Greek she'd learned as a child.

My most precious one,

I won't leave you there. Stay strong for me and I will free you just as soon as I can. I love you more than anything and I swear to you that I will come for you no matter what.

S.

She touched the words on the screen, grateful more than ever that she had him in her life. There was nothing she wouldn't do for him.

Soon she would be home again.

And the Guardian would still be trapped here . . .

Alone.

Seth stayed at his post, which was three steps behind Noir, as the ancient prick did his rounds with the prisoners Noir kept chained in the lowest pits of his golden castle. For now his master's attention was focused on their abuse and not his.

But how long would that last?

As if he heard the question, Noir glanced at him over his shoulder. "How goes your quest, maggot?"

"I'm close to having it, my lord. Of course it would be easier to find it if I could leave this realm, and—"

Noir ended his words with a vicious backhand. "You know better than to ask that of me."

Seth wiped the blood away that ran down his chin as he used his tongue to see if he'd lost any teeth from the blow. Though several were loosened, all remained.

And Lydia wanted to know why he didn't eat . . . It was hard to chew when his mouth and throat were forever damaged. Biting into anything, even something as soft and bland as a banana, hurt too much. Not to mention the juices and spices went straight into the cuts on his lips and into the tenderest part of his sore gums and throat—something that always set them to throbbing in the worst sort of way.

The unrelenting hunger and thirst pangs were so much easier to bear than any of that.

"Forgive me, Master."

Noir sneered at him. "There is no forgiveness for something as pathetic and stupid as you. No wonder your father refused to claim you. If I'd been your mother, I'd have left you to die, too."

Seth didn't speak as Noir continued to rail against him. It was a litany he'd heard so often that it played perpetually in his head even when Noir wasn't around.

But this time, he thought of Lydia in his bed and that image drove away the pain of Noir's words. The pain of his next blow.

Would she be reading right now? Or perhaps listening to her music while she . . . surfed, that was the word, the Internet?

He was so focused on the comfort of her, that he didn't see Noir stop at the door of one of the questioning chambers.

Noir grabbed him by the throat in a grip so fierce, it instantly dropped him to his knees. Seth knelt in front of him, wheezing through his damaged windpipe. His vision dimmed.

Don't lose consciousness. If he did, Noir might pull him into one of those rooms again.

Panic set his heart racing. He couldn't take another minute pinned to one of those tables. He couldn't.

"Are you paying attention to me, dog?"

Before he could answer, an alarm blared.

Noir let go, leaving him to gasp air back into his lungs.

"Summon my legion! We have intruders."

Coughing and still wheezing, Seth pushed himself up and disobeyed his master to go to his room, and make sure Lydia was safe from harm. He had a bad feeling about who was here and what they wanted.

Surely Solin wouldn't have been able to assemble an army so quickly. But what if he had?

He'd never see Lydia again. That thought hurt even more than Noir's beatings. Indeed, it felt as if someone was tearing his heart into pieces.

Seth shimmered in the corner and looked around.

She wasn't here.

No . . .

For the first time since he lay in the desert begging to die, he wanted to cry from the pain of it.

But after he'd materialized fully in the room, she ran out of the shadows with her breakfast knife held tight in her fist.

The rush of joy and relief in seeing her there overwhelmed him. Before he even realized what he was doing, he pulled her into his arms and held her close.

Lydia was absolutely stunned as she found herself crushed against those cold metal plates. The only person who'd ever held her like this was Solin.

As if she was the most precious thing in the world to him.

If she didn't know better, she would swear she felt the Guardian shaking while he held her. He had one hand cradling her head and the other arm wrapped so tight around her waist that she couldn't breathe.

She was so small next to him that her head only reached to the middle of his chest.

"You're . . . crushing . . . me." Her words came out in desperate gasps.

His hold tightened even more before he released her and stepped back. Panic radiated from his gaze as he bent down to inspect her for damage. "Are you all right?"

Whoa, that was actual concern.

From him.

"Uh, yeah. What's going on?"

He finally realized he was still touching her. The moment he did, he let go and moved back another step. "Someone's attacking us."

"Solin?"

"I don't know." He reached out to touch her face, then stopped his hand just before he made contact.

But before he could withdraw it, she took it into hers and held it tight. "Were you afraid he'd taken me?"

His brows lowered into one of his fiercest expressions. It was so dark and deadly that she thought he was angry at her—that he might actually damage her. "I was afraid you were hurt."

Seth had no idea why he let her know that. It was a weakness he shouldn't have. He shouldn't care whether she lived or died.

And yet . . .

He would do anything to keep her safe. He knew that now.

She wasn't a tool to be used against Solin.

Lydia was the woman who could be used to destroy *him*. He winced at the undeniable truth. *How could I have been so stupid?* Never had he cared about anyone or anything other than his books, and look at how Noir had tormented him over those.

The bastard had made him watch as he burned them in front of him and dared him to try and save them. Page by page, one by one. Noir took his only pleasure from making others suffer.

He would torture and kill Lydia and in turn, that would destroy him.

How would he be able to live if he knew he'd caused her harm? How?

Before he could gather his thoughts, the door he'd banished from his room reappeared to his left. He pulled Lydia behind him, then turned to face whoever was pounding against it.

An instant later it crashed open.

Lydia gasped as she saw the demons that were

spilling into the room. They definitely weren't Greek. She'd never seen anything like them in real life or in nightmares.

Suddenly, some unseen force pulled her back toward the bed and held her there as the Guardian attacked the demons.

She had a newfound respect for his prowess as she watched him battle them. They would get a wound in here or there, but he paid no attention to it as he cut them into pieces with his sword.

Dang, he was a great fighter. Probably one of the best she'd ever seen. How awful it had to be for a man so strong and skilled to be forced to subjugate himself to the cruel whims of Noir and Azura. She hadn't realized the true horror of his predicament until now.

To know you had the ability to fight like that and to be tortured the way he was . . .

How could he stand it?

He stabbed the last one through the heart, then turned toward her. The shield holding her fell and her high heels melted into a pair of running shoes. "Come, Lydia. It's not safe here anymore." To her complete shock, he held his hand out to her.

Hoping that wasn't a sign of the Apocalypse, she ran to him and took it.

He pulled her out into the hallway, where the sounds of fighting echoed loudly. An instant later, a full suit of armor covered her.

She looked up at the Guardian, who handed her a sword.

"Do you know how to use one of these?"

"Of course. Pointy end goes into the other guy, hopefully through the heart."

He inclined his head respectfully to her. She didn't miss the look in his eyes that said he half expected her to use it on him—like she'd done with her dagger the first time they met. The fact that he gave it to her when he didn't trust her said a lot.

"Who's attacking us?"

He sighed. "It looks like Thorn's people."

"Thorn?"

"He lives on the other side of the Divide. Normally he and Noir have a truce. But every now and again . . ." His voice trailed off as a winged demon swooped down at them.

Lydia caught the demon just as it went past, stabbing it through the heart.

The demon shrieked before it hit the ground behind her.

Without a single comment, the Guardian led her away from the fighting. She wasn't sure where they were heading until he opened a door and shoved her through it.

"What the hell?" a man growled in a tone so deadly, it startled her.

Her heart pounding in stark terror, she turned to see a tall dark-haired man on the other side of the room. He would have been every bit as handsome as the Guardian except for his eyes, which were so off-putting and unnerving they completely took him down several slots on the hotness scale. One was a vivid green while the other a deep, dark brown.

She shivered at the sight of them. And like the Guardian, the ferocity of his powers thrummed through the ether. She didn't know who he was or what he did here, but it was obvious he could eat her for lunch if he wanted to.

The Guardian locked the door and confronted the other man with his bloodied sword held out to his side. "You owe me, Jaden. Watch her and make sure she doesn't leave here."

Jaden laughed sarcastically. "Are you out of your freaking mind, Egyptian?"

The Guardian's nostrils flared. "It's the least you can do after what you did to me."

Whatever Jaden had done in the past caused him to wince. "I would ask if you have any idea what would happen to me if those assholes found her in my custody, but you know better than anyone the tab on that. Gods damn you for it."

"You're a little late, they already did." The Guardian glanced at her, then looked back at Jaden. "You're the only one here besides me who has the powers to protect her. Don't you dare betray me."

Jaden cocked his jaw as if he was considering betrayal after all. Or more to the point, putting the Guardian through a wall for daring to threaten him.

"It's pathetic when you and I have to become allies." He sighed in disgust. "My enemy's enemy, I guess . . . Fine, I'll watch her. But only because it's you. I wouldn't put my ass on the line for anyone else."

The Guardian inclined his head to him, then used an expression Lydia hadn't even known he knew. "Thank you. I won't forget this."

His face unreadable, Jaden looked past the Guardian to the doorway. Shouts and metal clanking against metal and stone echoed through the wooden door. "What's going on out there?"

"I'm not sure. I'll be back as soon as I can." The Guardian left them, then slammed the door closed, and bolted it from the outside.

Like the Guardian's, this room was dismal and bleak. Only Jaden had a fire blazing in his stone hearth, and his bed looked like he actually used it.

Jaden's gaze darkened as he scanned her from head to toe in a less than friendly manner. One that made her hackles rise.

"Seth doesn't know, does he?"

She scowled at his question. "Who's Seth?"

Jaden twisted his face up into an expression that questioned her mental capacity. "Hello? The Guardian who was just here, the big-ass guy with red hair, holding your hand and stupidly threatening me? Did you miss seeing him somehow?"

So that was the Guardian's name . . . Seth.

Strong and sinister, just like the man who bore it.

Jaden rolled his eyes. "He never told it to you, huh? Typical . . . Just typical."

"He said no one used it."

"They don't."

"Then how do you know it?"

Jaden laughed cruelly. "I know everything. Unlike Seth, I have my full powers most of the time. And you're really lucky he doesn't."

"How so?"

"'Cause when he finds out you're a jackal, he will kill you where you stand and bathe joyfully in your blood."

CHAPTER 10

Lydia scowled at Jaden and his dire prediction for her death at Seth's hands. One thing was certain. Even without her powers currently working, she wasn't about to describe any of them to an unknown being. "I don't know what you're talking about."

He tsked at her. "Yes, you do, little girl. And you can't hide anything from me so don't even try. I will know it for the lie that it is even before it forms in your thoughts."

Yeah, he was every bit as scary as Seth, but in an entirely different way.

Jaden crossed his arms over his chest and gave her a smile that said he might be considering her for lunch. "You're a Kattagari jackal. The scent of it is so strong on you that if Seth had recognized it, he'd have already cut your throat. The only reason why you're in human form right now, and can maintain it even when you sleep, is that you're also a Dream-Hunter. Lucky you. Unlike the rest of the Kattagaria, you have complete control over your animal half regardless of your physical stresses.

I'll bet you're even immune to losing them when you're shocked."

That was all true. It also helped that Seth had taken her powers, including her ability to shift.

"I heard that, and you're right." He laughed low in his throat. "Fascinating mixture of blood, isn't it? I wouldn't have considered it possible, but then it does make sense in a weird way when you think about it. Dream-Hunters are gods. Different genetics entirely than a human or Were. They've been able to impregnate everything from insects to trees to every species known. Given that, it makes sense that a god could impregnate a Were-Hunter even without the Fates mating them." An evil gleam sparked in his bicolored eyes. "That must have seriously pissed off those three bitches."

Lydia was stunned by his mini rant. How could he possibly know all of that? She had *never* breathed a word of her mixed heritage to anyone. She knew better. People didn't like things that were different and she was about as different as anyone could be. Her birth had been so unusual that, in human form, her mother had worn gloves to the day she died so that no one would ever learn she'd given birth without mating. There was no telling what the other members of her pack would have done had they discovered it. They might have been elated. Or horrified to the point they killed them.

Her mother had never been willing to find out the answer.

To Lydia's knowledge, only Solin had ever known the truth of her birth. And he would die before he told it.

Maybe Jaden was only bluffing or guessing.

Jaden's smile was so patronizing she wished she had some way to knock it off his face. "Don't bother denying it. I told you. I'll always know the truth no matter how deep you think you have it buried."

A chill rushed down her spine. She was desperate to know what she was dealing with right now—why he had the powers he did. "What are *you*?"

"Fubar."

She'd never heard of such a creature. Had his mother mated with a piece of steel or something? "Fubar?"

He wiped his thumb down the corner of his mouth as if he'd heard that thought, too, and was trying not to laugh about it. At least he had a sense of humor.

"Fucked up beyond all recognition." His features sobered back into the deadly sincere expression. "Kind of like you, only worse. I at least had a choice . . . Chose wrongly, big understatement there, but I did this to myself. You . . ." He let out a long bitterly amused breath. "Yeah. You were born screwed . . . just like Seth."

Which brought her back to one of many questions she had yet to have answered about her surly jailer. And this time she might actually get an answer—Gods love the chatty.

Thank you, Seth, for bringing me here.

"What is Seth, exactly?"

Jaden shrugged. "Like you, a demigod. Only in his case, his mother was human."

"And his father?"

"The Egyptian god, Set."

Well, that explained how he knew ancient cultures so well. Interesting that he'd neglected to tell her that himself. Most people would have bragged about having a pedigree that impressive.

But if his father was a major Egyptian god, especially one as powerful and feared as Set . . .

"What's he doing here?"

Jaden's answer made her blood run cold. "A pack of Katagaria jackals sold him to Noir when he was thirteen."

She sucked her breath in sharply. That explained why he'd kill her if he found out what she was. And who could blame him? There wasn't a hole in hell deep enough to even begin to make them pay for what they'd done to him.

Thank the gods, he'd taken her powers from her when he first saw her. Otherwise she would have transformed to fight him.

And he would have killed her for it.

But she still didn't understand why he was a slave here. Why would his father have allowed him to be sold to Noir, of all beings?

If anyone could have saved Seth from this horrific existence, surely it was *his* father. As a god of war, chaos, and total evil and destruction—which explained so much about Seth's personality and nature—Set hadn't been the kind of god to play around with anyone. He'd been known as the embodiment of total aggression, another thing Seth shared with his father. So much so that Set had killed his own brother, Osiris, and scattered his remains throughout Egypt.

If that wasn't bad enough, during an eighty-year war against his nephew Horus, he'd torn out the god's eye. Neither Horus nor Osiris were known for their weaknesses by any means. They'd both been strong gods, too.

Set's reputation had been one of lethal vindictiveness and the kind of cold brutality that only someone as sick as Noir could envy.

Even given all of that, she just couldn't wrap her mind around Set doing this to his own son. Her parents would have torn down Olympus to protect or save her.

The jackals must have had some nerve to risk Set's wrath by selling Seth. "Why did the jackals do that?"

"For the money Noir offered them. Why else? Greedy stupid bastards. And the sickest part? It really wasn't all that much. Barely more than pocket change and they spent every bit of it in less than a week."

She felt ill over that. Not that the amount mattered, really. But a low one would have kicked Seth's esteem down a lot harder than a fortune. "Why was he with them?"

Jaden let out a tired breath. "You sure you want to go there? Think long and hard before you answer. 'Cause once you start down this path, there's no turning back. No way to unsee the painted landscape that comes straight out of the lowest level of Rod Serling's *Night Gallery*."

Now there was an analogy. And maybe he was right. Maybe she should turn back before she heard any more. Because the more she learned about Seth, the more she was drawn to him.

I'm out of my mind. He would never accept kindness. And yet . . .

"I want to know." Actually, it was more than that. She had to know the truth.

Jaden moved to stand behind her. Before she could ask him what he was doing, he pressed his hands to her head. Suddenly, she was in another world. Another time and place.

A place bustling with activity. There were old carts being pulled by donkeys while men and women dressed skimpily in linen and flax rushed about to do their daily business. Most of the women had on black wigs with vibrant colored beads woven into them, while the men wore various styles of linen and braided headdresses. Almost all of them had their eyes rimmed in black and wore more makeup than a runway model. The higher ranking men had fake braided beards and wore all manner of jewels that sparkled in the bright sun.

So this was the ancient Egypt Seth had called home . . .

She saw him as a child around the age of six. There was no chance of missing him. His blue eyes glowed with innocence and a happiness she wouldn't have thought possible. His ringlet hair was longer back then . . . all the way down to his thin, frail shoulders.

Unlike the other children of that time and place, his hair wasn't shaved or concealed because of its unique color that he'd inherited from his grand-mother. A slave who had been captured in a far northern land and brought to Egypt, then freed. A mother she had adored and still mourned. He shared his eyes with his own father and his mother considered their celestial color a gift from Set so that she would always remember their brief time together.

And that hair, along with Seth's vivid blue eyes, made him stand out from those in the crowd around them as they walked quickly away from a temple.

His mother had painted his eyes black, very similar to the makeup he wore on his face here in Azmodea. Around his neck was a thick reed circlet that held the same colors as his swallow tattoo . . . and in the same order. He was dressed in a thin linen wrap that had been belted around his waist.

And in his left hand, he carried a small carved lion toy.

He was so adorable and sweet that it made Lydia's eyes mist.

"Mwt?" he breathed, trying to get his mother's attention. "I can't keep up. Please slow down."

She walked even faster.

He ran beside her. "Please, Mwt, you're hurting me."

"Shut up," she snarled at him. "I don't want to hear another word from you."

His face stricken, he cuddled his lion as if it might protect him from her wrath. "Did I do something wrong?"

She jerked him to a stop and slapped him hard, then yanked him forward again. "I said shut up."

His lips quivered as tears welled in his eyes, but he didn't cry out loud. Instead, silent tears streamed down his cheeks as he did his best to keep up with his mother's angry strides that carried them through town.

He didn't understand what was going on. First his father had insulted him when they'd gone to make an offering to the god, and now his mother was being mean, too. While his mother had never been the most loving of parents, she had never been quite this cruel either.

What did I do? He was only trying to understand.

Once they made it home, she slung him into the

stable, then forced him up on a donkey. She was so rough with him that his toy slipped from his hand. He reached out for it, but couldn't reach it where it lay in the hay since he was so small. "Mwt? I dropped my toy."

She hit his arm so hard, she left an angry red handprint there that stung long after she'd walked away. "Do not speak to me. Do you understand?"

More tears fell as he nodded. He wiped at his nose with the back of his arm while his mother gathered several strange items and then secured them to the donkey in a satchel she hung behind Seth.

Her black eyes glittered with hatred as she mounted her own donkey, then led him from the stable.

They traveled for miles outside of the town where they lived until they were deep in the desert. The heat was so oppressive and painful. Seth leaned over the donkey's neck, trying to keep the sun from blistering his skin. "I'm so thirsty, Mwt. Please may I have something to drink?"

She ignored his question.

His lips were so chapped and dry, they had started bleeding. Still his mother refused to take mercy on him.

It seemed like hours and hours had passed before she finally stopped and dismounted, then pulled both Seth and the bag down.

The hot sand went over and through his sandals, blistering his feet and legs. He tried to keep it out, but nothing worked. Even worse, he was starving. "Mwt, I'm so hungry. Do you have something for me to eat?"

She paused to glare at him. "I have nothing for you, do you understand? Nothing. You disgust me, you pathetic little dog."

"What did I do?"

She curled her lip. "You were born."

"But—"

She slapped him again. This time hard enough to knock him to the ground. Seth screamed in pain. The sand was as hot as lighted coals. And every-where he tried to go, he felt more of it.

Ignoring his cries for help, his mother pulled a large hammer from the bag she'd packed and re-turned to his side.

He looked up at her with a blistered angelic face that would have touched the heart of anyone who had one. His lips were covered with sand and blood while his red cheeks were streaked by his tears. "I'm sorry, Mwt. Whatever I did to make you an-gry, I'm so sorry."

There was no pity or love on his mother's face as she brought the hammer down over his legs, shat-tering his tiny kneecaps.

Seth screamed out in agony as he fell back into the hot, stinging sand again. But she wasn't fin-ished. Over and over, she hit his legs, breaking them so that he couldn't walk and follow her home.

Once she was satisfied that he would die here, she dropped the hammer beside him.

Then she looked to the sky over them. "Whore am I, Set, for birthing and suckling *your* repulsive, defective seed? Take the worthless bastard if you want him. I'm done with both of you."

And with that, she returned to the donkeys and left him in the sand to die.

Seth tried to crawl after her, but couldn't go far with his mangled legs. He called out for her to return, and for his father to help him, until his throat was too sore to make any more noise at all.

Neither of them came for him. Heartbroken and in utter agony, he lay in the sand with the heat of the desert sun baking his young body until his skin was as red as his hair.

All he wanted to do was die. But his father hadn't even given him that much of a gift.

Lydia heaved at the sight of his suffering. How could anyone do that to any innocent child?

How? The sight of him made her retch even harder.

Jaden handed her a bronze pot right before she lost the contents of her stomach.

When she was finished, he handed her a cold rag.

"You know the worst part?" he asked as he got rid of the pot.

Trembling, she placed the cloth at the back of

her neck. "There's something worse than what I just saw?"

"Yeah. The ancient Egyptians worshipped their children. They were notoriously loyal to family. But not Seth's. She should have been killed for what she did to him. Instead, his father rewarded her for it. After she left him there, Set had a newfound respect for her and took her in as his mistress."

Her own tears fell as the image of Seth in the desert haunted her. "Does he know about that?"

"Of course he does. He could even hear them talk about him and mock him when they were alive. The thing that haunts him most is how they would laugh over his weak, pathetic cries for help."

So that was why he wouldn't ask for help. No wonder.

And still Jaden took no pity on her. "He lay there for weeks, blistered by an unforgiving sun and chewed on by whatever found him. No food. No water. In pain. Unable to walk or fight."

Unable to die. She winced as she realized that was when he'd learned that he was immortal. What a way to find out.

Again, she understood why he'd refused to speak of it.

"After he'd spent a month in the desert, the jackals found him while hunting for food, and took him in to live in their small camp. He thought they loved him. At least that was the lie they told him."

"Until they sold him to Noir."

Jaden nodded. "When he asked his adoptive father why he was selling him, do you know what his father said?"

She was too afraid to even guess.

"You were never really one of us. How could we have loved something as pathetic as you? Not even your own parents wanted you. Why should anyone else?"

She pressed her hand to her lips to keep from sobbing for him. No wonder he'd been so feral when she'd used that one word. How many times had it been slung in his face and kicked down his throat?

"And you don't want to know what's happened to him since the day Noir brought him here, and dumped him in with his demons."

No, she didn't. She'd already seen the physical scars left by that. "So why does he hate *you*?"

CHAPTER 11

Jaden looked away from her, but not before she saw the shame and grief in his eyes. His breathing intensified as if he was fighting physical pain. "Seth hates *me* because I'm the stupid bastard who showed Noir how to drain his powers from him and keep him submissive."

Her jaw went slack as anger knifed her through the heart. How could he have done something like that? To a boy, no less? And here she'd thought he was decent.

In the end, he was even worse than Noir.

No wonder Seth hated people the way he did. He truly had had no one. Not once in his entire life.

She raked a repulsed sneer over Jaden's body. "Why would you have done that?"

He let out a laugh that was laced with bitterness and self-loathing. "Why does anyone screw someone else? I was trying to save my own ass. At the time, I didn't know Seth. I hadn't even seen him yet. Not that that's any kind of an excuse. Believe me, no one is more disgusted by my behavior than I am."

She wouldn't bet on that. It was a wonder Seth hadn't gutted him for it.

Jaden sighed. "My only defense is that I was in the detag area where I can't see out into the world. And Noir is one of only two people who can lie to me and I can't detect it. He told me that he'd found a bastard god who needed his powers drained. If I showed him how to capture the god and use his own powers to keep him weak, he'd allow me out of my hellhole, and I could kill the god for him." The shame in his bicolored gaze ran all the way to his soul.

"I'll never forget that moment when Noir threw him on the ground in front of me, and I looked down into the innocent face of a terrified, defenseless child who had no idea what had been done to him or why. Noir laughed like it was the funniest thing he'd ever seen. And I knew . . ." He ground his teeth and the agony on his face told her that he was being honest about his regret. "I knew I'd been lied to and that I'd just damned that poor child to more misery than any creature should suffer." He raked his hand through his dark hair. "I should have killed him that day. I should have. But I couldn't bring myself to slaughter a defenseless child."

"How could you have killed him?"

Jaden gave her an evil smirk. "There's nothing I can't kill. No matter how immortal."

"Then why don't you do us all a favor and kill Noir now?"

He glanced away from her and curled his lip in contempt. It wasn't until he spoke that she realized that contempt was directed at himself. "That's a long, complicated story, and it's one I will never tell to you or anyone else. Suffice it to say, not killing him when I could have was my biggest mistake and is my greatest regret. It never fails to mystify me how badly we fuck up our lives by trying to protect ourselves, and the ones we love, from hurt and from harm. Unfortunately, life is unpredictable and turns on you at the worst possible times. Too bad we can't club it in the head until it heels, or better yet dies."

Boy, did she ever know that. Whenever she thought things were going well, something always went tragically wrong.

"Why are you telling me all of this?"

"To save *your* ass. I've destroyed enough lives in my time. For once, I'd like to save one. Granted it doesn't even the scales, not by a longshot, but it's better than doing nothing." He jerked his chin toward the door. "In spite of what his parents and adoptive family did to him, Seth was decent when he first came here. Angry, understandably, but decent. Unfortunately, that didn't last. The unending misery and torture would have taken its toll on even the strongest of souls, and I give that boy credit, he lasted longer than anyone I've ever seen and that includes me. But after . . ." he trailed off as a dark cloud settled over his features.

Lydia frowned. "After what? You can't leave me hanging after everything else you've told me. How much worse could it be?"

"Ironically it's not," Jaden said with a heavy sigh. "It was just the straw that snapped the camel in two and left it bleeding on the ground. Seth made a pact with Noir's Malachai, Adarian. If he helped the Malachai go free, Adarian was supposed to come back and release him in turn."

She stated the obvious. "He didn't."

Jaden shook his head. "Better Adarian had ripped his head off and killed him than leave him here to face Noir's wrath."

She could only imagine how true that was. "I take it Noir wasn't happy."

"Lady, you have no idea. Noir draws the bulk of his power from the Malachai. When he found out why he'd been weakened and who was to blame, he did things to Seth that no one should suffer. Not just for a few weeks or even a year or a century. We're talking over a thousand years of torture so bad and grueling, I have no idea how that man is still sane. I honestly don't know why he hasn't gutted me for it. I wouldn't blame him in the least." He touched her again and this time she saw Seth as Jaden had seen him after his release.

He was perilously thin and weak. Gaunt. His eyes were sunk so deep into his skull that they made him look like a skeleton. But the worst was the huge bolt that had been pierced through his jaw.

It went from under his chin, through his mouth and tongue where the upper end was so large he couldn't swallow for it. Nor could he speak. If he tried, blood flowed from his mouth and choked him.

Now she understood the significance of the scar under his chin that he touched so often.

Jaden released her. "I was the one who removed the bolt and took him to his room to heal. Gah, I still can't believe what Noir had reduced him to. And what kills me most is that mankind owes Seth a debt they don't even know about."

"How do you mean?"

Jaden held his hand out for her.

Lydia started to hesitate, but she wanted to see the truth. So taking his hand, she braced herself for the images she was sure would haunt her.

Seth stood proudly in Noir's throne room as he told Azura and his master what he'd done.

Noir narrowed his gaze in warning. "What do you mean, maggot, that *you* let the Malachai go?"

Seth shrugged. "You can set Jaden free. He's not the one to blame."

Noir stood up with hell's fury burning deep in his dark eyes. "Surely not even you, as pathetic as you are, were stupid enough to defy me. Not in this."

Seth didn't back down or cower. He lifted his chin defiantly and braced himself for his master's wrath. He'd known when he agreed to help Adarian that there was a good chance the bastard wouldn't uphold his side of the bargain.

But he'd hoped. Slight though that hope was, he'd been desperate enough to want to believe that the Malachai had held a shred of decency somewhere inside him.

Now, Adarian had done what Seth had feared. He'd abandoned him to Noir's fury.

You could have saved yourself. You didn't have to speak up.

True. Noir had blamed Jaden for Seth's actions. And while Seth hated that son of a bitch with everything he had, Jaden hadn't turned him in for it. He could have easily spared himself by telling Noir the truth.

But he hadn't.

And while Seth's moral code wasn't what it used to be, he wouldn't stand by and see Jaden torn apart for something he'd told Seth not to do.

It wasn't right.

"What can I say, Master?" He sneered the title with an audacity that was as impressive and fearless as it was idiotic. "I am *that* stupid. Besides, it was a winning proposition for me. If Adarian had freed me, I would never have to be in your sickening presence again. If he didn't, then I would get to see your face when you realized that you are too weak to take over the human realm without him."

Seth actually smiled at Noir. It was cold, gloating, and cruel, but it was a smile. "After all these centuries of plotting and scheming, right when you were on the brink of seeing all those dreams fulfilled, you now have to watch as all of it slips away. Everything you'd hoped for is now gone. You can't do shit. And *that,* my lord . . . watching you fail to achieve the one thing you wanted most, *is* worth it."

Noir let loose a scream of bloodcurdling rage that echoed through the room. Then he blasted Seth through the wall behind him. His eyes glowing bright red, Noir stalked toward him with a deadly intent.

Seth lay on the floor with his skull split open and blood pouring out of his eyes, nose, and mouth. Still, he looked up at Noir and laughed through his pain, showing off a mouth full of bloody teeth. "I don't care what you do to me anymore. So go ahead and do your worst."

Now it was Noir's turn to laugh. "Trust me, little worm. I fully intend to."

Jaden released her.

It took Lydia a couple of minutes to get over the shock of seeing Seth like that. She'd assumed he was always submissive to Noir. That Noir had beat him like a tamed puppy.

The truth was far different. Even while knowing what Noir was capable of, he stood his ground. He was either the bravest man in history.

Or the dumbest.

"Does he always egg Noir on?"

"Unfortunately. He's never been able to help himself. No matter how many times they beat him down, he always finds the courage to get back up for another round."

She still couldn't believe he'd rubbed Noir's nose in it. And inside, she was so proud of him for what he'd done. "Why didn't you tell Noir the truth about who freed the Malachai?"

"How could I? Seth would never have been here, but for me. I figured it was the least I could do for him. I never dreamed the stupid little bastard would tell Noir the truth. Like I said, he has never learned when to keep his head down."

Obviously.

"And Noir delivered well on his promise. He rained down utter hell on that boy for centuries. He made it open season for any demon in the realm to do whatever they wanted to Seth."

"Thank you for not showing that to me."

Jaden inclined his head to her.

"So what made Noir release him after all that time?"

"He needed him. While *playing*," Jaden said that with complete sarcasm, "with the Dream-Hunters he'd turned against the Oneroi, Noir found out about something called the key to Olympus."

"Which is?"

"Something that can kill any and all of the Greek gods, including Zeus, and allow their powers to be channeled into one being. He who has the key doesn't need the Malachai to take over the world. He would be the most powerful creature in it."

And if that creature was Noir . . .

Yeah. It'd suck to be human or anything in his path.

"Before Noir could learn more, his Dream-Hunters escaped his hold and returned home. All but one, and he tortured that one for over a year, trying to get the location of the key."

"He wouldn't break?"

"No, he broke . . . into many pieces. But before he died, he told Noir that there was only one Dream-Hunter in existence who knew the key's location."

"Solin."

He nodded. "And since none of us can capture a Dream-Hunter, he went to Seth for it."

She scowled as she tried to figure that one out. "Why would Seth be able to capture one?"

"Son of chaos, war, aggression, and destruction, Seth has some epically impressive powers. Whenever Noir allows him enough of them, he has the ability to send the swallow on his neck out to do his bidding. It was the swallow that captured Solin in a dream and brought him here."

Shocked and stunned, Lydia tried to grasp that concept. While it wasn't uncommon for gods to have living marks on them, this was completely unexpected. "Where did he get it?"

"Now there's the kicker. His sorrow and pain conjured it out of the ether."

That didn't make a bit of sense. "How so?"

"In ancient Egypt, the swallow was seen in two

basic roles. It was a form the dead would often choose to revisit the earth and see their loved ones. Or one the gods would use, such as when Isis became one so that she could search the land for her husband's remains. While it was venerated and at times welcomed because it was a form the gods would take, the swallow was also seen as an omen of grief and sorrow."

Jaden paused for a minute as if he needed to collect his emotions before he continued. "When Noir brought Seth here, he . . ."

She knew it had to be bad. Jaden's breathing was ragged again. "He what?"

"He wanted Seth to understand his place in this realm. So he set the worst demons he had loose on the boy. For two days straight, they assaulted him and when Noir finally went to get him, the tattooed swallow was there on his neck. No one, not even I, knows how he conjured it. But he did. He'd used it so that he could mentally escape the horrors of what was being done to him. Noir tried to remove it so that Seth would never have that refuge again. But he couldn't. In the end, he discovered that if he kept Seth weak enough, he wouldn't be able to manifest it and escape. Now that swallow serves as a perpetual reminder to Seth that he can never get away from Noir. That Noir owns him, body and soul."

No wonder he'd clawed at it when she'd asked him why he had it. "Do the colors on it mean anything?"

He nodded and when he spoke, she wanted to cry for Seth. "Rebirth, victory, purity, death, the sun, and the sky . . . All the things that Seth longs for."

All the things that had been denied him.

And that made her so angry on his behalf that she wanted to go and stomp Noir into the ground.

If only she could.

"Why didn't the Malachai return for him?" she asked.

"Who knows. They are innately evil. I've never known one who could care for anyone other than himself. Why should he come back and keep his word?"

"Because you should always keep your promises."

Jaden scoffed. "Yeah, right. Trust me, babe, that seldom happens."

Perhaps, but the world shouldn't work that way. Ever. Then again the world was never perfect.

And that broke her heart even more.

Lydia squeezed her eyes shut as she again saw Seth as Jaden had found him—with that awful bolt in his mouth. She shuddered in revulsion. "I wish you hadn't shown me any of his past." Even though he'd warned her . . . She'd never be able to get it out of her head.

"And neither will Seth," Jaden said, reminding her that he could read her thoughts. "You asked him why he doesn't sleep. It's because he relives it all over again in his dreams. I remember when he was little, he'd wake up crying every night, only to be punished for it. Back then, he had no protection from the others. I did what I could to help him, but I'm limited, too. And like Seth, I spend more time in Noir's dungeons than I do being free to roam."

She felt for both men. Trapped here. Forever. She couldn't imagine anything worse. "Is there any way to break the two of you out of here?"

CHAPTER 12

The look on Jaden's face was heartbreaking. "I have no way to leave this place. Ever. To protect what I loved, I damned myself completely. But Seth wasn't so stupid. He can be freed. It won't be easy, but it can be done."

That sent the first bit of happiness through Lydia that she'd had in a while. Seth didn't deserve to be condemned to this place.

If I can free him . . .

"How?"

"You'd have to teleport him out, and then hide and guard him until his powers recharged to their full level. Until they do, Noir could summon him back if he located him."

"How long would it take?"

Jaden took a minute to think about it. "A month . . . maybe a little longer or even a little less. It would depend on how low his powers were when he left here."

But he could be freed.

That gave her hope.

Jaden leaned down to speak low into her ear. "And to answer the question you're too afraid to ask, yes. I think he can be saved. But it won't be easy. He has no reason to believe in or trust anyone. We've all betrayed him. Bitterly and repeatedly. We traded his innocence for our own selfishness and hung him out to dry over and over again."

Tears choked her as she thought back to what little she'd seen. How many more and worse stories were there? She was also too afraid to ask that question.

Jaden had been right. It was a miracle Seth was still sane. How he could show any form of compassion to her or any semblance of kindness to someone else was a testament to his strength.

She had to get him out of here.

"Just don't lie to him," Jaden warned. "He would never forgive you for it."

"Then I should tell him I'm a jackal and—"

"He will eat you for lunch." Jaden cut her words off angrily. "Listen to me, Lydia. He has centered all of his hatred on the family who lied to him and sold him. He hasn't forgiven me, but he never loved me or thought that much of me, so he doesn't hate me for what I've done. In his mind, a jackal is the symbol of treachery and ultimate betrayal. He will never trust you if he knows you're one of them. Since he doesn't know what you are, he has no reason to ask you about it. So, for the sake of the gods and yourself, don't tell him."

If only it were that easy. But her morals were different from Jaden's. "Omission is a lie in and of itself."

Jaden growled in frustration. "That's your decision. However . . ." This time, he projected Seth's past to her without touching her.

She saw Seth on his knees in the desert sand, clinging to his adoptive father's hand as he begged for mercy. "Please, It," the Egyptian word for father. "Please don't sell me. I'll do anything you ask. Have I not always been a dutiful son to you in every way?" He held his hands up to show the cuts and calluses on his palms and fingers from where he'd helped his family with chores. "Never once have I asked for anything. Never have I gone to bed and not told you how grateful I am to have all of you as my family. I don't understand why you would sell me."

His father sneered at him as he cruelly wrung his arm out of Seth's grasp. "You're pathetic, boy. No wonder your mother left you to die and your father couldn't be bothered to claim you." He kicked Seth back, into the arms of the demons who were there to take him.

Seth's tears flowed down his cheeks. "How can you do this to me? You told me that you loved me. That I *was* your son."

His father sneered at him. "You were never really one of us." Then his father turned into a jackal and ran off, leaving him to the demons.

The one on the right grabbed Seth by the hair

and leered at him. "We're going to have a lot of fun with you, boy. Don't worry. As pretty as you are, you'll have all the love you could ever want."

"Stop," she said, holding her hand to Jaden. "Please. I don't want to see any more."

"Don't you know, Seth feels the same way about it. But he had no choice except to endure it, and then to be damned to an eternity of remembering every demeaning, brutal detail. The slightest word or phrase. Sometimes it's nothing more than a fleeting smell or sound, and all of that floods right back to him with a clarity that leaves him ravaged and aching all over again as if it just happened to him. Just like your memory of the night your mother died. No amount of time fully eases that pain, does it?"

No, it didn't. As he'd said, one sound or the darkness and she remembered every detail of that night. No matter how hard she tried to forget, it never went away.

It was always there, stalking her and hitting her when she least wanted it to. There was no escape.

Not ever.

Only times of happiness between those memories. At first those times had been so brief as to not matter. But Solin had made her laugh and learn to live so that those moments would be longer and longer, until they finally outnumbered the bad memories.

For that, she owed him everything.

Seth had no one to make him smile. No one to

comfort him and tell him that he would learn to live again.

Not that he'd ever had a real life to begin with. He would have to start from scratch to even have a single decent memory to build from.

My poor demon . . .

All of a sudden, someone was at Jaden's door.

He stepped away from her as it opened. Prepared to fight, she held her breath, half afraid it was Noir or one of his other minions.

It was Seth.

She started to go to him, but there was an air of such rage and hostility around him that she was afraid he might hurt her if she did.

His armor and lips coated in blood, he had several new wounds and bruises on his face. But as always, he didn't seem to notice them. A tic beat a fierce rhythm in his jaw as his nostrils flared. He appeared to be one step away from going on a homicidal rampage.

The last thing she wanted to do was be the one who pushed him into it.

His icy glare went past her and straight to Jaden. "I'm being sent to guard the Nether Wall. Can you watch her until I return?"

Jaden gaped at his disclosure. At first she thought it was because he was asking Jaden to keep her longer.

It wasn't.

"Why are *you* being sent?" Jaden asked.

He gave Jaden a droll stare. "Since when does Noir answer to me?"

Jaden shook his head. "Who's going to stand at your back?"

Seth scowled at the question as if it baffled him. As if he thought Jaden was stupid for even asking it. "The same as always. No one." Finally, he looked at her and his features softened ever so slightly, as if he took comfort from seeing her there.

Then he returned his glare to Jaden. "Will you watch over her until I return?"

Jaden nodded. "I will."

He inclined his head in gratitude before he withdrew and locked the door again.

She turned back to Jaden as she tried to understand what was going on. "What's the Nether Wall?"

"It's the boundary between our realm and Thorn's."

"And why is that bad?"

Jaden snorted. "It's not if you don't have a soul. But if you do . . . Thorn's vultures flay you for it. Mentally and physically. Guarding that wall, especially alone, is one of the cruelest things to do to someone. It's like hanging out a single piece of steak at a rabid dog festival."

While she had no doubt that he wasn't exaggerating, she had a hard time believing it would be hard for Seth after everything else he'd been through. "Crueler than having your mouth bolted shut?"

Jaden's freaky gaze burned her with its sincere

heat. "Yes. Physical pain eventually stops hurting. It's the scars on the soul that never heal and never back off—those ride you with spurs. May the gods help him."

She knew the truth of that, which made her determined to help Seth any way she could. "Can you get me there?"

"Ah, hell no. Are you out of your mind?"

Maybe. Probably. It definitely wouldn't be the first time she had a moronic thought, and unfortunately, it wouldn't be the last. It was that kind of lunacy that had her here right now.

But it didn't change her conviction. "I can help him fight. Watch his back. You said it yourself, he doesn't need to be out there alone."

Jaden shook his head in disbelief. "And you will get him punished beyond belief if anyone sees you. Don't you understand, Lydia? By having you here without Noir's knowledge, he has all but declared war on Noir. If Noir finds out what Seth has done . . ."

"Why did he capture me, then?" Why put himself into more conflict with the god who hated him so?

"That is his job. He's supposed to capture anyone who comes here without an invitation. Then they are to be taken to Noir, who decides what to do with them."

She could just imagine what that demon did to anyone dumb enough to venture here.

By keeping her safe and hidden, Seth risked his own neck.

"Why would he take such a chance?"

"I have no idea. Honestly, I wouldn't have done it for anything. If I didn't owe him so much, I'd be handing you over right now." By the tone of his voice, she had no doubt he meant every word of it.

Thank the gods, he wasn't the one who'd found her, trying to help Solin escape.

Now, Lydia tried to understand what had motivated Seth to such stupidity. Yet for her life, she couldn't imagine why he'd risked his flesh for her—a nobody, an enemy—after all Noir had done to him.

It made no sense.

Seth took his post at the gate and widened his stance into his fiercest Guardian's pose. He dug the tip of his sword into the ground and rested his hands on the hilt. With any luck, the night predators would think twice about taking him on.

Though if the past was any indicator, they wouldn't give a shit. They would attack Noir himself. Anything for a drop of blood.

Here, demon, demons. Fresh meat. Come get some.

And all too soon, they would.

From here, he could see the tiniest bit of outline from Thorn's manor. It looked so harmless from a distance. But his one trip to it had tutored him well on Thorn's brutality. The ancient demon lord wasn't a bit kinder than Noir.

Bloody effing bastard. It hadn't been much of a fight, but Seth had done his best. Too young, too new to his powers, and drained from Noir's cruelty, he'd run there, hoping to find a haven.

What he'd found was a one-way trip back to Noir's lap . . . and his fist. Apparently the two demon lords had made a pact that they wouldn't keep runaways.

Look on the bright side . . . At least Azura wouldn't summon him while he was here, any more than Noir would. Given that lovely benefit, unlike Jaden, he didn't mind this duty as much as some of the others he'd been forced to do.

Yeah, it was emotionally grueling, but then so was life.

Even now he could hear Noir in his head. *"You pathetic wretch. You're worthless. Stupid beyond stupid. Go stand at the Wall for a couple of nights. Maybe then you'll learn how to fight."*

All in all, he thought he'd done pretty well, given the fact they were outnumbered twenty to one, and he was still drained by Noir and Azura's last feeding. Not to mention their latest round of Beat the Holy Shit Out of Him.

But what did he know?

And come tomorrow, he was sure Noir would beat him again for not having more information about the key he was supposed to find while protecting the Wall and doing everything else they wanted.

Yeah . . .

They're not what you want to think about anyway.

No, he wanted to think about glowing topaz eyes that danced with humor and sparkled with fiery spirit. Of soft, long black hair. Of moist lips that begged him for a kiss.

Closing his eyes, he conjured an image of Lydia in his bed. Yeah, that was what he wanted to focus on. Much better than all the other crap he had to deal with. He could almost smell the warm scent of her skin. It actually banished the chill from the cold winds that blew against his armor, freezing him to the marrow of his bones.

"Seth?"

He opened his eyes as he heard the sound of her voice. Glancing around, he saw no trace of her.

It's not her. She didn't know his name. Must be one of the predators screwing with him.

"Can you hear me?"

He realized it was inside his head. "Lydia?"

"Yes. Jaden explained to me what you would be facing. I wanted to come and help, but I understand why I can't. I don't want to get you into trouble."

Those words touched him so deeply that it left him temporarily immobile. *She doesn't care for you. How could she?*

It was most likely true.

It's definitely true, you imbecile. Noir's right. You are the dumbest idiot ever born.

Only a rank moron would think for even a second that his captive cared for him.

Even so, he wanted to hear her voice. Feel her next to him while he waited for attack. "How are you able to talk to me?"

"Don't be mad, okay? Jaden restored enough of my powers that I could sit with you while you stand post."

He should be furious over that. Yet he wasn't. He felt strangely grateful. "Are you really that bored?"

"No. I just needed to make sure you were all right. I don't want to see you hurt."

Those words and the faked sincerity in her voice struck him like a blow. No one had ever said a kinder thing to him. Not in all of his life.

But he knew better. "You don't care about me. Be honest. We're enemies, you and I."

"I'm not your enemy, Seth. I don't like being your captive, and I have to say that I'm still a little peeved over that fact. But I understand why you did what you did. And it means a lot to me that you're protecting me when you have no reason to."

A bad feeling went through him over those words. *Why the hell did I put them together?*

"How much has Jaden told you about me?"

"Probably enough that you'll beat him for it. But I'm glad he did."

Seth let out a disgusted breath. He couldn't stand for anyone to talk about him. Ever. It never boded well for his health. Physical or mental.

Not wanting to think about it, he turned the topic. "You should probably rest."

"Not until you do."

Her comforting voice took him back in time. Back to when he'd lived with the jackals and had had a friend. When he'd been able to trust the lies other people told him.

What he wouldn't give to be that naive again.

Don't trust her. She's using you to get free. If she weakens you, she knows you'll do something stupid for her.

All people were liars. He knew that with every part of himself.

And yet . . .

Seth wanted to believe in something again. He wanted to believe in someone.

Most of all, he *needed* to believe in Lydia.

"Tell me about your family, Lydia. What are they like?"

"They were wonderful."

"Were?"

"My mother died protecting me when I was a child."

He should have been so lucky. But he felt bad for her when it was obvious she'd loved her mother. "What happened?"

"Zeus had us attacked. Everyone was slaughtered. But my mother used her powers to send me away before they found me. She tried to send me to my father, but they killed her before she could get me all the way there."

"And your father?" *Please tell me he was better than mine.*

"He's wonderful . . . Most times. He can be very stern and demanding. But he does it out of love for me."

Good. One less being he wanted to mutilate.

Then he started to ask her about Solin, but stopped himself. There were some things he didn't need to know and that was one of them. It was actually at the top of his list. He didn't want to hear the love in her voice when she talked about another man when that man possessed the one thing Seth would sell his soul for.

It was cruel.

But she continued talking to him in that soothing voice of hers. "The hardest part was that I couldn't really see my father growing up."

"Why?"

"He has too many enemies who would kill me if they found me. So I've had to move around a lot. Never making too many friends for fear of them betraying me, whether by accident or intentionally."

"Like me."

"In some ways. It's why I understand you, I think."

Interesting thought, that. He didn't understand himself most days, so how could she?

"Tell me more about your mother. What's your fondest memory of her?"

"She would read to me every night and then sing me a silly song to go to sleep to. After she'd leave, many times I'd get up and try to sneak out to play with my toys."

"Did she spank you for it?"

"No. My parents never hit me. She'd tickle me back to bed and threaten to take away my dessert for a week. But she never did that either."

Seth felt the beginnings of a smile, but the moment he did, he felt an evil presence coming at him.

Out of nowhere, a reaper attacked. They were taloned and winged demons who would rip apart any creature they found. Lucky him, that he'd been here for their pleasure.

Seth cursed as it sank its claws into his shoulder. *That's what I get for not paying attention.* He should never have been talking to her.

"Seth?" The panic in her voice meant a lot to him, but he didn't have time to chat right now.

"I'm under attack, Lydia. I have to go."

"Seth!"

He ignored her as more reapers came for him and he fought them back as best he could.

But they weren't the only ones rushing him . . .

Oh yeah, this was going to really suck.

Lydia looked over to where Jaden sat on the stone floor, leaning against the wall by his fire.

"He's under attack. Are you sure we can't help him?"

Jaden sent her a mocking stare. "Sure. Let's go get him pinned to Noir's wall for a week, shall we? I'm quite certain it would thrill him to no end, and make us all feel better that you care so much."

"You don't have to be so sarcastic."

"Can't help it. I sucked sarcasm straight from my mother's breast."

She ignored his even more sardonic reply. "Is there nothing we can do for him?"

"We're doing it."

Lydia hated what they were doing. It wasn't in her to sit and not fight.

Getting up, she started pacing—something she did until she was too tired to keep going. Only then did she sleep. But her dreams, probably restored by Jaden, too, tortured her with the things she'd learned about Seth.

Most of all, they tortured her with thoughts of him standing guard alone and fighting against the monsters Jaden had described.

Please be okay. Please.

She woke up well past dawn, or at least what passed for dawn in this dismal realm. "Seth?" she tried again to contact him.

He didn't answer.

She looked to where Jaden slept by the fire. *I have to find him.* He was in trouble, she could feel it.

The only problem was she didn't know where he was or how to get there.

Suddenly, she heard a commotion out in the hallway. She went to the door and pressed her ear against it so that she might hear what was going on.

Rumbling voices thundered, but she couldn't make out their individual words.

Not until one spoke with a clarity that made her sick.

"Huzzah! The Guardian is dead!"

CHAPTER 13

Terrified, Lydia started to open the door to tear this place down until she found Seth, but Jaden grabbed her just before she committed suicide.

"Don't be stupid," he snarled in her ear as he held her still with his hand on her upper arm. "They'll tear you apart—and enjoy every minute of it. And what good would that do any of us? Believe me, I don't want to scrape bloody chunks of you off the floor and ceiling. Or get your remains smeared on the bottom of my shoes."

She curled her lip in distaste at what he described. That was basically the last thing she wanted, too.

Releasing her arm, he nudged her aside so that she'd be hidden by the door before he opened it.

She bit her lip as he left her alone in his room. He was right. What she'd almost done would have been the worst sort of stupid.

Thank the gods, he'd stopped her. But she couldn't think straight after hearing that news. Seth couldn't be dead.

Tears choked her as an image of him lying in pieces haunted her.

Why do I care?

She had no idea. And yet there was no denying the pain crushing her chest at the thought of him . . .

I have to know what happened.

Putting her ear to the door, she tried as hard as she could, but she couldn't hear anything else outside. No clue about what had happened or what was going on. *Come on . . . someone tell me something.*

Anything.

Time ticked by so slowly that it nauseated her. She was about to go insane before Jaden finally returned. He manifested in the room, right in front of her.

"Well?" she asked hopefully.

He hesitated and her heart stopped beating as she braced herself for the worst. The longer he delayed, the more her pain built until she had no idea how she was able to hold back her sobs.

"He's not dead," he said finally.

For that mean pause alone, she could have kicked him as she let out one audible sob at the good news. The relief from those three words was staggering. And for that, she was so grateful, she could almost kiss him.

Seth wasn't dead.

Oh thank you, gods, thank you!

"Where is he?" she asked Jaden.

He swallowed audibly. "I don't think you want

me to answer that." The note in his voice returned her terror tenfold.

What could have happened? Did Noir have him caged like they'd done to Solin? Her mind ran wild with horrific possibilities as she remembered all the images and stories Jaden had told her about this place and what went on here.

"Jaden," she chided. "C'mon. After everything else you've told me? I have to know where he is."

"It's *that* bad, Lydia. You're better off staying here for now."

Her heart pounding, she heard Noir cursing outside the door as he tried to open it. "Jaden! You worthless piece of shit, get out here. Now!"

Jaden vanished.

She pressed her ear to the door again, desperate for any nugget of a detail. She had to know something or she'd go mad.

"You yelled?" Jaden sneered contemptuously in a tone she was surprised didn't get him backhanded.

"Can you get that bastard dog down?"

"I can try. I'm not sure he'll be in one piece when I do, though. Hope that's okay with you?"

Was he serious?

What had they done to Seth now? She covered her mouth with her hand as horror for him consumed her.

"You better succeed, maggot. I need his power. Do you understand? You let him die and you'll take his place."

"Good luck with that."

This time, she heard the blow that sent Jaden slamming into the door that separated them.

"Bring him back alive. I need him."

She heard Jaden push himself up. "Then why did you send him out there alone?"

She heard the sound of another vicious slap.

"You better remember who you are now, worm. You're not my equal."

Jaden's voice was scarce more than a feral growl. "You're right, Noir. Free or enslaved, I'll always be superior to you."

"You better be glad I need you to fetch my dog. Otherwise you would pay for that."

"Yeah, fuck you very much, too."

Something hard struck the door, making her jump. But whether it was Jaden or Noir's fist, she wasn't sure.

"Don't let him get to you, babe." It was Azura's voice she heard this time. "We will have the key soon and then no one will stop us."

"I know I shouldn't let that smug little prick get to me, but I can't help it. He was always so arrogant."

"I know, brother. But let it go. We defeated, defanged, and emasculated Jaden a long time ago. All he can do now is raise your blood pressure . . . Your pet will be returned to you shortly, and it'll heal as it always does."

Lydia grimaced at the way the bitch spoke about

Seth like he wasn't human. Well, okay he wasn't fully, but he wasn't an animal or an object, either.

Damn them.

You better be glad I don't have my powers, puta. If she did, they'd be having a round right about now.

Azura laughed. "Then we can share another bite of it and we'll go after Zeus and his crew. Step by step, we will make it to the Malachai and then we'll be where we should be. Rulers of the world."

They walked away.

Flicking her nails at that door, Lydia was grateful they were gone before they sensed or discovered her. Or worse, she ripped the door open and did something stupid.

Ugh! One day those two would get their comeuppance. She only hoped she was there to see it happen.

But her relief at their departure didn't last.

After a few minutes, Jaden returned to his room without Seth. Something that made her panic all over again, especially since he was absolutely coated in blood that didn't appear to be his. Literally, from his forehead to his shoes. He looked like Carrie minus the painted-on prom dress.

Why wasn't Seth with him?

"Where is he?" she asked, terrified of the answer.

His face pale, Jaden was actually shaking as he made his way to his table and reached for an opaque,

green decanter without answering her or even looking in her direction.

This had to be bad.

And as he poured his drink into a jewel-encrusted
gold cup, Lydia frowned at the thickness of the
liquid and the color. If she didn't know better, she'd
swear it was blood.

After he knocked back all the contents of his
cup, he finally looked at her. "You don't want to see
him right now. Trust me."

"Don't be ridiculous. I have to go to him." He
would be alone with no one to tend his wounds,
and that was the last thing he needed.

Jaden crossed the room and placed his hands on
her shoulders. His eerie eyes burned her with their
intensity, anger, and disgust. "Lydia, listen to me,"
he growled between clenched teeth. "They almost
cut him in half. Do you understand? I . . ." he winced
as if he couldn't bear whatever flashed through his
mind. When he met her gaze again, she swore she
saw tears in his eyes. "Long ago I was one of the
most revered warlords ever born, with a lot of field
experience of god-war and massacre proportions.
I fought and survived battles that would make
Quentin Tarantino's movies look like a 1950s Dis-
ney musical, and I've never, ever seen anything so
gruesome. Do you hear me?"

Those words hit her like blows.

He couldn't be serious. Surely not . . .

Her own tears cut warm trails down her cheeks

as she imagined what he'd found. What was left of
Seth . . .

Releasing her, Jaden raked a trembling hand
through his hair and winced. "It's . . . it's sick what
they did to him. I didn't think anyone could be crueler than Noir. I stand corrected."

He snarled something in a language she'd never
heard before. "I should never have let him go alone.
I knew better. It's my fucking fault. All of this." He
lowered his head and fisted his hands in his hair.
"How could I have been so stupid? So selfish? Gah,
I'm such a fucking idiot."

She wasn't sure if he was talking about his guilt
over Seth or something else. But it was obvious,
his past was every bit as brutal and traumatizing
as Seth's.

Reaching out, she placed a comforting hand on
Jaden's shoulder. "You did what Seth asked."

Jaden shook his head and this time there definitely were tears in his eyes, and her own flowed in
response to seeing a man this strong hurt so much.
"I just wanted five minutes of not having Azura
and Noir breathing down my neck. Five minutes."
His gaze tore into hers with the hatred that he bore
for himself. "I condemned an innocent child into
an eternity of hell for that five minutes. I'm worse
than they are."

"No, Jaden. You're not. You think they have
given his pain any consideration at all?"

He curled his lip as he shrugged her touch away.

"Don't patronize me and tell what I am and what I'm not. I see myself for what I've become and I've never deluded myself or tried to spin my actions into something they're not. I know the beast in me and live with it every day."

And he hated it. He didn't say it because he didn't have to.

She knew there was no way to comfort him and even if there was, he wouldn't let her. He was too bent on flogging himself for his past mistakes.

Meanwhile, there was another man here who needed help. One who had somehow become important to her. If she couldn't help Jaden, the least she could do was go to him.

"Where is Seth?"

Jaden hesitated before he answered. "His room."

"Take me to him."

"I really don't think you need or want to see this."

She glared up at his peculiar eyes. "If you don't take me to him, right now, this second, I'll walk out that door and find him myself."

He growled low in his throat as he glared his anger at her. "And you would, too. You stubborn fool. Just remember, it was that kind of blatant stupidity that trapped me here. You should listen once in a while when someone warns you."

Lydia thought about that. He was right. She'd always been prone to leap and then think about the consequences on her way down the cliff, into the swirling ocean. Solin had dogged her hard over that her entire life. But she wasn't going to change today.

"He needs us."

Jaden shook his head. "Fine, but don't say I didn't warn you."

Before she could blink, they were in Seth's room, which was still bathed with that eerie blue glow. She took a second to get her bearings in the dark silence that heightened the sound of her own heart beating. The jackal in her smelled his blood, not that she couldn't see it plainly enough.

How did he have any left inside his body?

Completely naked, Seth lay on the bed so still, he didn't seem real or alive. With his head turned away from her, his straightened auburn hair spilled over the black pillow.

Bracing herself for the worst, she walked across the room slowly.

His breathing was so shallow, she could barely see his chest moving. His skin had a deathly ashen pallor to it and was covered with a fine sheen of sweat. Sweat that made the swallow on his neck glisten, reminding her of how he'd gotten that tattoo.

She choked back a sob over the pain of his life, wishing she could make him forget it.

He lay with his long legs stretched out and one arm draped over his chest, just above . . .

She froze in horror. "Oh my God," she breathed as she finally saw what Jaden had warned her about.

Never in her entire life had she seen a wound so foul. It looked as if a sword had gone through his stomach, just above his hip and below his bottom rib, stopping only when it hit his spine.

How could he still be alive? How? It defied any kind of logical explanation and she couldn't imagine how excruciating it had to be.

Worse, he was still conscious. Against all odds and all reason. His eyes were mere slits, but they glowed with his agony as he turned his head to look at her.

His breathing became ragged as he gave her that familiar scowl that was redundant with his face paint.

How could he stand it and not scream? How? But then she knew.

He was used to pain.

It was all he knew.

She wanted to scream for him over what they'd done. There was no sense in this. Damn them all for it. Why wasn't someone tending him? Doing something to alleviate his pain?

But then she knew the answer to that, too.

No one cared. No one except her.

Taking his bleeding hand into hers, she knelt on the floor beside him. The last thing she wanted was to jar the bed in any way and cause him more pain. "What happened?"

His grip was weak as he swallowed. He didn't answer her question. With his gaze locked on hers, he spoke to Jaden, who stood just to her left. "I'm returning her powers to her. I need you to send her out of here, back to her own world."

Lydia shook her head in denial. "I won't leave with you like this."

His glared intensified. "You *have* to, and you need to go now."

"No. I—"

"Listen to me, Lydia." He tensed and grimaced as if pain tore through him. For several seconds he panted from the weight of it. Then his tight grip relaxed and he opened his eyes again. "I wasn't attacked. I—I was tortured."

It took several heartbeats before she understood what he was saying. But it made no sense. "Why?"

He broke out into another round of sweat as if talking was straining him too much. "The Greek gods are looking for you. Not to take you home. They've been sent here to kill you."

Her jaw fell under the assault of disbelief that hit her hard. "What?"

"He's telling the truth," Jaden said from behind her. "I found him bolted to the Wall. It looked like they'd spent all night, trying to force him to take them to you."

Seth coughed up blood, something that made the rest of his body bleed even more. Tears of pain gathered in his blue eyes. "I told them nothing. But they know that you're in this realm. It's why they breached my room. Somehow they could tell you were in here." He had to pause to catch his breath. "Jaden had you shielded last night in his room so they couldn't locate you."

His words stunned her. None of it made any sense. "Why would they want to kill me?" What had she ever done to them? She'd purposefully stayed away from the Greek gods.

"They wouldn't say. But you have to go and hide from them. They won't stop until you're dead." He lifted her hand to his bloody lips and kissed her knuckles. The moment his lips touched her skin, she felt a rush go through her as he restored all of her powers.

When he released her hand, the blood was gone from her skin. "Go."

When she didn't leave, he glanced past her to Jaden. "Get her out of here."

Jaden nodded, then pulled her toward a corner, out of Seth's line of vision. Before they left, he leaned in to whisper in her ear. "You should know something."

"What?"

"He could have stopped his torture at any time by telling them where to find you. The only reason it stopped was that his morning relief saw that it was Greek gods and not Thorn's people attacking him and called for reinforcements. Otherwise, he'd still be bolted to that Wall . . . protecting you."

With his blood and flesh.

Her heart shattered as she heard those words.

Seth didn't believe in protecting anyone except himself. How many times had he said that? Yet there he lay, torn apart because of her.

How could she leave him to this?

"Can you do something to heal him?"

Jaden shook his head. "I don't have those powers."

And neither did she. Nor did she know anyone with them.

"What's going to happen to him after I leave?"

Jaden fell silent as he considered it. "He'll eventually heal. The pain will be unbearable until he does, but . . . he'll live. However, if Noir finds out he was tortured and not attacked by Thorn's people, and why he was interrogated by Greeks . . . his punishment will be a lot worse than this. By keeping you here, he's brought enemies into Noir's home. That's not something the King Asshole and Queen Whore take lightly."

She couldn't imagine anything worse. Her stomach heaved at the thought.

And in that moment, she knew what she had to do.

No matter what it cost her.

"How do I get him out of here?"

CHAPTER 14

Jaden hesitated before he answered. "Yes, you can teleport him out of here, but you have to understand something before you do. In the condition he's in, he won't be able to help you in any way. None. Noir and Azura have his powers sucked down to virtually nothing, and by returning yours to you, he is literally drained to the level of a human. He's defenseless right now. He can't even move."

It didn't matter. She wasn't about to leave him here. Not like that. Not after he'd sacrificed himself to keep her safe. Only a heartless bitch could do such a thing. And she might be a lot of things in life, but that had never been one of them.

She blinked away her tears. Later she'd cry. Right now, she had to stay on task. "I don't care. I won't leave him."

His features softened. "Thank you."

She didn't understand his gratitude. "For what?"

"For being the woman I thought you were. You've no idea how rare a beast that is."

Before she could stop herself, she hugged him for his kindness.

Jaden held her tight, as if he were trying to commit this to memory because he knew he wouldn't have anyone else hug him for a long time.

If ever again.

Lydia stepped back from him. "Are you sure you can't come with us?"

"Positive. If I break my word and leave against Azura's wishes, someone a lot more important to me than I am will be hurt. I can't do that."

She understood and she hated it for him. He didn't deserve to be here any more than Seth did.

As she started back to the bed, Jaden stopped her. "Where will you take him?"

"I don't know. I doubt it'll be safe at home. If the ones after me found me here, then they most likely know where I live. Same thing for Solin's place."

"Do you have any friends?"

"Not really." In spite of her talks with Seth, she had a hard time trusting people, too. Plus being immortal made it difficult to have humans as friends. They tended to notice when she didn't age.

"Then you should go to Sanctuary."

She frowned. "Sanctuary?"

"It's a bar in New Orleans that's owned by a group of Ursulans."

Her heart clenched in fear. By nature, both the Katagaria and Arcadian branches of Were-Hunters were highly territorial. They couldn't stand for another species to enter their domain. Many times, such an action would start all-out war. That was the last thing she needed.

Not to mention, bears and jackals were mortal enemies.

"I can't go there. They'll kill me."

"No, they won't. I swear. The Peltiers are different. It's run by an Arcadian bear named Aimee and her Katagari mate, a wolf named Fang. They have doctors there who can help you with Seth. It's your best shot."

"An Arcadian mated to a Katagari?" She'd never heard of such a thing, never mind the fact that they were two different species.

"I told you, they're different."

She wanted to believe him, but . . . "You're sure they won't hurt us?"

"Positive. They'll welcome you both, and do you no harm."

Please don't be lying to me.

But why would he? He really did seem concerned about Seth. *You keep telling Seth to trust other people. It's your turn to put some faith in them.*

Realizing the truth of that, she nodded, then returned to the bed where Seth lay.

He opened his eyes and cursed obscenely when he saw her again.

"Nice to see you, too, beast." She smiled at him

and brushed the hair back from his bruised cheek. "I told you if you returned my powers that I'd get you out of here. Just so you know, *I* keep my word."

Seth didn't know what stunned him most. The fact that she'd come back for him or the feather-light kiss she brushed against his lips.

Even through his vicious, biting pain, both of those warmed him completely. And when she pulled back, he suddenly found himself in a strange room with red brick walls and no windows. He lay on a small, thin bed that was surrounded by strange steel and glass cabinets, the likes of which he'd never seen before.

Where was he?

Was this another hell realm?

The door behind Lydia flew open so fast, it rattled on its hinges. Three large men came in, ready for battle.

Grinding his teeth against the pain he knew would come, he put his arm out to block Lydia from them and sat up.

Too late, he realized that was a bad mistake as unimaginable agony ripped through him and stole his strength. His head swam and vision dimmed. But he refused to pass out and leave her to them.

He groaned out loud as the pain increased even more. It was absolutely killing him.

"Seth!" Lydia wrapped her arms around his shoulders and laid him back against the bed with a care that amazed him. Her lips touched his ear as she held him close and trembled against his body.

In that moment, he wanted to die with her like that. Wrapped around him, offering him comfort. Especially if it was a lie and she really didn't care about him. He didn't want to live and discover the truth.

The men came forward and surrounded his bed.

Seth tried to summon his strength to fight. How could he protect her?

I'm worthless.

The one with long black hair braided down his back placed a hand on Lydia's arm. "We'll take care of him."

Seth shoved him away. "Don't touch her!"

Instead of making him mad, the man offered him a smile as he moved her further away from the bed. "My name is Carson and it's all right. We won't hurt her or you."

Seth wasn't sure if he believed him. But what choice did he have? It was bad enough that he was injured to the point he could barely move. He was also bare-assed naked. Gods, just what he needed.

More humiliation. And in front of guys he could beat down like punks if he wasn't so injured. Damn. Would his degradations never cease?

Lydia moved past Carson to return to Seth's side. "Can I stay with him?"

The beefy man with long, curly blond hair scoffed. "Girl, I don't think you want to see this. Carson's a whiz at medicine, but dayam." He gestured toward Seth's injuries. "This is some seriously nasty shit. Unless you're a doctor, too, you'll just be in the way, and you'll probably lose some lunch before all is said and done."

Lydia bit her lip in indecision.

"C'mon," the blond man said more gently this time. "My name's Dev, and we won't be far away. Just in the next room, okay?"

Still she held on to Seth's hand and that succeeded in bringing tears to his eyes. But he blinked them back before anyone else saw them.

"I'll be okay, Lydia. Go with him."

Her topaz gaze glowed with her reluctance. But finally, she nodded. "If you need anything, call for me and I'll come."

He let go even though it pained him to do so.

Dev took her out of the room.

Carson glanced at the man with short, black hair. "Colt? Can you let Margery know it's safe to come in now?"

"Sure, Doc. I'll also let Fang and Aimee know we've got company."

"Thanks." Carson draped a warm, thin blanket over Seth's loins to give him a modicum of modesty.

He hated to admit it, but he was grateful for Carson's action, and he despised the fact that he couldn't dress himself or conjure enough powers to do it.

The Greek Phonoi and Dolophoni had stripped

his armor off not long after they'd driven him into the Wall. Those bitches. If he ever laid hands on either group, he'd tear them apart.

But last night, he hadn't stood a chance. Not when his powers were already low and they assaulted him with reapers and dagnytes first. He still had no idea why Thorn would have aligned himself with the Greeks. Normally he stayed out of such things. The dark lord despised demon politics.

Not that it mattered. The important thing was that Seth had to get enough strength back to protect Lydia before they found her.

Seth glanced over to the door Colt had left through to see a tiny woman with red hair several shades lighter than his and blue eyes, come in. She wore some kind of blue shirt and a white jacket with a long white skirt that had running shoes peeking out from beneath the hem. Her hair was coiled into a bun and she had a pair of cat-like glasses.

She offered Seth a kind smile. "Glad to know the danger's past." Pushing her glasses further up on her nose with her knuckle, she joined Carson beside him. "The woman's named Lydia, by the way."

"Yeah I know," Carson said as he laid out things Seth couldn't identify. "He called her by name before she left. Our guest here is Seth."

She smiled at him again. "Hi, Seth. I'm Margery, Margy or Marge, Mars or about a dozen other nicknames people use for me. I'll answer to just about anything so long as it's not an insult. And in case you're wondering, I'm the other doctor who works here with Carson. We're going to get you patched up real fast, okay?"

Frowning at her outgoing ebullience, Seth wasn't sure what to make of these individuals. His powers were so weak that he felt exposed and unsure. Defenseless. He hated to be this vulnerable when he didn't know who or what he was up against.

What their abilities were.

Never mind their intentions.

Carson shined a light into his eye that had the broken blood vessels.

Cursing, Seth grabbed his hand and shoved the light out of his face.

"It's okay," Carson said patiently. "I'm just trying to assess what all has been done to you."

"Isn't it obvious? I had the shit beat of me." What kind of physician couldn't tell that by looking at him from across the room?

Did they not know what they were doing?

Carson laughed. "Yes, I'm aware of that. But I need something a little more specific before I treat you." He stepped forward again. "May I look in your eyes? I want to see if you're in shock or have a concussion."

Seth nodded, and did his best to not strike out at him. But it was hard when Carson's merciless light made his head hurt even worse than it already did.

Once Carson finished with that, he slid the light

into his jacket pocket. "Do you mind if we wash the paint off your face?"

Yes, he did. Greatly. "Why?"

"Well, it's going to make it a lot harder to clean and dress the cuts you have and I'm pretty sure you're going to need sutures on one of them. Not something we want to do over greasepaint. That's if you don't mind?"

What did it matter at this point? Could he really look any weaker to them than he already did?

"Okay."

Margery came forward with a warm cloth to clean his face while Carson examined the cut one of the Phonoi had made through his stomach.

One day, he was going to find that bitch and pay her back tenfold for that cut. She'd had the nerve to laugh after she did it.

Once Margery had his face clean, Carson felt the bones around the eye Noir had punched. Seth could only imagine how beautiful that "kiss" was after last night's punch.

Carson sighed. "All right, Seth, I know you're not a shapeshifter. And by the severity of these wounds and the fact you're still alive, never mind fully conscious and not screaming your head off, I'm going to assume you're some kind of immortal. Not a Dark-Hunter with those eyes. So what are you, then? Demon? Vampire?"

Seth choked on the word he hated. "Demigod."

Carson exchanged an unidentifiable look with Margery that Seth wasn't so sure about, then asked, "Greek?"

"Egyptian."

"Ah. Okay, I'm a little rusty on your pantheon. We don't come across you guys much here. And let's face it, I can't exactly Google real facts about ancient gods. So I'm hoping you can help me out a little. Do you know, offhand, if I can give you anything to relieve your pain?"

That question confused him. "I don't understand."

Margery patted him gently on the shoulder. "Do you know what medicines can ease your pain?"

Oh . . . He remembered his adoptive father had used salves and some kind of root plant to soothe pain, but he had no idea what any of them had been. It was too long ago to remember.

And since then . . . Noir, Azura, and the others had only wanted to give him pain, never take it away.

"No. Whenever I'm injured, I eventually heal without anything."

"Has anyone ever tried to give you anything?" Carson asked.

Only a hard time. "No."

Carson rubbed his jaw as he thought it over. After a few seconds, he nodded at the other doctor. "All right, Marge . . . I'm going to give you the honor of choosing for him. Have fun."

"Oh thanks a lot, Carson. I appreciate it." She winked at Seth. "If it doesn't work, remember the one you want to be mad at is the male doctor, not the woman."

Carson snorted at her, then turned his attention back to Seth. "Do you mind if I knock you out?"

Hell yes, he minded. Last thing he wanted was to be hit anymore. He was tired of it.

Anger ripped through him as he glared at Carson. "Why would you want to do that?"

"So that we can work on you without causing you pain."

Yeah, right. No one cared about giving pain to others. They lived for it.

And now that he thought about it, he realized how stupid it was to be here with them. What had he done?

How could he have let them separate him from Lydia? Dear gods, they could be doing anything to her right now. Anything. What if she needed him?

What if they were hurting her?

Panic laid hard talons into his conscience. He had to find her before it was too late. "Where's Lydia?"

"She's safe," Carson reassured him.

Bullshit.

"I don't trust you . . . Lydia!" He tried to sit up, then groaned as the pain in his stomach and head made him sick.

The doctor forced him back down, but he wasn't

about to go. Not until he was sure they weren't rap-
ing or torturing her. Or worse, handing her back to
Noir.

"Lydia!"

She came running through the door.

Only then did he breathe easily. He shoved at
Carson so that he could reach for her.

Lydia took his outstretched hand and held it
tight. Frowning, she glanced around at all three of
them. "What's wrong?"

He couldn't answer for a few seconds as he struggled with the misery that tore into him from every
angle. The only thing that grounded him was her
soft touch . . . the concern in her warm eyes.

"I didn't know what they were doing to you," he
said at last.

"They were feeding me."

Really? He found it impossible to believe. "You're
all right, then? No one hurt you? You're sure?"

Lydia's heart broke at the panic in his suspicious
gaze. She cupped his face in her hands, desperate
to calm him down and soothe him before he hurt
himself any worse. "Not everyone is cruel, Seth. I
told you that. It's all good. They're not going to
hurt us. I promise." She pushed him back onto the
bed.

Seth growled in fury as another round of agony
shot across his stomach and down his back. Gah, it
hurt.

Lydia took his hand into hers and placed her

head next to his on the bed. He closed his eyes as he savored the first bit of real pleasure he'd ever known.

"I'm right here, Seth," she whispered to him as she brushed his hair back from his face. "I'm not going anywhere." She kissed his cheek, then looked up at Carson. "Do whatever you need to."

"You sure? 'Cause he's better off untreated than having another episode like that one."

"He won't fight you." She tightened her grip in his hand. "Will you, sweetie?"

Seth couldn't speak as he heard her endearment. No one had ever used one for him or if they had, he couldn't recall it. In that moment, he knew he was lost to her.

There was nothing she could ask of him that he wouldn't do. Nothing.

"I won't fight," he breathed.

The doctors returned while Lydia stroked his hair. He'd never felt anything better than her fingers against his scalp. Her tenderness left him even more raw and bleeding than his wounds. It shattered something deep inside him that craved her.

Suddenly, something sharp bit into his arm. Cursing, he reached for the doctor and grabbed him in his fist.

Lydia pulled at his hand. "It's all right, Seth. It's just medicine. It'll help you. I promise. Please let go."

Seth did, but only because she asked him to.

Lying back, he tried to focus on Lydia's face.

He couldn't. His eyelids were so heavy now. The pain was fading and as it went, it pulled him with it.

Seth tried to fight it, but in the end, he took one breath and surrendered himself to the darkness.

Lydia let out a relieved sigh as Seth finally relaxed. "I'm so sorry about that," she said to Carson.

"Think nothing of it. Believe me, we've seen just about everything you can imagine, and a few things I'm sure you can't, shoot through our doors at one time or another." Carson inclined his head toward Seth. "And he's not the only one with a really bad past. Believe me."

Margery brought a tray of medical instruments over to the bed. "You might want to go finish eating now, hon. He should be out for a while."

Lydia wouldn't put money on that. Not from what she'd seen of his stamina. "Or he could wake up in a few minutes and reach for your throats again. If you don't mind, I'd rather stay like I promised. He doesn't trust easily and I don't want him to stop trusting me, you know?"

Margery's glance went straight to Carson before she caught her slip, then quickly turned it back to Lydia. "I do know. But if you're squeamish, you might want to face the wall while we work."

"That I will do."

Carson brought her a chair.

Sitting down, Lydia listened to them as they started patching Seth up. She would have commented on the germs, but then given Seth's immortality it probably wasn't that big a concern.

"So how long have you two been doctors?"

Carson laughed. "About a hundred years for me. Margery, a little less."

Margery snorted. "A lot less. I'm human and I've been working with Carson for over a decade, but haven't had my medical license all that long."

Fascinating.

"So what clan do you belong to?" Carson asked.

Lydia had no idea what he was asking about. "Clan?"

"You're Tsakali Katagaria . . . what clan are you?"

Her heart pounded as she swung around to face him. "You can't say that to anyone. Ever. Okay?"

He arched his brow. "Ah . . . okay. But that's going to be a little hard to keep secret here. Any Were-Hunter who comes into contact with you will know it instantly."

Crap! Why would Jaden send her here after telling her not to breathe a word of her jackal status to Seth? Surely someone as powerful as he would have known that other Were-Hunters could sense her and identify her species. Had he done it intentionally? Was that why Seth was so mistrusting of him?

She suddenly felt like a complete blind fool for ever listening to Jaden.

And I even hugged him. She could beat both of them. Him for doing it and her for listening.

Her entire body started shaking as she feared Seth's waking up to hear this. "Then we can't stay. We have to go."

Carson scowled at her. "What are you so afraid of?"

Death. Dismemberment. Noir finding them. Solin getting hurt. Seth dying when he couldn't.

Greek gods out to kill her.

The list kept growing by the second.

Don't tell him any of it. It was none of his business. Especially since Seth's paranoia had started to infect her.

But she had to make sure they kept their mouths shut. For everyone's well-being. "You can't tell anyone that we're here or tell them anything about us. Do you understand?"

Carson's gaze turned dark and dangerous. "Who are you running from?"

She bit her lip as she debated what she should let out and what she should keep between her and Seth.

"Listen," Carson's tone matched his dour expression. "The people and animals here are my family. If you pose a danger to them, I need to know. We've already been attacked once and nearly destroyed. If we have another enemy coming, then we need to know immediately. We have children and infants here to protect."

Children. Here.

That changed everything. She didn't want anyone ever having the memories she had. No child should hear or see their mother die.

Please, don't kill me. She wasn't sure who that was directed at exactly. Seth or Carson.

But she couldn't put the kids in harm's way. "He's a servant to Noir, and I freed him. When Noir finds out that he's gone, he will come after him, no holds barred. It will get extremely bloody."

"And you?"

"I was told that some of the Greek gods want me dead. It's how Seth was injured. They were trying to find me. I don't know why, though. I really don't."

Carson cursed, then turned to Margery. "Tell the others."

Grabbing a towel to wipe the blood from her hands, she quickly left the room.

Lydia rubbed her head, which was starting to ache from all of this. "I didn't mean to endanger you. Jaden said we'd be safe here . . . that you could help Seth."

"It's all right. We can cope as long as we're forewarned. Just don't let us get blindsided." He returned to working on Seth. "Man, whoever did this to him certainly knew what they were doing."

"How do you mean?"

"I mean he was interrogated by someone who

knew exactly how to wring as much pain as possible out of him and not kill him. Poor bastard."

"Will he be all right?"

"He'll heal. I don't know about the 'all right' part. That's not my department. I can only fix bodies. Hearts and minds are another matter."

Lydia turned to look at Seth's bare face, which was still covered with bruises and cuts that marred his otherwise flawless handsomeness. She wanted to cry, but Solin had taught her to keep that inside.

When they know what makes you cry, they know what hurts you most. Don't give your enemies that.

Closing her eyes, she reached out to talk to him and see what was happening.

But Solin didn't answer. And that scared her even more than her current predicament. Here, in this realm, with her powers restored, he should be easy to contact. She'd never, ever had trouble finding him before.

He'd only be silent to her if he couldn't answer because he was fighting.

Or he was dead.

She couldn't even contemplate the latter. It would destroy her to lose him.

Suddenly, she felt another powerful presence coming into the room. Warm and at the same time freezing, it thickened the air on the other side of Seth's bed.

Carson pulled back and grabbed a scalpel from his tray as if ready to battle who or whatever it was.

Lydia did the same, 'cause whatever it was, it would be fierce if it chose to fight them. And she had a sickening feeling that it was coming here for her.

But most of all it wanted Seth.

CHAPTER 15

A golden mist shimmered in the air like beams of sunlight first thing in the morning, then slowly turned into a beautiful, tiny woman. Her café au lait skin glowed and accentuated the greenness of her almond-shaped eyes. Her dark brown sisterlocks were pulled back from her face and held with a leopard-print scarf that matched her long skirt.

Lydia was stunned by the elegance of the woman who was so beautiful, it was hard to look at her.

Making a sound of total disgust, Carson relaxed and dropped the scalpel back onto the tray. "Menyara, you scared the shit out of us with that over-the-top entrance. What are you doing here?"

At first, she didn't seem to hear him. She stared at Seth as if she were looking at the ghost of a loved one.

Taking her cue from Carson, Lydia stood down as well. Obviously Menyara was a known entity here.

When Menyara finally spoke, her voice was incredibly deep and powerful for her dainty size. "I felt the blood call of one I thought was long dead.

I couldn't believe he was here, in this realm, after so long." She approached the bed almost reverently so that she could stare down at Seth and study his pale features. "But *he's* not the one I feel." She reached out and traced the line of his swallow tattoo. "Still . . . they are very similar and yet so different. I don't understand how this is."

Lydia started to speak, but Carson motioned her to silence. "She is Ma'at," he whispered. "The Egyptian goddess of justice."

Menyara turned Seth's face toward her, then frowned as she smoothed down his left eyebrow. "Where did he come from?"

"He serves Noir," Carson answered.

"Is he a demon, then?"

Lydia cleared her throat, testing to see if Carson would let her answer yet.

He nodded at her to continue.

"He's not a demon. He's an Egyptian demigod. Noir bought him when he was a boy, just coming into his powers, and enslaved him."

Menyara winced as if the mere thought caused her pain. "His mother was human?"

"Yes."

"His father?"

By the way she asked the question, Lydia could tell Menyara knew the answer, but wanted it confirmed before she spoke it out loud. It was almost as if she feared by saying it first, it would somehow make it true even if it wasn't.

Lydia licked her lips before she answered. "Set."

Menyara spoke rapidly under her breath in a language Lydia had never heard before. But it sounded like she was cursing someone. She hoped it was Set and not Seth.

After a few seconds of her anger, she calmed down, then closed her eyes and hovered her hand over Seth's heart.

Seth's eyes immediately flew open as he sucked his breath in sharply and arched his back. It was as if someone had a hook in his chest and was trying to lift him from the bed. He panted in pain as every muscle in his body tensed and bulged.

"Stop it!" Lydia snarled. "You're hurting him." She rushed for Menyara, but Carson caught her.

Still, Menyara chanted in that lyrical language, not caring how much agony she caused Seth.

He groaned and cursed as if he were being tortured all over again.

Shrieking at them, Lydia wanted to stop her, but Carson wouldn't let her. "Damn you, let me go!" She tried using her powers on both of them, but somehow they deflected them, making her feel weaker than she ever had before.

How could she not be able to stop this? How could they hurt him more? Couldn't the goddess see he'd been through enough already?

Suddenly, light streaked out of Seth's wounds. One by one, they began knitting themselves closed. The bruises and cuts on his face and hands slowly faded.

Lydia froze as she watched it.

When the last one was healed, he fell back flat on the bed where he lay panting. At first, he stared up at the ceiling as if waiting to feel pain again. Then he turned his head toward her and she saw the relief that filled his beautiful blue eyes. Eyes that were no longer haunted by his battle with physical pain.

It was the first time she'd seen him without any injuries or marks. Only the tattoo showed on him now.

She smiled in amazement. While she'd known he was unbelievably handsome, she'd never quite imagined the exact beauty he would hold once he was whole.

Now . . .

He was stunning. His coloring so unusual and exotic. And those curls . . . They made him irresistible.

"You need a shave, hon," she teased, walking over to him so that she could playfully scrape her fingers against the auburn whiskers that darkened his cheeks. Even they didn't mar his looks. They only made him appear more rugged.

More masculine.

And if they were alone right now, she'd be nibbling her way down that angular jawline until she tongue-bathed him all over.

"What happened?" he asked in a low whisper as he reached up to finger his lips and eye that had been so damaged by Noir's cruelty. "Why don't I hurt anymore? Where did it all go?"

Those words brought home the fact that this was probably the only time since Noir had bought him that he hadn't been in excruciating agony.

Lydia indicated Menyara with a tilt of her head. "She healed you."

Frowning, he turned his head. The moment he focused on Menyara's features, he curled his lips in disgust.

Whoa . . . that was *not* the reaction she'd expected. By the look on Menyara's face, it was evident she was expecting something a little kinder too.

"What are *you* doing here?" he growled at her.

Menyara's gaze turned dark with sadness. "Shh, child," she said soothingly. "I won't hurt you."

His cold expression showed every bit of his denial. "Your presence here offends me."

Menyara winced. She reached out to touch him, then stopped herself as if she feared how he might react to it. "What was done to you by your father was so wrong, and for that I apologize even though I know no amount of apology will ever take away the pain of what he did. I weep for that, too. But I am *not* my brother and I would *never* deny my kin."

The pain and accusation in his eyes was tangible. "You didn't come when I called for you and I screamed for all to have mercy on me until my throat bled."

"I didn't hear you, or I would have come."

"I don't believe you. You are a goddess. One of

order and justice. When I called for you, your silence judged me unworthy, and you left me to suffer unspeakable horrors."

Lydia wasn't sure if she believed Ma'at either. But either way, it didn't matter. No apology or anything else would ever be able to undo the hell they'd all damned him to.

Menyara swallowed as if she heard Lydia's thoughts. "You look so much like my brother." She held her hand out toward his face as if she imagined she was cupping his cheek. But she didn't make contact with him. "It's been so very long since I last saw his face. In spite of what you think, Set wasn't always bad or evil and I did not judge you. While your father was born of darkness, he also fought against it every night by our father's side, making sure that Ra would rise and drive the evil back for another day . . . Like you with Noir . . . You have the better part of his nature."

"Don't you dare defend him to me. Ever."

Menyara nodded sadly, then looked at Lydia. "The two of you must go. It's why I've healed him. Your enemies won't let you rest. Not until Seth's powers are fully regained."

Lydia frowned. After what Menyara had just done for Seth . . . "Can't you give them back?"

"Unfortunately, I'm not the one who has them. They have to leave Noir and return to Seth and there's nothing any of us can do to rush that happening." Taking a step closer to the bed, she reached out, this time intending to touch Seth, but he grabbed her wrist before she could make contact.

"Don't touch me."

Menyara's eyes misted as she dropped her hand. "Noir has already sent out his hounds to find you. It won't take them long to catch your scent here. They will sense it just as I did. I've healed your body, but—"

"You'll forgive me if I don't thank you."

"I will indeed." She stepped back and whispered under her breath.

An instant later, a tall, extremely muscular man appeared by her side. His short hair was dark brown with blond highlights, and there was something about it that reminded Lydia of a lion's mane. His green eyes were a perfect match to Menyara's, making her wonder if they weren't related as well. His skin tone was much closer in color to Seth's.

Dressed in a pair of jeans and a dark blue T-shirt, he stood as if ready to tear someone's, anyone's, head off.

"Maahes," Menyara said sweetly, in a tone that made his name sound like Me-uhs, "this is my nephew, Seth. I want you to watch over him until his powers return."

Maahes brought his right hand up to his left shoulder and bowed his head reverently to her. "I will guard him with my life, my lady."

Seth sneered at them. "I am the High Guardian of

Azmodea. The last thing I need is someone watching over *me*. Trust me, I know how to fight."

Menyara sighed. "That is the same arrogance that cost your father his life."

"I'm *not* my father."

"No, you're not. But you are my family, even if you deny it. And now that I've found you, I have no intention of seeing you hurt if I can help it." She pulled the necklace from around her neck and kissed it. She held her hand out toward Seth. The necklace vanished from her fingertips, only to re-appear around his neck.

He scowled at it before he tried to snatch it off. The chain wouldn't break.

"The kiss of Ra cannot be removed by violence. Only by love. It will protect whoever wears it from any physical harm."

Seth ground his teeth at her words, hating her for them. It was too little, much too late. His aunt Ma'at was one of many gods he despised. "Where was your kindness when I needed it?"

She glanced away, but he didn't miss the guilt in her eyes. She knew he was right. "Sadly it wasn't there for you. And for that I am very sorry. But things change. People change. There aren't many of us left anymore. And I'm tired of losing the people I love. Of burying my family."

Ma'at looked at the god of war who stood next to her . . . another relative Seth had no use for and no desire to be near. "Travel with Maahes. If not for your safety, then for Lydia's. He can protect her should, Ra forbid, you fall. And unlike you, he's familiar with this world. He'll know best where and how to hide her from harm."

Seth started to argue, but she was right. He knew exactly what Noir would do to Lydia if he caught up to them. And he was woefully ignorant of the human realm. Everything had changed so much since the last time he'd walked it as a boy. There was absolutely nothing in this room that was familiar. Not even the peculiar bed he lay on.

Reluctantly, he nodded.

His aunt smiled in satisfaction. "May Ra be between you and harm in all the empty places where you must walk." And with that, she vanished and left them.

Seth looked down at his undamaged body, amazed by it. Nothing, absolutely nothing hurt. Nothing throbbed. Nothing pinched. It was incredible. He honestly couldn't remember the last time he'd seen it this way. The last time he'd felt no physical pain whatsoever.

So used to pain as a constant companion, he kept waiting for it to kick in.

But it didn't.

Unable to comprehend why Ma'at would be kind to him now, after all these centuries, he conjured his armor to cover him, then scooted off the bed. Thank the gods he finally had enough power to at least clothe himself.

Lydia stopped him as he started for the door. She pressed her lips together into an adorable smile that did make one part of him hot and aching again. She swept his body with a bemused gaze, but he'd much rather have her sweep it with another part of her body. "Sweetie . . . honey . . . sugar-pie, you can't walk around like that. There's not a Ren Faire in town. And people will notice."

There she went with her foreign terms again. "A what?"

"Exactly." She put her hands on his chest and his armor turned into a strange short-sleeved black shirt and a pair of very uncomfortable blue pants like Maahes wore.

Holding his arms out, he looked down at it in disgust. "What is this?"

"T-shirt and jeans. It's what modern man wears."

"But I feel naked in it."

"You'll get used to it."

He wasn't sure he wanted to. It offered no protection whatsoever. "Where do I put a sword?"

"You don't," she said with a hint of laughter in her voice. "*That* will get you arrested."

He was completely perplexed by her words. "People have no weaponry here? How do they protect themselves from roaming animals and barbarians?"

"We do have weapons, we just don't carry them out into public, and while some of my past dates would lead anyone to believe barbarians are still

alive and well, and thriving, the real thing is something of the far distant past."

Maahes laughed at them. "Good gods, boy, how
long has it been since you were in the human realm?"

Seth had to think about it for a minute. "When
Neferkare was pharaoh."

Maahes arched a brow. "Which Neferkare?"

"There was more than one?"

Maahes snorted, then laughed. "Damn . . . you're
old. Not compared to me, but . . . you are definitely
long in the tooth, and setting you loose in the current
world after all this time should be entertaining as
hell." He laughed until he coughed.

When he realized no one else was amused, he
sobered.

Sort of.

Lydia gave Maahes a chiding glare. "How long
ago was that?"

Carson answered, "Second Dynasty."

And that meant absolutely nothing to her.

When she deepened her scowl, Maahes clarified
the description, "Around 2686 BC."

She gaped at Seth, unable to comprehend how
long Noir had kept him. How long he'd been tortured.

That was over forty-five *hundred* years. Forty.
Five. Hundred. Years. She could barely get her mind
wrapped around it. And she'd stupidly thought herself to be old. She was an infant in comparison.
Good thing she'd never thrown that in his face.

"Dang, you're old." She'd been right. Seth did predate Rome.

By a lot.

"How long?" Seth asked.

Suddenly she felt bad for being even the least bit amused. "You really don't know?"

"You've been to Azmodea. You know it's always hard to tell the days apart, and then during my confinement . . . I honestly have no idea."

Even Maahes sobered as he realized the horror of Seth's existence. "It's been over forty-five hundred years since Neferkare was pharaoh."

Seth couldn't breathe as that sank in. No wonder it'd seemed like an eternity.

It had been.

And he wasn't sure how to deal to with the knowledge. He was strangely numb. It wasn't like he'd expected to come out of Azmodea ever again, but . . .

Lydia leaned into him. "It's okay, Seth."

Was it? He really wasn't sure about that. It was a good thing he'd agreed to having Maahes with them. He'd be all but worthless here.

Lydia exchanged a concerned glance with Maahes. "He's going to seriously wig when he sees what's out there."

"Wig?" Seth asked.

"Lose your mind. Wave it bye-bye."

He frowned. "I still don't understand most of what you say."

"And now I truly understand why. C'mon, Grandpa, we need to get going."

They started for the door.

"Wait."

Lydia paused to look back at Carson who was putting together a quick bag for them. One that held bandages, medicine, his wallet, and a cell phone that he'd kept in a drawer. He handed it to her.

"What's this?" she asked.

"In case you need it. Make sure you don't use your own credit cards or accounts. You don't want to create a trail for anyone to follow. There's enough cash in there for you, and feel free to use my cards." He picked the cell phone up. "This is a burn phone with my number already programmed into it. If you need a cavalry for anything, call me. I can get to you in a blink and I will bring as many soldiers as I can, and our army is by no means small."

His offer touched her. "Are you sure?"

"Absolutely. I can't stand to see anyone hunted. Good luck to you guys."

She inclined her head to him. "Thank you, Carson."

"Walk in peace," he said, stepping back.

Lydia took Seth by the arm and teleported him to the alley behind the house they'd been in. She and Maahes started for the street, until she realized that Seth wasn't moving.

Arching her brow at Maahes, she turned back to

find Seth staring up at the sky with the most incredulous expression she'd ever seen on anyone's face. His features were filled with boyish wonderment and awe.

And it reminded her of his staring at the sun on the computer in his room.

He turned around in a slow circle while he tried to take everything in. The trees, the sky, the buildings, and what to him had to be all the alien sounds of faint jazz and zydeco, cars, and people talking and laughing as they went by on the other side of the brick wall.

Her heart breaking, she walked over to him.

"It's so beautiful," he breathed reverently. "And warm."

"New Orleans usually is."

"New Orleans?"

"That's the name of this city."

"Oh." He finally looked down at her, and she realized he was squinting to the point she was amazed he could see anything at all.

No wonder. He'd lived in darkness for so long, his eyes weren't used to light anymore.

She conjured a pair of sunglasses for him, then put them in his hand.

He scowled at them. "What are these?"

Oh yeah. He wouldn't have a clue.

Maahes folded his arms over his chest. "In your day, Egyptians used kohl to protect their eyes from the harsh sun rays. Today, we use these . . . they're called sunglasses."

Lydia took them from him and put them on his face. *Boy, did I choose well.* He looked great in them. She glanced back at Maahes. "Is that really why Egyptians did that?"

"It is indeed."

"Wow, and I just thought they did it for fashion."

Maahes didn't comment on that. "We need to get going. I have no idea where I'm taking you, but it doesn't seem wise to stand out here in the open when we have preternatural trackers trying to find us."

He made a really good point. "Where are going?" she asked.

Seth shrugged. "As long as it's not Azmodea, I don't care."

In that moment, she felt completely lost. She really had no place to go. Home was out of the question. Solin was MIA.

All she had were the two men with her.

"Hey now," Maahes said. "Don't be making that face. Okay? You start crying, I start crying, and I look like a total freak when I cry. Nothing worse than a big-ass man blubbering like a baby. Totally kills my chances with the women. You know?"

"I wasn't going to cry. But it was sweet of you to be concerned."

"No problem."

Seth scowled at the easy way they conversed with each other. Especially since they'd only just met. Worse was the jealousy inside him that wanted to punch Maahes straight in his arrogant jaw.

"Well," Maahes said finally. "I guess the best place would be mine. It's isolated and should be safe should something scary go down."

Lydia couldn't think of anything better. "It sounds perfect."

As they started to leave, she realized Seth had wandered off again.

This time, he was at the wall, looking at the parked cars lined along the curb. Smiling, she went to wrangle him.

As soon as she reached him, a car went flying by. Eyes wide, Seth jumped about ten feet.

She put her arm out to settle him. "It's okay, Seth."

"What was that thing?"

She answered him with a question of her own. "Didn't you see a car online?"

"No."

Maahes made a sound of disgust in the back of his throat. "This is going to get annoying fast if he freaks every time he sees something he's not used to."

Curling his lip, Seth started to attack. But Maahes caught him with what appeared to be a Vulcan death grip and pulled him into his arms.

Seth froze instantly.

After a few seconds, Maahes released him.

Staggering a bit, Seth pressed his hand to his forehead as if he was dizzy. He curled his lip at Maahes. "What did you do to me?"

"Brought you up to date. I don't want you piss-ing in a sink or doing anything else to draw attention to us. We need to blend in and not look like refugees from a badly written time travel movie."

Seth still felt sick to his stomach, but he now had a whole new vocabulary and an understanding about the world he was in. For that, he could almost thank the bastard.

Almost. He still really wanted to slug Maahes, though.

Lydia reached up and laid her hand on his cheek. The moment she did, he completely forgot about his need to put his foot in an uncomfortable place on Maahes's body. "Hey."

Seth looked down at her.

"We'll get through this. Trust me."

"I do trust you." And he did. But then he cut a glare to Maahes. "That son of a bitch is another story. I don't trust anyone who serves a god, and especially not one whose most celebrated epithet was Lord of the Massacre."

She widened her eyes at that. Her face pale, she met Maahes's smug look. "Is that true?"

"It is."

"Do I want to know why they call you that?"

Seth answered for him. "He's the hand of retribution. Ma'at's personal slayer for anyone she wants punished."

It didn't have the effect on her that he'd hoped for. Instead of being angry at his enemy, she was rational with him.

Seth hated rational.

"So he's kind of like you, then. I would think you two would get along."

The taunting smirk on Maahes's face was definitely not helping his mood. "I'm also the one invoked by the innocent to protect them."

Lydia sucked her breath in as Seth's eyes darkened in a way that let her know Maahes was about to bleed.

When he spoke, his tone was deadly calm and razor sharp. "But only when it suits you."

There was so much buried rage in those words that it made the hair on her arms stand up. When Seth had been wounded and in pain, he'd been scary.

Whole, even without his powers . . .

He gave the full god in front of him a run for his money and Maahes knew it.

The cocky went straight out of Maahes as he caught Seth's meaning. "Are you saying you called for me and I ignored you?"

Seth didn't answer.

Instead, he brushed past him, driving his shoulder in to Maahes's and headed for the street.

Maahes frowned at her. "What didn't he tell me just now?"

Lydia sighed as part of her wished she was still as ignorant about Seth's past as he was. "When he was a small child, his mother," she choked on using that title for the bitch, "took him into the desert, broke his legs, and left him there to die. From what

I've heard, I'm pretty sure he called on all of you to help him and not one of you could be bothered."

Horror played across his face as he thought through what she told him. "Why did she do something like that?"

"Set thought he was pathetic and worthless. He insulted the mother for bearing him, and most of all for giving Seth his name."

Maahes cursed. "So she took him into the heart of Set's domain to die in front of him. No wonder we didn't know."

"What do you mean?"

He didn't answer.

Instead, he ran after Seth and pulled him to a stop. "Before you continue to hate us, let me explain something. Set was the god of the desert. That was *his* domain, not ours. We were never allowed to venture there unless he invited us. He would violently attack any god who dared to encroach on his territory and need I remind you what he did to Osiris and Horus? Your mother took you into the desert not just to hurt you in front of your father, but to keep us from finding out about it. Because I can promise you that had any of us learned of her cruelty, we'd have killed the bitch for it."

Seth fell silent as he digested those words. Honestly, he'd never expected an apology from any member of his family. As a rule, the gods never admitted to any kind of fault.

Now both Ma'at and Maahes had offered him one.

But in the end . . .

"It changes nothing."

Maahes nodded. "You're right. It doesn't change whatever happened to you, and that is a tragedy. However, it should comfort you to know that we would have helped you had we known."

Oh yeah, that was great comfort to him. Especially given how many times he'd called them, for what was it again . . . ?

Forty-five hundred years? Oh wait, he hadn't called for them quite that long. He'd probably given up after a thousand or so years of them ignoring him.

He sneered at Maahes. "You offer me empty words that mean nothing. It's easy to say what you would have done, if only. But neither of us really knows what action you'd have taken. Believe me, the one thing I've learned about the gods is how fickle all of you are. Praising a person one moment, and then damning them in the next. So don't try to alleviate your guilt by offering me what you think will make me feel better. I want nothing from any of you except to be left alone." Seth turned and continued down the street.

Lydia patted Maahes on the shoulder. "I know how you feel. He's kicked me like that, too."

"Yeah, but you probably didn't deserve it."

"And neither did he deserve what was done to him. Unlike you, I've seen the horror of his existence. He's entitled to his hatred."

"Then I will stay behind you two and try not to offend him with my presence."

Lydia started to respond, until she realized that Seth had stopped on the sidewalk about a block from them.

That wasn't what concerned her.

Rather it was the tall, skinny puta pawing at him that made her blood boil. Her vision turned dark as she quickly closed the distance between them. Why wasn't Seth sending her away? *Look at her, Lydia. She's gorgeous.* Which only made her ache all the more.

The blonde ran her tongue around her index finger while she looked up at Seth from beneath her long, over-mascaraed eyelashes, then bit and sucked it in a suggestive manner. She continued to run it around her lips as she spoke. "So you're visiting, huh? How long will you be here and where are you staying?"

Lydia wrapped her arms around his and glared at the woman. "He's staying with me. Right, pookie?"

Seth wasn't sure what to say. Lydia's voice was sweet and at the same time brittle . . . like her eyes as she stared up at him. He wasn't quite sure what was going on, but he had a bad feeling he was in trouble for it.

Lydia turned her gaze back to the woman who'd stopped to ask him directions. "Now if you don't mind, we're late for a meeting with his 'special' doctor. We have to make sure he doesn't run out of cream for his genital rash. After all, it's highly contagious, and burns like crazy when left untreated."

The blonde rushed off.

Seth kept opening and closing his mouth as he mentally ran through what she'd just done. He was stunned, appalled, and at the same time, oddly amused. And he had no idea which emotion was strongest.

Had she really just said that about him? To a perfect stranger?

Why?

Lydia snarled as she moved away from him. "You are such a man!"

He wouldn't have thought that was a particularly bad thing, except for the tone of her voice, which said it was. "What did I do?"

She raked him with a glare. "Chasing after the first piece of skank you see? Really?"

Thanks to Maahes, he understood the words. But her fury left him completely lost. "Why are you angry at me?"

"Why do you think?"

"I honestly don't know."

She rolled her eyes. "Yeah, right. You all but drooled on her."

"At no time did I drool." His mouth was completely dry and had been the whole time he conversed with the woman.

"Your eyes drooled. I saw them."

He was totally perplexed by this argument. Was he not allowed to speak to anyone? "I'm wearing dark sunglasses. How can you see my eyes?"

"She's jealous, Seth."

He looked at Maahes for an explanation. "Why?"

Lydia broke off into her hand gestures.

"Are you yelling at me, now?"

Maahes laughed. "Oh yeah, kid. She's calling you a lot of names."

That surprised him. "You understand her?"

Maahes gestured back at Lydia in the same language.

For some reason, it angered and hurt him that they'd cut him out of the conversation. "Are you mocking me?"

Lydia flicked her nails at him, then turned and stormed off.

Seth had no idea what he should do. He didn't understand human emotions or relations. Not really. It'd been too long since he had any.

Maahes let out a heavy sigh. "You hurt her feelings, boy. You need to go apologize."

"How did I hurt them?"

"Think about it, Seth. She risked her life to bring you here, to save you from hell, and what do you do the first minute she leaves you alone? You let another woman flirt with you."

That was flirting? Really?

He'd thought the woman attractive, but she was

nothing compared to Lydia. She hadn't made his blood race or given him thoughts of her draped over his body.

Only Lydia did that. She was the only woman he was willing to bleed for. How could she not know that?

Seth ran to catch up with her. "I didn't mean to hurt you if I did. She asked me for directions, and I told her I couldn't help her. That's all that happened."

"I don't care."

"Then why are you mad at me?"

Lydia didn't have a rational explanation. She knew she was overreacting and behaving badly. Yet . . .

"I don't know, okay? I just know it hurts inside."

His features tortured, he cupped her face in his hands. "You are the one person I would never hurt."

Lydia went to kiss him, but he snapped his head back before she could touch his lips with hers. His rejection cut her so deep, it felt like her soul was bleeding. "I don't understand you, Seth."

And the sad truth was, she wasn't sure if she ever would. Her heart aching, she walked back to where Maahes waited for them.

Seth sighed as he tried to understand what had just happened. *You should have let her kiss you.*

But he liked the fact that, for the first time since he was a boy, his lips didn't hurt or sting or bleed.

Idiot. Women liked it. He knew that. He wasn't sure what pleasure they got from biting him so hard, but . . .

I suck at this world, too. And in that moment, he realized the sad truth he'd never wanted to face.

He didn't belong anywhere. Especially not in this world.

It was just as well. She wasn't his anyway. She could never be his.

Once his powers returned, he'd leave her and go . . .

He had no idea. There was no home for him here. No one to call friend. Suddenly this world was even more terrifying to him than Azmodea.

Why are you panicking? Either there or here, the results are the same.

He'd be alone. At least here, he wouldn't have to worry about Azura and Noir.

But as he went back to where Lydia stood and she refused to look at him, he discovered a pain even worse than their torture.

Seeing the hurt in her eyes and knowing he was the one who'd given it to her.

Solin slammed his hand against the clear door, knowing it was useless, but unable to stand in here and do nothing.

Madoc paced behind him. "You're not accomplishing anything."

"It makes me feel better and it keeps me from beating the shit out of you. So you ought to be grateful that I'm banging on it and not your head."

"Whatever."

Ignoring him, Solin looked around at the small group that was caged with him. In addition to Madoc were Deimos, Phobos, Zeth, and Delphine. It seemed as if they'd been locked in this pit for days.

Like him and Madoc, Zeth had black hair and blue eyes. Phobos and Deimos were twins and, until they were locked in here, were the leaders of the Dolophoni who were now in pursuit of Lydia.

Delphine was one of the rare Dream-Hunters who had blond hair. "We need to figure out who betrayed us," she repeated for the millionth time.

Solin growled. "We've been over it and over it again. I don't care about your traitor. What we need to find is a way out of here. Preferably before they kill Lydia."

But at least he took comfort in knowing none of the people in this room had betrayed him. Hence why they were his jail buddies.

But who had? What god would be so stupid?

Deimos patted him on the back. "We'll get to her in time."

"What if we don't?" Solin couldn't bear the pain of the thought of losing her. She was everything in his world. "The Guardian said he'd kill her today if I didn't get back to him."

Phobos, who was sitting on the floor with his head on his legs, looked up. "Maybe he'll suck you back to Azmodea and then you can locate her."

"Yeah," Deimos agreed. "How did he nab you last time?"

"Through my dreams. He sent a lure in to trap me."

Deimos cursed. So long as they were imprisoned here, none of them had any powers. Not even the ability to travel in dreams.

They were totally screwed.

"Look on the bright side," Phobos said with a cocky grin as he cut his gaze to Delphine. "Sooner probably than later, Jericho will notice his wife's not around and he'll find us and kick the door down."

"He's right. My baby won't play."

Yeah and as the son of Warcraft and Hate, Jericho was a formidable god.

Still, Solin had looked into the painted face of hell and seen what it was capable of.

And right now, that beast had his daughter, and he had no idea what the Guardian was doing to her.

Hold on, baby. I'll get to you. I swear it.

Solin only hoped that his enemies didn't kill him first.

CHAPTER 16

Lydia stood in her newly adopted bedroom in Maahes's impressive home, staring out the floor-to-ceiling windows at one of the most beautiful views in the world. When he'd said his house was isolated, he hadn't been joking.

What he'd failed to mention was that his home was in the middle of an island he owned. She'd always loved looking out at the sea, but this . . .

Wow. It reminded her a lot of Solin's home in Greece. She'd be hard-pressed to decide between them as to who had the better view.

And she would have enjoyed it a lot more if she wasn't still angry at Seth.

Bastard.

Was she really so repugnant that he couldn't even kiss her? She didn't know why she was so fixated on that, but it had stomped her hard in an ego that had never been all that much to begin with. She knew she wasn't the prettiest of women. That her overly large eyes were a freakish color. One of her past boyfriends had even made the comment that he'd broken up with her because she reminded him of a troll doll with its big spooky eyes . . . Something that gave him the willies.

She wanted to kill Seth for bringing back all of this pain that she usually kept buried.

I'm not your yo-yo, buddy. She was tired of trying to guess his moods, which never made any logical sense to anyone but him.

Gah, how frustrating could one man be?

And what the hell was the thumping in his room? It'd been going on for the last few minutes, to the point that she was ready to go beat him with her shoes. Wasn't it bad enough he hurt her feelings? Was he now trying to make her insane?

But as she stood there, contemplating his murder, a weird sensation tickled the back of her mind.

Something's not right.

She couldn't explain it, but she had an overwhelming need to get to him and make sure nothing was wrong.

Of course he's okay. Really? You're freaking out over nothing.

Still, that feeling persisted. In fact, it was growing stronger by the heartbeat until it became a full panic that he was under attack and needed her.

You're so stupid. Just go check on him so that you can see what an idiot you are.

And she was, too. She had no doubt. Why else would she be worried over someone who could take care of himself?

Fine. Whatever. "I've had enough." What would the harm be? At least he wouldn't laugh at her.

He didn't know how to do that.

Furious at herself, she left her room and knocked on his door.

He didn't answer.

And still that thumping droned on.

Glaring at the wood that separated them, she used her powers to unlock and open it. But the minute she entered the room, she stopped dead as she saw him lying on his bed.

Asleep, he was in the middle of a nightmare and it appeared as if he was trying to fight someone off him. The thumping came from him hitting the wall with his arm while he flailed against whatever was in his dream.

She went to him and tried to wake him. "Seth?"

He didn't respond at all.

Her bad feeling intensified. Had something grabbed him in the unconscious realm? "Seth!" She shook him even harder.

Still, he slept on.

Lydia ducked as he almost hit her. She had to do something to wake him. Fast.

Fine, if she couldn't get him this way, she had another. Lying down beside him, she closed her eyes and used her powers to walk into his dreams.

It took a few minutes to get past her fear for him so that she could make the connection she needed.

Eventually, the haze cleared and she found herself in Azmodea again.

She cringed. Why would he come here? But unfortunately, that was what people did. They either visited things that were familiar or things they wanted to see. Seth had so little experience with anything outside of the hellhole that it actually made total sense for him to be here. Where else would he go?

And he better be hurt after bringing her back here, or else he would be once she found him.

Then, they would have a nice long chat on acceptable dream locations for future unconscious traveling.

With white gossamer wings, she flew over the dark landscape, trying to locate him. At first she didn't see anything in the darkness.

"Where is she?" The angry voice came from her right.

Lowering herself into the shadows, Lydia followed it to a small sinister meadow.

A mocking, masculine laugh rang out. "You hit like an arthritic three-year-old girl." That was Seth's voice.

Her heart clenched. *Oh no . . .*

He *was* in trouble.

"You really think you can hurt me?" he challenged whoever he was talking to. "Think again, bitch."

Tucking her wings in, Lydia crept through the shadows until she found him. Her stomach lurched as her gaze focused what was happening. *Not again . . .*

He was speared against a tree. Literally. Three long-handled spears were planted in his stomach and chest, holding him there while he was surrounded by four women.

The one she'd heard earlier grabbed his hair and wrenched it hard. "Call for her. Now!"

"No."

She slammed his head back against the tree. "Have we not done enough damage to you already?"

"Is that what this is?" Seth asked derisively. "I thought it was foreplay."

Lydia couldn't believe what she was seeing or hearing. Those were Dream-Hunters torturing him. They must have been waiting for him to sleep so that they could grab him and drag him back into this hell.

Damn it. She hadn't even thought to warn him about a danger she'd known from birth. Stupidly, she'd assumed everyone knew to be wary of Dream-Hunter powers.

But Seth wasn't Greek.

The Dream-Huntress sank her hand deep into his hair again so that she could yank his head down to hers. "Shame we didn't know how pretty you were the other night when we had you. Even the Phonoi would have been impressed."

"Fuck you."

She smiled at him, then jerked his lips to hers.

Seth growled as she pulled back and left his lips pouring blood. He spat the blood at her, but she dodged it and laughed before she backhanded him.

Lydia felt sick as she realized why he hadn't kissed her earlier.

How could I forgotten? After all she'd seen?

But then she'd been so wrapped up in her own damaged past, she'd lost sight of the fact that Seth didn't know kisses could come without blood and pain.

Even I bit him when he kissed me.

No wonder he'd pulled away. He hadn't meant to hurt her. He'd only been trying to protect himself from more harm.

Somehow she'd forgotten about biting him. But she'd lay money that Seth hadn't. How could he? He'd only been trying to give her a voice and she'd hurt him for it.

Strange how you always remembered the pain someone gave you, but seldom the hurt you caused them first.

"Here, Maia." One of the Dream-Hunters passed his tormentor a knife. "What say we castrate him? You think it would carry from his dreams into his real life if we did?" She looked up and tsked at Seth. "What? No smart retort for that?"

Seth didn't say anything as he tried again to pull one of the spears out of his chest.

The damn thing wouldn't budge.

He glared at the four women who'd dragged him to this realm against his wishes. "Do whatever you want. You're just wasting your time anyway. Lydia won't come for me."

He wasn't the one she loved. And even if by some miracle he was, she was still furious with him. Hell, he was lucky *she* hadn't pinned him to the tree.

When he'd tried to apologize again at Maahes's house, she'd slammed her door in his face.

Devastated, he'd gone to his room. And with nothing else to do and no one to talk to, he'd made the mistake of trying to sleep.

He should have known better. Why would he have ever thought himself safe? Slumber had never once in his life given him peace. It'd only left him weak and open to attacks.

The Dream-Huntress lifted the knife to his neck. "Where would you rather I stab you this time? Hmm?" She hovered the blade over the hollow of his throat. "This is always a painful place to be stabbed."

She trailed it down to his chest, raising a bloody stripe under the blade. "Then there's always the heart, or . . ." She moved it to his cock. "So what's it to be? If we harm you badly enough in a dream, you'll carry those wounds with you back to your waking state. So if I were you, I'd call her while you're still able."

He shook his head in steadfast denial. "I won't do it." He would never put Lydia in harm's way.

"It sucks to be you tonight." She pulled her arm back to stab his cock.

Seth tensed and held his breath in expectation of the pain he could already feel.

For once, it didn't come.

Before she could stab him, a blur came running from the shadows and tackled her to the ground.

At first, he thought he was imagining things. But there was no mistaking the flash of topaz eyes glowing in the dark.

Lydia was on the woman, beating her down with a ferocity he hadn't known she was capable of. The other three launched themselves at her.

"Lydia, behind you!"

She came to her feet and manifested a staff that she twirled around her back to the front. She caught one of the women with the hard end of it against her face, then knocked a second in the head. The third, she punched in the middle.

He had to give her credit. She knew how to handle herself with a skill he wouldn't have thought possible. It was a good thing he'd taken her powers when he captured her. With her abilities, she might or might not have defeated him, but she would have definitely put a hurt on his body.

In a matter of minutes, she had the bitches on the run. As they fled, she shouted after them. "Send the word out, you whores. If you want to fight me in this realm, you better practice more and bring serious backup."

Her breathing labored, she turned to face him.

Never in all of his life had he seen anything more beautiful than her tousled hair falling into those eyes that touched a part of him he thought was gone forever.

His heart.

Brushing her hair back, she threw her staff to the ground and ran to him. "You still with me?"

He looked down at the spears in his torso. "Sadly, I can honestly say, that compared to other sessions I've had this one wasn't so bad."

She sighed wearily. "You find your humor at the strangest times." Her brow furrowed, she reached for the bottom spear. "This is going to hurt. I'm so sorry."

He stopped her before she could yank it out. "Why are you here?"

Lydia paused at the odd catch in his voice. He really had no comprehension. "Don't you know?"

He shook his head. "You were so mad at me. I didn't think you'd ever speak to me again."

She took his hand into hers and held it tight. "Baby, I would always come for you."

"But I didn't call you."

"You didn't have to. I knew you needed me. Now hold on." She jerked the spear out as fast as she could, hoping to spare him as much pain as possible.

Seth bit his lip as she freed him of the other two. Instead of letting him hit the ground, she caught him against her and held him close.

"Hold on," she whispered in his ear as she draped his arm around her shoulders. "I'll take you home."

Seth came awake slowly. For a full minute, he was afraid to open his eyes lest he find himself back in his room or, worse, in Noir's torture chamber.

But as he caught the scent of his precious lily, he knew he was safe.

When he blinked his eyes open, it was to see the most beautiful woman in existence.

Before he could move, she started tearing at his shirt, pulling it up to expose his stomach and chest.

"What are you doing?" he asked.

"Making sure those bitches didn't hurt you so much that you brought your wounds back with you. I swear if they did, I will stalk them down and kick their teeth in until they beg me to stop and even then I'll . . ."

Lydia froze as she heard the most incredible thing of all.

Seth's laughter.

Stunned, she sat back on her legs to scowl at him and marvel at the way his smile lit up his entire face and made him all the better looking.

He truly had an adorable smile that could melt the iciest heart.

But she was completely bemused by his mood. "You find *that* funny?"

"No," he breathed. "I find it a miracle." He reached up and cupped her face in his hand. "You really came for me."

Closing her eyes, she rubbed her cheek against his palm, savoring the feel of his skin on hers. "I told you I would."

But he'd never believed it. Not for a single heartbeat. Words were cheap.

Actions cost.

Even so, she had fought off his attackers and brought him home. Just like she said she would.

She released his hand and went back to searching his body for injuries. Something he wouldn't have minded so much if it wasn't turning him on so badly that he couldn't stand it.

And when she leaned over him, spilling her soft hair across his chest that she'd bared, he almost came just from the scent of her alone.

Lydia hesitated as she saw the fire in those blue eyes that followed her every movement. More than that, she felt his desire for her swelling against her thigh.

Neither of them moved as they stared at each other, both afraid to move. Afraid of how the other would react if they did.

They knew one wrong word or action would shatter this moment, and it was something neither of them wanted to accidentally spoil.

But Lydia had never been timid in anything. She dissolved his shirt completely so that she could run her hand over his bare chest and feel the wall of cut muscles there. He had the lightest dusting of red hair over his pectorals. Hair that vanished over his eight-pack abdomen only to pick up again below his navel, where it was thickest of all, as it led her gaze down to the part of him that was swollen for her.

However, it was his tattoo that stood out so brightly on his skin. That was what beckoned her first. The one thing he'd manifested in an attempt to give himself comfort.

The first haven Noir had stolen from him.

Now she wanted to be the one who gave him comfort and took away his pain. To show him that he didn't need a bird's wings to escape what was happening around him. That there was pleasure to be had in his own body.

Let me love you, Seth . . .

But would her stubborn demon lord ever accept that from anyone? Even her. Or was he so badly damaged that nothing would ever make him whole again?

Seth ground his teeth as Lydia leaned forward to run her tongue over his swallow mark. It was the first time since it'd appeared that he didn't hate it and what it signified.

Closing his eyes, he surrendered himself to her mouth and warm touches that reached far below his skin and soothed him on levels he'd never imagined he possessed. His senses on fire, he was actually dizzy from the pleasure of finally having her in his arms.

He ran his hands under her shirt and over her back, delighting in how warm and soft her skin was. How good it smelled. Everything around them faded as he surrendered himself completely to her caresses. Caresses that were far sweeter than anything he'd imagined them to be.

And how could he? No one had ever touched him like this.

Like he mattered.

There was no pain in her gentle touch. No fingernails shredding his skin.

But her top was beginning to frustrate him as he tried to feel more of her. "No fair," he whispered in her ear. "You still have a shirt on."

It vanished instantly.

Seth sucked his breath in at the sight of her perfectly formed breasts. Her skin tone was so pale compared to his. Something that didn't make any sense since she was from the world of bright sunlight and he'd lived in darkness for so long that he could barely tolerate the sun at all.

His mouth watering, he cupped her breasts that overfilled his hands and smiled at the bounty of them. He lifted her up so that he could run his tongue over the tight nipple of her right breast and finally taste her.

Mmm . . . she was even more succulent than his best fantasy, and he wanted to taste every inch of her body until he was drunk from it.

Lydia shivered at the way Seth's tongue played against her breast as he rolled her over onto her back without withdrawing from her.

Then he moved from breast to breast, tickling her nipples with his tongue and then his whiskers in turn. Something that made her entire body convulse with unbelievable bliss. Who knew a man could do that? Her demon lord was extremely talented. So much so that she actually came a few minutes later just from that alone.

Throwing her head back, she laughed in ecstasy as her world exploded.

Seth smiled as he felt her shuddering against him. The sound of his name on her lips . . .

It was the sweetest of songs and he was so grateful he'd given her that voice.

He'd never taken delight in pleasing his partners before. In the past, he'd developed that particular skill as a way to get them off him quicker so that he could find his own release and be done with them.

But with Lydia, he wanted it to last and he wanted her to be pleasured like she'd never been pleasured before. He was desperate to make sure that when she left this bed, she didn't regret a single minute of being with him.

Lydia licked her lips as her body settled back down and Seth continued to run his hands over her breasts while he gently nipped her skin with his teeth. She lifted herself up to kiss him.

He pulled back again.

"Seth—"

"I'm sorry," he whispered. Staring at her, he swallowed hard, then lowered his lips toward hers. His entire body was tense and rigid. He all but cringed in expectation of her kiss.

Lydia ran her finger over his mouth while he watched her. "A kiss isn't supposed to hurt, Seth."

He frowned as if he thought she was insane.

"Trust me."

Seth nodded, even though he didn't believe her

for an instant. Kisses didn't hurt women. But they always hurt him. No matter who gave them, the result was ever the same.

He braced himself for the coming pain as she pressed her lips to his. She buried her hands in his hair while she lightly tongued his lips, sending chills all over him. And when she slipped her tongue into his mouth to stroke his tongue and tease his teeth, he swore he saw stars from it.

Lydia smiled as she felt him relaxing against her, and getting more into the kiss, until he finally took control of it.

Now it was her turn to be amazed. While she'd had her share of boyfriends and dates over the centuries, none of them had ever kissed her like this.

Like she was the air he breathed. She sank her hands into his soft curls and let them wrap around her fingers in the sweetest of caresses. She didn't know why, but those curls always made her smile. Probably because hair like his was rare. Not just the unusual color of it, but also the silkiness of his curls. The way they spiraled in a mad chaos that was unruly and yet controlled and formed. Ever a contradiction.

Just like him.

And in that one moment, as their breaths mingled and he groaned against her, she made the most startling discovery of all.

She loved him.

Truly. Deeply.

And with the whole of her heart.

Yes, he made her crazy. He had a way of infuriating her to the highest level of madness and motivating her into wanting to murder him.

And at the same time, he broke her heart and made her crave his touch even while she was trying to figure out where to hide his body.

But most of all, whenever he looked at her, she felt like a goddess. Pure and simple. And when he held her like this, she could almost believe she was beautiful.

I love you, Seth.

If only she dared say that out loud. Yet she knew better. He wasn't ready to believe her. He'd been too hurt. But in time, she was going to make him see it. Somehow.

Seth's head swam at the way Lydia held on to him and kissed his lips without hurting him in the least. Never had he imagined anything sweeter. More succulent.

Now he understood why people craved this. Why they were willing to die and to kill for it.

And as he breathed her in, a need came from the darkest part of his soul.

Love me . . .

He was desperate for her heart and he had no idea why. But whenever he was with her . . .

Nothing else mattered. He felt no pain.

Only her. Her smile warmed him all the way to the coldest part of his soul. And she had no idea how much power she had over him. Noir may have owned his body.

But she owned his heart and his beleaguered soul.

In her arms, he had the ability to dream again. To believe that maybe, just maybe, he wasn't a worthless piece of shit to be used and discarded.

That maybe for once, he was worth keeping.

In that moment, he felt more exposed and vulnerable than he ever had before. Because he knew a truth he could never deny.

Lydia was the one person on this earth, above or beyond, who could destroy him with one single word.

How could he have done this to himself? He knew better than to let anyone close to him. Yet he couldn't keep her out. She was too vital, too sweet, and the way she looked at him . . .

Like he mattered.

In her eyes, he saw the man he'd always wanted to be and he never wanted to disappoint her.

Lydia playfully rolled him over so that she could stare down at that gorgeous body that rippled with raw power. She kissed her way from his chest to the juiciest hipbone ever made.

But when she brushed her hand lightly against his cock, he jerked away from her and grabbed her wrist to keep her from stroking him.

That reflex caught her completely off guard. She'd never had a man do that to her before. Usually they begged to be touched.

Once again, he surprised her.

Mystified, she met his uncertain gaze.

He pulled her hand up and laid it against his chest before he finally explained. "I can perform a lot better for you if you wait until the end to hurt me there."

She didn't know what made her hurt the most, the sincere honesty in his voice or the expectation of pain she saw in his eyes. He spoke as if he were nothing more than a trained monkey with no other purpose than service her and go.

Her hand trembling, she brushed his curls back from his forehead. "Has no one ever made love to you?"

Scowling, he cocked his head. "Made love? I don't know what that is."

Of course, he didn't. Because no one had ever touched him with a loving hand. They had used him, abused him, and then thrown him away his entire life.

But that was going to change.

She smiled up at him. "You're about to find out, but you have to trust that I'm not going to hurt you."

"I don't know if I can."

The saddest part was that she believed him. "Then I'm going to teach you."

Seth had no idea what she meant by that until she manifested five silk scarves. She looped one about his wrist, then tied it to the bed.

Panic gripped him at her intent. "What did I do to displease you?"

She laid her head on his chest and shook it. Then

she locked gazes with him so that he could see the sincerity in her eyes. "Baby, this isn't about punishment. It's about pleasure. *Your* pleasure. Trust me."

She kept saying that.

Did he dare?

Trying to make her happy, he forced himself to submit to what she was doing even though it terrified him.

Once she had his arms and legs tied down, she hesitated. "Are you okay?"

He wasn't sure. He hated this feeling of vulnerability. Of being at anyone's mercy. Ever.

But he'd made her a promise.

"I think so," he lied.

She narrowed her gaze at him as if she sensed his dishonesty. "Trust. Me. You really are going to enjoy this." And with that she blindfolded him.

Seth held his breath as he feared what she'd do to him now that he couldn't protect himself at all.

Until he felt her long soft hair on his chest. Ever so light, it teased his flesh like a butterfly's kiss. His eyes rolled back in his head as she gently beat him with it. But there was no pain.

Only sweet torture.

Slowly, teasingly, she began kissing him again. First his lips, then his neck and ears. Ears that she licked and blew into until his body was on fire from it. Her naked breasts were plastered against his skin while she slid herself down his body, nibbling his flesh the whole way.

Okay, this was good.

Actually, it was far beyond good. Anytime Lydia wanted to tie him down and torture him like this, he would be her most willing slave.

Then he felt her warm breath against his cock. He tensed involuntarily.

Her fingers started dancing over the tip of him, until he was leaking from it. His breathing ragged, he bit his lip as blind pleasure consumed him. Slow and easy, she rubbed his moisture down his shaft until she played with the curls at the center of his body. Her fingernails brushed through them ever so lightly and then she slid her hand down until she cupped him in the gentlest caress he'd ever known.

Arching his back, he growled at how good it felt.

Then he felt something even better.

She took him into her mouth and tongued him until he thought he'd die from it. More than that, he heard her murmurs of pleasure. She actually enjoyed tasting him.

He couldn't believe it.

No one had ever done that to him before. No one.

He tried to hold himself back so that he could please her in return. But she was relentless with her mouth, tongue, and hand as she licked, sucked, and stroked every inch of him.

Before he could stop it, he came.

Still, she didn't pull away. Rather she continued to taste and please him until she'd sucked the last shudder from his sated body.

Only then did she let go of him. With a gentle hand, she slid his blindfold off and smiled. "You still alive, baby?"

He would never get used to the way endearments for him rolled off her tongue. "No, *sšn*." How could he be after that?

She jerked back as if he'd slapped her. Then her eyes darkened with a fury he didn't understand the source of. "Um . . . um . . . Seth?"

That icy tone made him extremely wary. Especially since he was still tied down and at her mercy. "Lydia?"

"Did you just call me Su-san?"

He scowled at the foreign word. "Susan? What's that?"

Her voice was still coated with icy venom. "A woman's name."

"I've never heard of such a name."

"Then what did you just call me a minute ago?"

It took him a minute to figure it out. "You mean *sšn*?"

Lydia narrowed her gaze as he said it again. And as before, it made her want to kick him because it sounded kind of like Ses-sahn—the way someone with his accent might say the name Susan or Suzanne. "Yes. Who is that?"

"Not a who. It means lily in Egyptian."

"Lily? Really?"

He nodded.

What an odd thing to call her. "Why lily?"

"It's the most sacred and beautiful of all flowers in Egypt. They bloom in mud and shine in the darkness like a gift from the gods to remind you that no matter how bad something is, it will get better. That no matter how dark the night, the light will come for you. If you partake of them, they have the power to calm and soothe you, and to heal your wounds." When he spoke his next words, they were laced with emotion and sincerity. "You are, and will always be, my *sšn.*"

Lydia pressed her lips together as tears gathered in her eyes. Those words set her heart pounding as she realized that *sšn* was so much more than a random endearment that he'd tossed at her.

He'd given it thought and chosen it with purpose.

Seth writhed on the bed as if he was trying to reach her. "I didn't mean to sadden you, Lydia. I'm sorry if I did. If you'll untie me, I'll please you now."

She sniffed back her tears and offered him a shaking smile. "You haven't made me sad. Not at all." She moved his necklace aside so that she lick his nipple again. "This isn't about you pleasing me. It's about me giving *you* pleasure. And baby, I'm about to rock your world."

Hours later, Seth lay on the bed with Lydia curled against him while she slept. He'd wrapped himself completely around her so that her hips pressed against his groin and her breasts rested on his arms.

All he could smell or feel was her, and it was all he wanted.

He still couldn't believe all the incredible things she'd done to him this day.

It was . . .

Words failed him.

Now he was completely sated and calm in a way he'd have never thought possible. Everything was right in the world and he didn't possess hardly a single god power.

Who would have ever thought that could happen?

He, the most feral of Guardians, the only one who had withstood the worst torture Noir could dish out, was tamed by the tiniest woman he'd ever seen.

And she hadn't done it with beatings or insults.

She'd broken him with a single kiss.

It didn't make a bit of sense. He'd been sold to Noir against his will and had fought that possession every day since. But he'd willingly given himself to her. Without question or regret.

Seth rubbed his cheek against her hair and smiled. This day had been the only happiness he'd ever known. And unlike her, he was afraid to close his eyes and sleep.

He was terrified that if he did, he'd awaken to find it all a dream. Or worse, have it all snatched away from him again.

Never had the gods allowed him to be happy. Why should that change now?

Suddenly, Lydia jumped up in the bed as if something had shocked her. Her breathing ragged, she reached for him and started searching his bare body.

Her actions worried him. "What are you doing?"

She clenched the necklace Ma'at had given him in her palm, and finally calmed down a degree. "Why didn't this work?"

"I don't understand."

She tightened her grip on it. "Remember what your aunt said when she gave it to you? That it would protect you—and yet it didn't. The Dream-Hunters attacked you and hurt you while you wore it."

He pulled on the chain until she released it and it fell back on his bare chest. "But only in my dream was I hurt. The one Dream-Hunter told me before she started to stab me that I should have been harmed outside the dream, too, but I wasn't. So maybe it did work."

Lydia calmed down a degree as she considered that. Perhaps he was right.

And yet, she couldn't shake the bad premonition she'd just had while she was sound asleep. It was of Seth being dragged back into Azmodea by Noir and put in a room like the one she'd found Solin in.

Over and over, she saw his abuse so clearly . . .

In every detail.

The last time this had happened to her, her mother had died just days later.

And in the exact manner she had foreseen.

CHAPTER 17

Lydia laughed as she watched Seth trying to figure out how to work her iPod. Only he could look that sexy with a frown so stern while wearing a set of black in-ear headphones that trailed down both sides of his head.

"This was made by a demon, too, wasn't it?" His voice thundered in the room.

Lydia pulled out one of the earphones. "You're talking really loud. You should always take one of these out when you speak so that you don't accidentally shout at people."

"Oh. Sorry." He sighed in frustration. "I don't get how this plays music."

"Well, it doesn't just play music. You can use it for all kinds of things. I have pictures in here, games, even movies."

"What kind of pictures?"

Lydia shrugged. "I have some of my house in England." She scrolled through her album until she found one of her living room, then she held it out to him so that he could see.

Seth studied the sedate room that was decorated in greens and yellows. It was very understated and yet also feminine. "It's nice."

"I like it." She scrolled to another photograph and held it out to him. "That's my backyard."

It reminded him of a jungle. Still it was serene and inviting. In all honesty, he felt a little guilty over keeping her here with him when she could be home right now had he not kidnapped her.

She would have been safe. But for him.

"You must miss it."

Without responding, she leaned forward to show him again how he could toggle around the photos. "Just press this and it'll scroll right through."

He did as she said, and discovered more photographs of her home and of her neighbor's yard. But when he got to one of Solin and her with their arms wrapped around each other, all the happiness inside him died.

How could he have forgotten about Solin?

Because you wanted to.

Yeah, but that didn't make it right.

Lydia placed her hand on his. "Seth? What's wrong?"

I'm a jerk and a sucker. That's what's wrong.

Most of all, he was a fool.

Seth couldn't speak at first as guilt overwhelmed him. When he found his voice again, he glared at her. "How could you . . ."

She continued to play the wounded innocent in this. "How could I do what?"

Seth showed her the photo of her with Solin. The love and happiness on their faces . . . He deserved to have the crap beat out of him over it. He should never have touched her. "How could you cheat on Solin after everything he's done for you?"

She gaped. "Excuse me?"

His temper mounted at her feigned indignation. She had no right to be angry at him for defending the man she'd screwed over. "You heard me."

Lydia was so stunned by his assumption about her relationship with Solin that she was at a complete loss for words.

His gaze narrowed even more. "Are you trying to think up a lie to excuse it?"

Now that, that set her temper off, fast. It took everything she had not to slap him. When she spoke, it was through clenched teeth. "I don't have to think up anything." She raked him up and down with her gaze. "I . . . you—I—I . . ." She kept sputtering and stuttering in outrage.

"He loves you so."

"And I love him!" she snapped.

"Then how could you have had sex with me, knowing that?"

She gestured at Seth's lower extremities. "Because I can't have sex with *him*." She almost choked on the word.

The very thought of sex and Solin nauseated her. "Why not? Is he impotent?"

She shivered in revulsion. "No . . . I don't know. Why would I know? Ew! Gods! Stop that! Ew! Ew! Ew! I don't want to think about that area of his body. As far as I'm concerned, he doesn't have one of those, and nothing other than his feet exists below his waist." She made a gagging noise as she slung her hands in the air, repulsed beyond endurance and disgusted by the very thought of Solin having sex with anyone. "Yes, I know I'm being childish, but I don't care. That's how I feel about it. Yuck! Who wants to have sex with their father? Gross, gross, gross . . . Gross!"

Seth sat back on the bed, unbelievably stunned. And not over her outrage and overreaction. Was any of that true?

"What?" he asked.

"Yeah," she snapped, jerking her head at him, "you heard me. Incest doesn't run in my family, buddy. Just so you know."

Okay, now he had the distinct impression that she was insulting him. "What are insinuating?"

"You're the one with the family tree that doesn't branch." She illustrated said tree with her fingers. "How many Egyptian gods slept with their brothers' and sisters' wife's mother's uncle's dogs? Hmm? I ask you?"

He wasn't quite sure if he should be offended or amused by her attack on his family. Honestly, he had no real feelings for any of them other than hatred and disdain but . . . "Have you visited *your* pantheon lately?"

"We're not talking about my pantheon, here. Are we? No. We're insulting *yours*."

Seth was definitely amused now. "Well, just so long as we have that straight . . ." Which brought him back to what had started all of this. He sobered instantly. "Is he really your father?"

"Yes . . . and you are absolutely the only single living person besides us who knows this. So if you tell anyone, I will know it and I will choke you until you . . . do something that makes me happy."

Why did he find her vague and odd threats so amusing? Other than the fact that they were at least creative, he had no idea.

But he had to come back to one thing in her tirade. "Why did you tell me, then, if no one knows?"

"You were accusing me of being a whore. Thanks, by the way. I'm so glad to know you've been paying attention and taking notes in the Trust classes I've tried to teach you."

Now that reignited his anger. He didn't like for anyone to put words into his mouth. He always spoke plainly so there was no reason to misinterpret his meanings. "I didn't call you a whore."

"You implied it."

"I did no such thing."

"No?" She cocked her neck at him again, letting him know just how angry she still was. "Then I want you to run all of your words backward in your head and listen to them. Then put on my ears and listen to them again, and then tell me what you hear. If that doesn't spell whore in any language, I don't know what does."

She *might* have a point with that. But he didn't want to admit it right now. "Can we go back to when we weren't fighting?"

"Little late for that now, buddy. You should have thought about that before you opened your mouth." She started signing angry gestures at him.

He tried to follow and understand, but it made no sense to him whatsoever. "I've got to learn your language one day." Although, he definitely understood the last gesture she made at him. "You sure you're not too sore for that after everything we've done? I know I don't mind and I'm certainly willing to accommodate you."

She made a sound of ultimate disgust as she got off the bed and headed to the bathroom, then slammed the door.

Seth couldn't resist calling out after her. "Does that mean I should still be naked when you return?"

She stuck her head back through the door. "You know, I think I liked you better when you were menacing . . . and quiet." She slammed the door shut again.

Those words took him back to how he'd lived in Azmodea and he felt all the amusement drain instantly out of his body. In some ways it seemed like a lifetime ago.

And in others, it was still right there, a painful wound that he was afraid would stir again and start throbbing.

But there was one undeniable truth. "I didn't like me then," he said under his breath. He much preferred talking, even fighting, with her than living that miserable life.

Subdued by his somber thoughts, he lay back on the bed that was covered with her sweet scent. He should shower too, but he didn't want to wash her off him.

Not yet.

He wanted to sit here and just breathe her scent in for as long as he could. He picked up his shirt from the floor where she'd dropped it last night after they'd returned from a run to the kitchen to find something to eat.

It, too, smelled like her. He lifted it to his nose to breathe her in at the precise moment she returned.

She wrinkled her nose in distaste. "Well, at least you're not sniffing your body parts, I guess."

Now there was an odd place to go. "What?"

"Nothing. But if you ever do that with my underwear, I will be so grossed out, that I will never, ever touch you again. Just so you know."

He would definitely commit that to memory. Not that he'd had any plans to sniff her underwear, far from it. But he didn't want to do anything to annoy her. "Any other rules I should know about?"

"Keep the toilet seat down at night, and don't eat the last potato chip. Ever."

"I will remember the seat, but have no idea what the other is." Maahes had forgotten to give him that knowledge.

"Good. Keep it that way and we'll get along famously."

She flounced back to bed.

"Are you still mad at me?"

"I am. Will probably be so for some time. Did you really think I was so slutty that I'd put one man at risk to save me and then turn around and sleep with the one who'd promised to hurt him?"

Seth felt a little trapped by the question. The one thing he'd learned with her was that if he said the wrong thing, she closed him out.

If he said the wrong thing and it *really* annoyed her, she wouldn't let him touch her at all.

He cared for neither scenario.

But before he could stop his mouth from opening, he spoke. "I'm rather surprised you slept with me given that he's your father."

Lydia raked him with another grimace. He would never learn to stop when he was behind. "You're impossible! I swear you learned your social skills from monkeys."

Seth's face fell as if she'd slapped him. He pulled the earphones out and set them and the iPod down.

Without a word, he went to the window to stare out at the sea. Completely naked and oblivious to that fact, he made a striking pose there with his arms crossed over his chest.

She was still having to get used to his perfect unscarred body, and the fact that he had no modesty whatsoever.

Her heart thumped hard against her breastbone as she watched him. With no idea what had hurt him, she got up to join him there.

She pressed herself against his spine and wrapped her left arm around his lean waist. "I'm sorry if that hurt you." She rubbed her fingernail down his shoulder blade and kissed a spot on his bicep. "Could you at least tell me why?"

A tic started in his jaw. "It reminded me of something my adoptive mother used to say, and . . ."

"And what?"

Seth fell silent as he wrestled with emotions he'd never expected to feel again. He cared for this woman. He didn't want to hurt her, but most of all was a fear that he hadn't known since he'd been a child.

Fear that something or someone would take her from him and he'd be unable to protect her. But the worst was the terror that she'd become so disgusted with him, like everyone else had, that she'd leave him for it.

Please don't throw me away, too.

Just once, he wanted to be worth keeping.

"Seth?" She placed her hands on his hips to twist his body back and forth playfully.

He looked down into those haunting topaz eyes that branded him as hers every time he saw them. "It's nothing."

"Okay, but which word do I remove from my vocabulary, oh great knight who formerly said Ni?"

He drew his bows together as he tried to decipher her strange words. "Huh?"

She smiled at him. "It's a movie reference. So what word?"

"Monkeys."

"All right. No monkeys of any kind. Just remind me to move my sock monkey collection off my dresser when we get home."

When we get home . . .

Those were the sweetest words he'd ever known. It meant that she saw a future for them.

So why couldn't he?

But every time he tried, he could only imagine himself with Noir again. Was he so scarred that he couldn't believe in anything else?

Or was it a premonition that told him he would never be worthy of happiness.

She trailed her hand slowly down the front of his body until she cupped him. Her fingers worked magic on his body as she massaged him back to life.

He had no idea how he could possibly get hard again. Not after the hours they'd already had together.

But it didn't take her long to have him stiff and ready to fill her again.

Turning in her arms, he cupped her face in his hands and kissed her like she'd showed him. Then he scooped her up in his arms and returned her to bed so that he could taste her fully.

Lydia shivered as he laved her ear, then moved down her throat to her breasts. He seemed obsessed with those. But his attention this morning was for other things, she realized, as he nibbled a blazing trail down her stomach to the part of her that really should be sore by now.

Yet it wasn't.

She parted her legs, giving him access to do whatever it was he wanted.

His eyes half closed, he dipped his head down to taste her. She let out a pleasured yelp as he slid his tongue over her, then scraped her with his whiskers. Burying her hand in those soft curls, she watched as he teased her. It was as if he couldn't get enough of her body.

She certainly couldn't get enough of his touch. She rubbed herself against him as he delved deep inside her with his tongue. Biting her lip, she moaned as his fingers joined his tongue in tormenting her with pleasure.

"Seth?"

Seth glanced up at her to see the fire in her eyes and the smile on her face while he licked her. He loved that she said his name whenever they did this. It let him know that she wasn't thinking about any-one else.

And now that he knew the truth about Solin, he was even more possessive of her.

She was his.

All his.

He gave her one long, slow lick. "Come for me, Lydia. I want to taste you on my lips again."

Lydia gasped as he returned his mouth to her and quickened the movements of his fingers. Reaching down, she laid her hand against his cheek so that she could feel the muscles of his working while he tasted her.

And in that moment, she obliged his wish as her body spasmed.

Then he crawled up her ever so slowly until he slid himself deep inside her while she was still cli-maxing. The sensation of his warm, thick fullness made her gasp as he began to rock himself against her hips. Fierce, long, hard thrusts that heightened her pleasure all the more.

Arching her back, she met each of his strokes with the same desperation he had.

"That's it, baby," she breathed as he found the perfect rhythm that never failed to leave her beg-ging for more.

He laced his fingers with hers as he stared down at her while he thrust himself against her hips. She loved feeling him like this. Inside and outside of her.

Seth clutched her hand in his as he watched her staring up at him with the kindest gaze he'd ever known. No one had ever looked at him the way she did. Without disgust or condemnation. She was so small in his arms that at times he was afraid he'd hurt her by accident. But she'd been able to stand up to the worst of him.

Which made no sense because he knew that in the end, she was the best part of him. The only good part.

And he lost himself to her. With a pleasure so profound it burned his soul, he buried himself inside her up to his hilt and let his release flow. He held himself perfectly still as his body convulsed.

Sated and weak, he lowered himself over her, taking care not to put too much weight on her. But he didn't want to pull out of her quite yet. She wrapped her arms and legs around him and cradled his entire body with hers.

"What are you thinking about?" she asked him as she brushed his hair back from his face.

"Absolutely nothing except how much I like being inside you."

She wiggled her hips against his. "You do feel good there."

He kissed her, then pulled away to sit back on his legs so that he could study her body.

Lydia frowned as she watched him fingering her. "What are you doing?"

"I'm looking at the part of me that's on you." He touched the wetness between her legs and rubbed it into her with his thumb. "I don't ever want another man with you . . . like this."

She shivered at the possessiveness in his tone. "What are you saying?"

I love you. But Seth couldn't bring himself to speak the words out loud. He didn't know how.

Still, she smiled up at him and then she started singing in the most beautiful voice he'd ever heard, a song that reached so far inside him that he couldn't breathe as tender emotions overwhelmed him. "I hunger for your touch. Alone . . . and time goes by . . . so slowly . . . and time can do so much . . . "

While she sang to him, she reached up and laid her hand on the hollow of his cheek. He knew they weren't her words, but the way she sang them . . .

It felt like they were and they went straight to a part of him that had never been touched before. They said exactly what she meant to him. And why he'd learned a new level of hell.

It wasn't the physical pain of Azura or Noir's cruelty. It was living a life without any beauty in it. Living a life with no laughter or teasing smiles.

A life with no Lydia.

Lydia lay there, staring at him as emotions played across his face. In that moment, she knew what he'd wanted to say and couldn't. And it was okay, because she didn't need the words. She could see it plainly in the way he looked at her as if terrified he was dreaming and at the same time so hungry that his light gaze seared her.

Taking his hand into hers, she folded his two middle fingers down and spread out his thumb, index finger and pinkie so that they were standing up straight.

"What's this?" he asked quietly.

"What you're not saying, but I hear it anyway." She kissed his folded down fingers and placed hers over his.

Seth stared at their combined hands that strangely reminded him of two halves of a heart that formed a whole one when placed together.

She was right. It was exactly how he felt whenever he was with her.

Her smile brightened the darkest part of him as she buried her hands in his hair and brought his lips down to hers. "I will never leave you alone again, Seth," she whispered before she kissed him. "I promise. Not unless you want me to."

And that he would never crave. How could he?

But as she made him blind with the ecstasy of her touch, he couldn't shake the feeling that this wouldn't last.

How could it?

He'd been cursed by his own father and thrown away by his mother. Even so, he wanted to believe in her promise.

If only he could. Yet in the back of his mind lingered the bitter doubt that all of this was only temporary.

He dipped his head down to taste her again. Just as his lips brushed hers, unimaginable agony tore through his entire body. Before he could do anything, it lifted him from the bed and threw him into the wall.

CHAPTER 18

Seth felt the first stirring of his god powers returning to him as he hit the floor hard enough to splinter an internal organ. Thank the gods he wasn't human, or he'd be dead right now. But what he truly hated was the metallic taste of his blood in his mouth.

Revolting.

With his tongue, he checked to make sure his teeth were still in place, then looked to see what had attacked him.

His blood ran cold the moment he realized what Noir had done. What the bastard had sent after him.

Damn it to hell . . .

Verlyn who at one time had been a god of ultimate good. Noir had corrupted it and turned it into the twisted embodiment of evil in front of him now. Seth had no idea how Noir had accomplished it. All he knew was that Verlyn was one of the deadliest creatures in existence.

So much so, that even Noir hesitated to release him for fear that one day he wouldn't be able to put Verlyn back into whatever cage Noir kept it in.

Standing an impressive seven feet in height, Verlyn couldn't be bargained with. It merely did what it was told.

And obviously its orders now were to bring Seth back to hell.

Seth closed his eyes and summoned as much of his powers as he could. A small kiss.

Just a token. A little more than what he'd had at Sanctuary.

But it was enough to put his armor in place and to set fire to it. Pushing himself up, he knew this was about to get ugly.

Lydia dressed herself in a pair of jeans and a T-shirt as she stared at the mountain that'd just appeared in their room. Dressed in a long, black coat with a high-standing collar that was trimmed in silver . . . silver that appeared to be stained by blood, the man had shaved his head smooth and symbols were tattooed down the center of his skull, culminating into a sharp point right between his eyes.

His right eye was ringed with black and from the bottom of it was another set of symbols that went down his cheek to his chin. The only color on his body was a splash of a bright green shirt he wore beneath the black coat.

But the most shocking thing came when he turned to assess her as a threat.

He had the same eyes as Jaden. Only in reverse. Where Jaden's eye was brown, his was green and vice versa.

There had to be a story there between them. Were they relatives? But this wasn't the time to try and do an interview. Not when the mountain turned away from her and headed for Seth with a deadly stride that promised Seth a major ass beating.

She launched herself toward the mountain.

"No!" Seth growled, throwing his arm out toward her.

He manifested one of his force fields around her to hold her back from the fight.

Seething, she glared at him. "What are you doing?"

"Saving your life. He won't attack you, unless you attack him, and then he'll kill you."

She scoffed. "I doubt that."

"I don't."

Lydia held her hands up in a choking gesture. Why wouldn't he see her as a capable fighter? She was just as able to battle as he was.

But then given his age, she was lucky he wasn't more of a chauvinist. All in all, he did pretty well with it.

Sometimes.

However, this wasn't one of them.

Seth backed up against the wall, making sure to keep Verlyn in front of him. That was the only safe place when dealing with an enemy this deadly.

Verlyn's eyes started glowing red. "You have been summoned, Guardian."

"Yeah," Seth said slowly. "It's what I figured. But I'm going to have to disappoint Noir and you."

Verlyn tsked. "Poor choice that."

"Yeah, well, what's new there?"

Baring his jagged teeth, Verlyn rushed him.

Seth caught the beast and flipped him to the floor. He tried to pin him there, but it was impossible. Verlyn probably outweighed him by a good hundred pounds of solid muscle. Muscle that shouldn't be as flexible as his was.

"Damn you, you fat bastard. Lose some weight." It was like trying to control a full-grown rhinoceros.

Verlyn twisted around in a way that shouldn't be possible for something with an internal skeleton and snatched Seth off his back. He slammed him against the floor hard enough to daze him. And then Verlyn slammed him there a couple more times for good measure.

"I think you need some help there, baby," Lydia called to him. "Want to let me out?"

"No," he choked through his windpipe that was being crushed by Verlyn's hand, which happened to be twice the size of his. "Won't be able to play with you later if you're bruised and I'm feeling guilty that I caused it."

"You are so sick."

And right now, he was getting his ass kicked. Seth kept punching at Verlyn, but it was like hitting a brick wall with a bare hand.

Not to mention, he was getting tired of having his

head dribbled on the hardwood floor. Why hadn't Maahes carpeted the damn place?

Speaking of that bastard, where was Mr. I Would Have Protected You Had I Known? So much for his worthless vows.

Yet again, he was nowhere around when Seth needed him.

Then Seth smelled it. That fetid stench that signified Verlyn was opening the channel between the human realm and Azmodea.

If he didn't do something fast, he was going back there.

Lydia saw the panicked despair in Seth's eyes as he locked gazes with her. That scared her, but when her shield suddenly went down so that she could join the fight, she knew she had only heartbeats to save him.

Her only thought his safety, she ran for Verlyn. When he would have grabbed her, she shifted into her jackal form and latched onto his forearm with everything she had.

Verlyn screamed out in pain, trying to pound her into releasing him. But she wasn't about to let go. Not until he was gone and they were safe.

Out of nowhere, a bolt of lightning went through the room, striking Verlyn right through his heart. Lydia released him immediately. Unfortunately, the bolt didn't kill him, but it knocked him through the glass window and sent him to the sea below.

Maahes ran to check on them.

Seth wasn't ready for that as he stared at Lydia's true form.

She was a jackal.

A fucking jackal.

And as he stared at her, something about her tugged at his memories. Like déjà vu. But he couldn't place it. Not right then when he was grappling with so many other rancid emotions vying for his attention.

Why hadn't she told him?

Unaware of the turmoil he'd interrupted, Maahes pulled back from the window. "C'mon. We need to get out of here. I'm pretty sure our friend down there isn't dead."

Verlyn wasn't, but in a few minutes, Lydia might be.

His gaze never wavering from her canine body, Seth pushed himself up from the floor.

Lydia returned to her human form even though she had second thoughts about it. One look at Seth's face and she knew just how badly she'd screwed up.

He would never forgive her for this. And she couldn't blame him for it. Not really.

But right now, they had to get away from Verlyn and she still had her promise to keep. She wasn't about to allow Noir to take Seth back.

"Where do we go now?" she asked Maahes.

Maahes stepped away from the shattered window. "Out of here, 'cause he's getting up and he don't look too happy about it. Does he have any friends?"

Seth's tone was stoically dry. "He makes his own friends."

Moving to stand next to Maahes, Lydia didn't understand what Seth meant until she scanned the landscape below where Verlyn had fallen, and saw that he could split himself into multiple beings. Multiple beings who could fly and climb up . . .

Fast.

Maahes cursed. He grabbed Lydia by the arm, then Seth. One second they were in his house, and in the next, they appeared in the throne room of a huge golden Egyptian temple. Lydia turned around slowly to take in the beauty of it. From the luminescent way it appeared, she was sure they were no longer in the human realm, but another. The walls shimmered from sheets of gold. There was a huge dais in the center where a gilded throne was flanked by two god statues. She had no idea which two, though. One she could swear must be Maahes's. Not that it looked like him. It was merely an impression she had.

"Now I dare that bastard to come here," Maahes said proudly.

Lydia hoped he was right, but she wasn't feeling so cocky. "Where are we?"

"Ma'at's house. Her temple, actually. She doesn't really live here. She thinks it's too ostentatious." He all but sneered the last word.

Yeah, he would say that, given the overstated

luxury estate he lived in. Obviously, Maahes didn't have a problem flaunting excess wealth.

"We'll be safe here," Maahes said confidently.

Seth snorted. "I wouldn't bet *my* house on it. Believe me, he'll find us. It's what he does."

"Yeah, but—"

Seth gave him a withering stare. "He was one of the original six primal gods. Believe me, this won't even slow him down."

Maahes cursed under his breath.

"Exactly," Seth added sardonically.

Lydia refused to be so pessimistic. "Then how do we escape him?"

"We don't. Ever."

Maahes narrowed his gaze. "I don't believe that. There's always a way to defeat anything. You two make yourselves at home, and I'll be back in a few." He vanished instantly.

Alone now, Lydia felt awkward as she turned toward Seth. His face was stoic, but it was the torment in his eyes that cut to her soul.

"I'm sorry. I should have told you what I was."

Still, he gave her no clue about his mood. "Why didn't you?"

"Jaden told me not to. Given what happened to you, we were afraid of how you'd react to it."

He rubbed absently at his neck where the swallow would be under his armor. "Does Jaden make all of your decisions for you now?"

She screwed her face up in distaste. What was

he trying to say? She wasn't exactly sure, but she knew it was making her angry. "That's not fair, and you know he doesn't."

He moved to stand in front of her, reminding her of just how huge and intimidating he could be, even when he wasn't trying. And even though he appeared completely calm and composed, his blue eyes screamed at her. Or maybe that was the weight of her own conscience.

The one thing she was sure about was that she'd hurt him. And that she'd never meant to do.

"Then why didn't you tell me?" he asked quietly.

That answer was complicated so she settled on a simple one that she hoped would placate him without hurting him more. "I was afraid he was right."

Seth ground his teeth as she stabbed him straight through his heart. For a full minute, he couldn't breathe from the pain of her words that hurt him so much more than any physical blow. So, he'd been right, even though deep inside, he'd been hoping he was wrong.

Still, he refused to let her know just how much damage she'd done to him with that.

Not now.

You're a monster. Why would she ever see anything else? You're stupid and revolting . . .

He cleared his throat to make sure no residual emotions would be there to betray him when he spoke. "Have I ever given you any reason to fear me?"

Her jaw dropped with incredulity. "Uh, yeah."

Then she ticked her list off her fingers. "You took my powers. Made me your prisoner and threatened to kill me *and* my father. Have you forgotten that you tortured my father, and I don't mean a little bit either?"

No, he hadn't. The guilt of that tore at him every time he looked at her and saw how much she loved her father.

Nor had he forgotten his own list of ills against her. "You stabbed me. You bit me until I bled, and you invaded Noir's sanctum to free a god Noir wanted questioned. Had I not taken you prisoner when I did, he would have nailed you to the wall and eaten your entrails. Trust me, you would never have gotten Solin out of there in one piece. And you would still be there, begging for someone to kill you."

"Yeah, okay," she said angrily, "a little touché there, but—"

"There's no but. Yes ... I am pissed off that you're a jackal. I can't stand them. But that's not why I'm mad."

"Why, then?"

"You, who have done nothing but lecture me on trust, didn't trust me with the truth. You withheld it, and you purposefully hid it." Because she had thought of him as less than human.

Less than caring.

That was what stung him deepest of all.

He didn't deserve that. Not from her. Not after all he'd done to protect her. "I thought . . ."

No, he wouldn't say it. There was no need. Her actions told him everything he needed to know.

"Thought what?" she asked when he didn't finish.

"Nothing." Seth started away and then stopped as his anger mounted to a level so high, it blinded his vision. He wanted to lash out and sting her as deeply as she'd kicked him. "No, it *is* something."

He raked her with a sneer. "I thought you saw me. But you're just like everyone else. I'm nothing but an animal to you and that's all I'll ever be. Something to be feared or kicked or caged or put down."

But never kept.

Never trusted.

Never loved.

Seth winced at the bitter truth. "All of you think that I can't control myself. That I'm . . ." he caught himself before he said the one thing he thought of himself.

. . . my father. Incapable of feeling or caring.

His adoptive father had said that so many times. *There's something not right with that one. You can never trust the gods or their by-blows. They're tricky, sneaky bastards.* And they'd all mistrusted him when he'd given them no reason to.

Just like her.

Looking back, he wasn't surprised that he'd been sold at thirteen. He was only surprised now that they'd kept him that long.

But he'd expected better from Lydia. He didn't know why. Not when everyone else had kicked him.

Still, he'd hoped.

And yet again, he'd learned better.

She reached for him, but he wouldn't let her touch him and weaken his anger. Not this time. He needed it to keep from being hurt any worse. Anger might not be worth much, but at least it kept him warm when nothing else did. And it kept him safe, cocooned away from the world and from being around those who lied to him.

Tears glistened in her eyes. Something that kicked him in the groin with steel spikes. "I *never* treated you like an animal."

"Didn't you? In the beginning, did you not set out to tame me?"

She sputtered indignantly. "No, not exactly."

"No or not exactly? Which is it?"

"It's both." Her cheeks darkened as her temper kicked in to match his. "Okay? I'll admit that. I didn't know you then. And do you not own a mirror? Have you seen what you look like when you're painted up and standing nine thousand feet tall with this gigantic aura of I-hate-everything-around-me? You know, you're just not real approachable like that, buddy. That whole fuck-off-and-die attitude you've armor-plated yourself with tends to unnerve people. Excuse me for feeling the very thing you were striving to make me feel. You're a little too good at it. Maybe if you'd learn how to smile once in a while it might help. Certainly couldn't hurt. So yes, in the beginning, I did bite you and I was trying to win you over to my side. But then, I did see you. I did."

"And yet you still fear me, don't you?"

Lydia pressed her lips together as she debated how to answer. "What do you want me to say?"

"I want the truth."

"Fine then. Yes. There's still a part of me that's scared of you. I'll admit it. I've seen where you've lived and what's been done to you. Horrors like that take their toll. They have to. You can't walk through hell and not be scarred by it. And while I've seen the good in you, I've seen the worst. The worst does terrify me. So given all of that, I decided to listen to Jaden's advice and not tell you I'm a jackal. I didn't want you to lash out and hurt me for something I can't help."

But it was okay that she'd just done that to him.

Because she didn't see the man in front of her.

She only saw Noir's mindless slave. The animal Noir had made him. She didn't think enough of him to believe that he could have his own sense of right and wrong. That he could walk through hell, and while he was definitely scarred from it, he was still whole.

Still worth *something*.

Yes, there were times when the scars opened and he bled anew . . . like now.

But he wasn't a monster. He didn't lash out at anyone without reason.

And he'd never once lashed out at her. She had no reason to doubt him.

Yet she did.

There's something not right with that one. You can never trust the gods or their by-blows. They're tricky, sneaky bastards.

But it wasn't just the gods.

It was everyone. All beings served their own agenda. No good deed was served without them expecting something back in return.

And he was through being hurt and kicked for no reason. "You know, I'm really not as stupid as everyone thinks. I am. I can tell the difference between you and the jackals who fucked me over . . . But then maybe not. Because right now, I'm thinking what you've done cuts me a whole lot deeper than what they did."

I expected better from you.

Seth headed out of the nearest set of doors he could find. He had no destination, other than to get as far away from her as he could.

I can't believe I was so stupid. After everything he'd risked for her. She still didn't trust him.

Why do I bother?

"Maybe I should just go back to Noir," he breathed.

At least in Azmodea, he knew the rules and they never changed.

There, he knew how to protect himself.

Yeah, okay, so he sucked at it, but he knew what to do to not get thrown through a wall. There, he saw the punches coming and he decided beforehand if he wanted them or not.

But here . . .

It was a minefield where he was assaulted when he least expected it. And the blows Lydia gave him hurt so much more than the worst torture Noir could devise.

"Seth?"

Why did the sound of his name on her lips weaken him so? He didn't want to stop or turn around.

But he couldn't walk away. Not from her.

Against his will, he paused and waited for her to run up to him.

Lydia slowed down as she reached his side. He stood as proud and powerful as ever with that mop of riotous curls softening a countenance that was as deadly as it was beautiful. All of her life, she'd dreamed of finding someone who made her feel the way he did.

Someone who could make her laugh when she shouldn't, and who would talk to her about absolutely nothing. Someone she could sit with and not speak for hours, and that would be okay, too.

Most of all, she'd dreamed of a man who made her feel beautiful when he looked at her. Not with words. But with the light in his eyes that would shine only for her.

The tenderness in his touch.

Who would have ever dreamed that man would be Seth?

She moved to stand in front of him, but he still wouldn't look at her. The way he bounced his gaze around to look at anything else would be funny, if she didn't care about his pain.

But she did.

"I wouldn't hurt you for anything. Not now. In the beginning, yes. But . . ." She braced herself for whatever off-the-wall reaction he might have. "I love you, Seth. I just wanted you to know that."

Seth froze as he heard the last thing he'd ever expected someone else to say to him. The one thing no one ever had. "What?"

"I love you. And only you."

He stared at her in total disbelief as those words echoed in his heart. Were they true?

Did he dare hope or believe that they were?

How should he react? He honestly didn't know. A multitude of indecipherable emotions exploded through him all at once, paralyzing him.

She looked at him expectantly. "Aren't you going to say something?"

What? What was he supposed to say? Nothing in his screwed up past had ever coached him on how to deal with something like this. Pain he could handle. Contempt he was well versed in. Insults rolled right over him.

But love . . .

What did someone do with that?

Lydia waited for some kind of response, but all he did was stand there, eyes wide, like a statue that strangely made her think he was waiting for a pigeon to come crap-bomb him.

Suddenly, he started looking around again. At the sky, the yard, behind them, in front of them. Everywhere.

"What are you doing?" she asked with a light lauth at his strange behavior.

He leaned toward her to whisper in an awed tone. "I'm looking for something bad to happen."

She frowned. "I don't understand."

"You can't love me. No one does." The sincerity in his voice and expression was heart-wrenching. He truly couldn't fathom anyone caring about him.

Not even her.

Laughing, she pulled him into her arms so that she could bury her hand in the curls at the nape of his neck and hold him close. "You silly man. Of course I can love you."

Seth wrapped his arms around her, stunned and shocked, as she swayed him back and forth. He couldn't even begin to sort through his rapid-fire emotions right now.

But at the bottom of it all was an equal amount of euphoria . . .

And holy ranking terror.

What did people do when they loved each other? He tried to remember the few years he'd lived with the jackals, but it'd been too long ago, and he'd banished all those memories to the darkest part of his mind.

Now he trod a whole new landscape where nothing was familiar. The only thing that kept him grounded was the woman in his arms who'd rocked his entire existence.

The woman he would die for.

"What does this mean, Lydia?"

Lydia smiled up at him as she finally understood his bizarre question. For a man with so much worldly experience and a thorough understanding of the worst things in the universe, in many ways, he was like a small child who was baffled by a simple act of kindness.

"Well, when people love each other, they usually make a commitment to each other . . . or the man runs for the door in stark, raving terror."

His look turned to steel. "I don't run from anything."

"I know, sweetie." She stood up on her tiptoes to kiss the stern frown from his brow. "It's one of the things I love most about you." She held her hand up with the sign she'd taught him in bed. "This is how you say 'I love you' in my language."

He duplicated the gesture and laid his hand against hers like they'd done earlier. The unspoken happiness in his gaze set her heart pounding even faster.

"How do you say it in ancient Egyptian?"

He actually had to think about it. Something that made her eyes water as she realized why he had to struggle to remember. After a few seconds, he shrugged. "I don't know. I never heard those words said together."

She sniffed back her tears. "You will always, *always* hear them from me. Every day. I promise." Lydia's gaze dropped to his neck where she'd planned to kiss him, but something else caught her attention.

Was that . . .

No. Was it?

Standing on her tiptoes again, she pulled the neck piece of his armor down so that she could get a better view and double-check what it was she thought she saw.

Seth stepped back. "What are you doing?"

"The swallow . . ."

"What of it?" he asked after a few seconds when she didn't continue speaking.

Lydia was aghast at the sight. She couldn't get over it. "It's different now."

"How so?"

She traced the tail feathers with her fingertip. "The heart inside its tail . . . It's no longer broken." She used her powers to conjure a mirror so that she could show him. "See . . . the heart's whole."

Seth leaned his head back so that he could see his mark. She was right.

Finally, after all this time, his swallow could fly again.

He was whole.

Because of *her*.

He leaned down to kiss her lips, but before he could, something bright flashed around them. It came and went so fast, that he wasn't sure if it'd been real or imagined.

Not until Lydia arched a brow. "Was that lightning?"

"I don't know."

It flashed again. Then four more times in rapid succession.

This time, Seth recognized that pattern and what it signified. "It's Maahes. He's in battle."

And there was only one person Maahes could be fighting here in this realm.

Verlyn had found them.

CHAPTER 19

Seth hesitated outside the throne room. In battle, it paid to get your bearings before running in half-cocked. That was the quickest way he knew of getting gutted, and he'd been gutted enough to verify it for a fact.

And while he knew he would survive a good gutting, Lydia might not and he wasn't about to take a chance with her safety.

As he listened, the familiar sounds of violence and battle rang out around him, reminding him of the life he'd had to endure all these centuries past.

I don't want to go back to that. Ever.

He wasn't a coward. But he was tired of fighting for every little thing. Of being on guard with every creature he came into contact with, knowing they wouldn't hesitate to strike out at him if given a chance.

Lydia had spoiled him with another world, and it was one he never wanted to leave.

Which meant he had to get rid of these assholes so that they could . . .

Make a commitment to each other. That's what Lydia had called it. And that was the life he wanted now. One with her in it.

That was the life, the only thing, he was willing to fight for.

Closing his eyes, he tapped into the powers that Noir had been stripping from him since puberty. They were stronger now than they'd been even an hour ago, and they still weren't at full strength. It made him wonder what they'd be like at maximum capacity. They'd have to be impressive, given what he felt right now.

No wonder Noir had kept him under heel. At full strength, he would have the ability to give the bastard a good run for his money.

The jackals should have asked for a higher price when they sold him. Stupid bastards.

And with those powers, he was able to see everything going on inside the throne room.

Verlyn and Maahes were there and engaged in a bloody fight as they stood toe-to-toe. But they weren't alone.

Far from it.

Solin, along with other Dream-Hunters and a Greek god he didn't recognize, were fighting another group of their own kind. And as he watched and listened, he finally understood why everyone was after them.

Why the gods were after Lydia.

His stomach churned. Verlyn wasn't here for just him.

There was someone even more important to everyone in that room. He looked back over his shoulder.

The same person who was everything to him.

In her jackal form, Lydia started to run past him, but he caught her against his chest and held her tight before she made a serious mistake.

Struggling against his hold to free herself, she flashed back to human. She crouched beside him to give him a nasty glare. "What are we waiting for?"

Sanity.

But it was a little late for that. What the hell? Not like he'd ever had any to begin with.

He inclined his head to the combatants inside. "The Phonoi and those bitches from my dreams are in there."

Lydia felt the blood drain from her face as she heard his news. The Phonoi? Here?

Why would they have come for Seth when he was Egyptian and Noir's property?

As the Greek embodiment of Murder, Slaughter, and Killing, the Phonoi were the triplet goddesses Zeus sent in whenever he wanted someone killed.

But why kill Seth?

"Are you sure?"

Nodding, Seth's jaw muscle worked furiously.

He pinned her with a stare that made her stomach clench. "You're the key, Lydia."

She drew back with a scowl. "The key to what?"

"The key to Olympus that they're trying to find."

The man was nuts. "There's no way. You're wrong."

He stroked her cheek, looking at her as if he'd never seen her before. But that wasn't what scared her. It was the light in the back of that icy blue gaze that sent a shiver over her because she didn't know what it signified.

"Think about it, *sšn*. It's the only thing that makes sense. Don't you see? It's why Solin was the only one who knew where the key was. Why the Greek Dream-Hunters came for me, demanding I give you to them. Why else would they want to kill *you*?"

Even though it made sense, she refused to believe it. She couldn't. "I can't be the key to Olympus. I know nothing about it. I've never been there. Never met Zeus or any of them. I . . ."

Lydia's voice trailed off as a long-forgotten memory flashed through her mind. She saw her mother on that awful night that was forever branded in her heart. Smelled the fire and heard the screams and shouts of her family dying.

"Where is it? Give us the key and we'll spare the rest of you."

She'd never seen who attacked them, but now she remembered the angry voices that had been right outside their small home.

Their attackers had been looking for a key that night, too. Her grandfather and uncles had gone to fight them while her mother grabbed her from bed and dressed her to run.

"Stay calm, Lydia. Don't panic." Her mother had kissed her on the cheek. *"I know you're scared. So am I. But this is something you have to do alone. I can't go with you. Now that they have my scent, they'll be able to hunt you down and find you if I do."*

Lydia had tried to speak, only to learn that she couldn't. And that terrified her even more. Why couldn't she make even a whisper?

Her mother's hand had shaken as she stroked her hair to soothe her. *"I did that so that you can never speak of this night to anyone. You understand? Trust no one . . . Now, I'm sending you to your father. He'll guard you always. You are the key that men will kill to possess. Whatever you do, listen to what your father tells you. One day, you'll understand."*

Then her mother had tried to transport her to Greece.

Lydia hadn't made it. Their enemies had killed her mother before she could finish the transport.

Instead of Greece, she'd landed in the desert. Alone. Terrified. Bereft. For days, she'd staggered through it until one man had come out of a sandstorm to save her.

She wouldn't know he was her father until long after she'd grown up.

And then only because, as a young woman, she'd been desperate to learn something about the man she'd thought had abandoned her and her mother. Ready to confront him and give him nightmares until he begged for mercy, she had been shocked to her foundation to find Solin.

The man who'd raised her like a daughter because she *was* his daughter. A daughter he was terrified of claiming lest one of his enemies hurt her because of him.

She still remembered that night of discovery as if it were yesterday.

"I tried everything to make your mother love me. At first she thought I was a human and then when she found out I was a Dream-Hunter, she hated me.

"Even then, I didn't give up hope. But in the end, I had to leave. She wouldn't allow me to stay no matter what I said or did.

"I didn't find out about you until your third birthday, and I promised her that I wouldn't try to see you. She was afraid that if anyone learned I was your father, that they'd hurt you for it. And I knew she was right to be afraid, so I agreed to stay away from you."

All her mother had ever said to her and her grandfather was that Lydia's father had been a god who'd seduced her. She'd never named Solin.

"I am the key," she breathed to Seth, facing the truth that scared her. As Seth had said, it all made sense now. "What are we going to do?"

Seth had no answer for that as a thousand thoughts went through his head all at once. And all of them had the same outcome.

Watching Lydia die.

Now that Verlyn had been called out, he wouldn't stop until he had them both locked in Azmodea, and while they could run for a while, they would be pursued constantly until they made a mistake.

And then they'd both be in Azmodea. Sooner or later. No matter how hard they tried. There was no way to run forever.

Honestly, he didn't care about himself. His own life had no meaning or value to him. It never had. But hers . . .

She *was* everything. For her, he would fight.

For her, he would die.

And now that they knew who and what she was, the Greeks would never stop hunting her. Not until she was dead and posed no threat to them.

Neither would Noir. If Seth knew nothing else about the gods, he knew that much.

And the more he chased his thoughts, the more he kept coming back to the only solution that made sense. But that solution made him ill.

You can't. Noir will kill you.

If only. But Noir wouldn't kill him. He'd only make him wish he was dead.

Bracing himself for what he had to do to free her of this, he offered her a grim smile. "I have an idea."

* * *

The moment Seth entered the throne room with Lydia in his arms, all the fighting stopped. One by one, the others turned to gape at him.

He held his head high while inside he was so cold and aching that he wasn't sure how he could move.

I had to do this. There was no other way.

But knowing that didn't make it easier to bear. Like his father, he was a god of tragedy and sorrow. Ever condemned to destroy whatever it was he might love.

Condemned to never know love at all.

Seth kept his gaze on the Greek gods as he took Lydia toward the Phonoi and Solin, who'd been fighting each other. It was so quiet now, he could hear the blood rushing through his veins.

With his jaw slack, Maahes lowered his sizzling lightning bolts. Fury blazed in the god's eyes, but Seth was too numb right now to care what the ancient god thought about him. "What have you done, boy?"

Seth didn't answer as he walked past Maahes and placed Lydia on the ground at Solin's feet. "I told you I'd kill her if you didn't return. I just kept my word."

With a cry born of ultimate grief, Solin drove a short sword straight through Seth's side.

Grimacing in pain, Seth shoved him back, then wrenched the sword out. He faced the Phonoi and Dream-Hunters around him, then dropped the weapon on the ground. "All of you can stop fighting now. She's dead."

The Phonoi moved to check.

Seth struggled to keep his composure. But in his mind, all he could see was the look on Lydia's face when he'd stabbed her and apologized for it. The fear and accusation in her topaz eyes had torn him apart.

"Why?" she'd breathed, her eyes filled with the pain he'd given her as she placed her hand to his cheek. He still had her bloody handprint there.

Unable to answer for the agony that shredded whatever remained of his battered soul, he'd merely held her against him, choking on his grief as he watched the fire fade from her eyes. And when she'd gone limp in his arms and her hand had fallen away from his skin for the last time, he swore he'd died with her.

He'd never hated himself more.

Not that it mattered. Lydia was gone.

Now they would leave her in peace.

The Phonoi glared at him in unison as they verified her death to the others.

When Solin went to attack him again, Verlyn grabbed him to keep him from hurting Seth. Solin struggled against him, calling Seth every name he could think of and inventing a number of insults Seth had never heard before.

But Seth ignored him.

Besides, there was no insult Solin threw at him that he hadn't already thrown at himself, and worse.

The Phonoi approached him as a single unit. "Thank you for your service."

Seth's breath caught as he heard the gratitude in their voices. He'd finally had someone thank him, and what had it been for?

Killing the only thing he'd ever loved.

But still he said nothing as they faded out of the room.

The other Greek gods who'd been fighting by Solin's side to save her, stared at him as if he were the dirt they stood on.

Seth met their condemnation every bit as stoically.

Closing the distance between them, Verlyn grabbed him by the hair and snatched his head back while he immobilized Seth's limbs so that he couldn't fight or flee.

But why run now?

Grimacing in pain, Seth kept his gaze on Lydia's body as they faded from the room.

I love you, Lydia. Please forgive me.

With the blink of an eye, Seth was back where he'd started.

In hell.

Well, more precisely, he was in Noir's study, where the dark lord rose to his feet to confront him.

Verlyn shoved him forward, then returned to wherever it was he stayed when he wasn't serving Noir.

Heartbroken, and more tired that he'd ever been

before, Seth faced his master, knowing he'd screwed himself straight to the wall this time. There would never be another moment of peace in his life. Not another moment free of misery.

It was what he deserved.

"On your knees, dog," Noir growled at him.

Seth shook his head. He wasn't about to bow down to anyone.

Noir curled his lip. "Ever defiant. Did I not tell you what I'd do if you failed to bring me the key?"

"You did."

"Did you think I was bluffing?" Noir grabbed him by the throat and dissolved his armor.

There was no need to respond. There was nothing Noir could do to him now that would compete with the agony of living without Lydia.

In fact, he hoped the physical pain would be able to distract him from the misery in his heart. Because right now, that burned more than any injury he'd ever sustained.

"I'm going to enjoy this," Noir snarled at him.

Seth laughed bitterly and then did what he did best.

He pissed off his master. "Go ahead. Do your worst."

"I'm so sorry."

Solin ignored Delphine as he cradled his daughter's body against his chest and wept. His soul screamed out that she, the only thing in his life that had ever meant a damn to him, was now gone, and he felt so incredibly lost.

In a life marked by scarring pain and soul-searing agony, nothing compared to what he felt right now. Nothing.

All he could do was see images of Lydia as a child, reaching out to him. Remember the frustration they'd both had as they struggled to learn sign language so that she could talk to humans. The frustrations they'd had when she'd started dating, and he'd disapproved of every man she'd brought home.

Oh the nightmares he'd given some of those pricks. No one had ever messed with his girl that he didn't make them pay.

Until now.

And what hurt the most was that he'd never see her again. Never watch as she sang to him with her hands.

Because I failed her. It was all his fault. Had he been stronger . . . faster . . .

Why couldn't the Guardian have killed him instead?

Delphine reached to comfort him.

"Don't touch me!" he growled.

There was no comfort to be had. Not now. Not ever again.

Did Delphine really think that some stupid, paltry touch would soothe him when his heart had been ripped out?

Jericho, Delphine's husband, moved forward as if he was going to attack him over hurting her feelings, but Zarek stopped him. The two of them had been the ones who'd finally heard Delphine's call and had released them so that they could chase down the Phonoi to stop them from hurting Lydia.

But not in time. If only they'd found the phonoi sooner. Maybe then they could have saved his baby.

I wish the Guardian had killed me the first day he captured me.

Anything would have been better than the agony of living without his daughter.

Maahes moved forward. "Is there anything I can do?"

"Fuck off and die."

Instead of getting angry, Maahes walked away and left him to his pain. As did the others.

Except Zarek.

He waited until they were alone before he approached Solin. "I'm not going to insult either of us with some mambi-pambi bullshit. Life sucks. No one knows that better than I do. But if you want to go break ass over this, I'll be there for you. Just shout. The bloodier, the better."

Strangely, that did make him feel better. And he knew Zarek meant it.

"Thank you." But he'd never take Zarek up on that offer. He'd never put the demigod in harm's way. Unlike him, Zarek had a family. The one thing Solin had always wanted.

The one thing he'd always been denied.

He'd never even heard his own daughter call him father.

Not once.

Zarek inclined his head to him respectfully, then vanished.

Alone now, Solin looked down at Lydia's pale face that had never failed to make his heart swell with pride.

Until today. Today there was nothing but blinding misery that cut so deep, his soul bled from it.

He brushed at her skin, trying to clean her. There was so much blood. How could anyone have done this to such a kind, sweet being?

How?

I'll kill him, he swore to himself. He didn't know how, but he was going to get that bastard and rip him to pieces.

It's what you get for trusting someone. If anyone knew better, it was he. They had a traitor in their midst, and that betrayal had cost Lydia her life.

He would find the turncoat Dream-Hunter, too, and bathe in their blood.

But first he had a daughter to bury.

Lydia groaned as she blinked open her eyes. She felt so incredibly sick. What had she eaten?

Where am I?

She looked around the lush bed with linen curtains surrounding it. The sound of the sea and smell of saltwater was thick in the air. Over the top of the bed was a gold medallion and a crystal chandelier that, when lit, would cast dancing deer on the ceiling.

She frowned as she realized where she was. Solin's house.

But why was she here?

Why was she dressed in this garish white gown?

Oh good grief! She was in lace and ruffles. Ick! It was something her father would put her in, and something she'd only agree to wear if she had a severe head injury . . . or was dead.

"Damn it, George, I wanted the white ones for today! White! Do you hear me?"

She jumped at Solin's angry shout. How strange. She'd never heard him fuss at poor George before. He normally had infinite patience with his valet, who was more family than employee.

Yawning, she stretched and sat up at the same time Solin came into her room.

He froze to gape at her, then a heartbeat later he flashed himself across the room to grab her into a hug so tight, she couldn't breathe.

"You're crushing me." Lydia didn't know who was most stunned when those words came out.

Her or her father.

Shocked to the core of her being, she stared up at him as he looked down at her, gaping. "Was that you?"

She touched her throat, almost too afraid to try again. "I think so."

Dear gods, she could speak . . .

But how?

And still, why was she at Solin's? She kept coming back to that because she had no explanation whatsoever. "What am I doing here?"

Solin scowled as he tried to grasp what was happening. Lydia was alive.

Alive!

He'd planned to entomb her body in only a few hours. But here she stood, whole and hale, and . . .

Alive.

He kept repeating that one word because he couldn't believe it. The Guardian hadn't killed her?

It was inconceivable. She'd been here for two days while he made preparations. No pulse. No heartbeat. And now she was just as she'd always been.

"Don't you remember the last week?"

Lydia shook her head. "I was at home. I remember that I was angry about something, but I don't remember what. Then I woke up here. Did you teleport me?"

"No, baby, I didn't. You really have no memory of . . ." he didn't want to mention Azmodea if she didn't remember it, "coming after me?"

She shook her head. "Why did I come after you?"

Solin's eyes misted as he realized what the Guardian had done for her.

He'd freed Lydia forever so that she could finally live her life without either of them having to fear that the other Greeks would find her. Everyone thought she was dead now.

For the first time in her life, she was completely safe.

But why would he have done such a thing?

Why do you think?

The Guardian loved her. There was no other reason for it. None. He'd given his own freedom, his life, for Lydia.

Solin stood there, amazed and grateful. Never in his life had anyone done anything like this for him. "Do you remember anyone from the last couple of days?"

She arched her brow. "Like?"

"A man with red hair?"

"Haven't been to McDonald's in a long time. Are you okay? You're looking at me really strangely."

"Never better." He smiled at her. "I'm just grateful you're awake. You've been extremely sick the last few days . . ." He'd have to explain eventually why she was missing several days out of her life. What better way than illness? "We were worried about you, that's all."

But inside, he felt like shit as he debated what to do. He hated to keep a secret from her, especially one that involved someone who obviously loved her as much as the Guardian did.

She had a right to know what he'd done for her. But if she had no memory of the Guardian, why disturb her with the truth?

Obviously, her safety had meant more to the Guardian than anything else. Who was he to interfere?

So long as she didn't remember, he would never speak of it.

"Are you hungry?" he asked, touching her warm cheek—something he would never again take for granted. "I can have George make you anything you want."

Lydia smiled at his offer. "Banana pancakes would be wonderful." She didn't know why, but she had a strange banana craving.

"Get dressed and I'll have them waiting in the atrium." Solin kissed her hand as if it were a holy relic and hesitated before he finally let go and left her.

Yeah, okay, her father was in a very, very strange mood.

As she went to the armoire and opened the door to get something a little less hideous to wear, there was a shadow in the back of her mind.

A world beyond a world.

Why did that seem important?

She opened and closed the armoire door. The way the blue wallpaper flashed on the ceiling reminded her of something. But what?

It was on the tip of her tongue, but she couldn't quite grasp it.

Blue on the ceiling?

What did I get into? She felt woozy and had a voice. But what really confused her was when she pulled her gown off and saw . . .

Was that a swallow?

What on earth?

Frowning, she fingered the weird tattoo on her shoulder just below her collar bone that hadn't been there before. It was incredibly colorful and beautiful, but she had no memory of having it done. And if that wasn't strange enough, she had some weird Egyptian cartouche around her neck.

Okay, remind me to never, ever drink again.

"You're so pathetic."

Seth didn't bother to look up at Noir as the bastard came to drain his powers again. He was so weak he could barely breathe. Since his return, as part of his punishment, he hadn't been allowed to charge them at all.

And for that small mercy he was actually grateful.

Without his powers, he had no way whatsoever to see Lydia. There was no temptation to even try . . .

Which kept her safe.

Still, he would give anything to have one more second with her. To see those beautiful topaz eyes . . .

Noir laid his chest open, bringing him out of his numbed state as pain seared him. His overlord had become even more sadistic in his attempts to make sure Seth suffered as much as possible. And in guaranteeing that Seth would never escape again.

Not that he would.

He had no reason to go anywhere and every reason to stay. So long as he was here, Lydia was safe.

That was all that mattered to him. At least that was what he kept telling himself. But over the weeks, it'd gotten harder to remember the sound of her voice. The softness of her touch.

It terrified him that the day might come when he'd have no memory of her whatsoever.

And that was a far worse torture than anything Noir and his demons could dish out.

But his initial torture on his return here had at least clarified one thing in his memory. He knew why Lydia's jackal form had seemed so familiar.

Her mother had been one of the jackals in his adoptive family.

Her grandfather was the one who'd sold him to Noir.

The irony of that stayed with him. But it didn't stop the part of him that loved her anyway.

Noir raked his claws down the side of Seth's face as he finally pulled back. "You are too repulsive to look at."

Seth had no response as he closed his eyes and tried to escape in his mind.

But he'd given Lydia his swallow and cartouche to keep her safe whenever she awoke, and without those he had no choice except to stay here and feel everything.

Lydia floated in the dream realm on her white gossamer wings. She didn't know why, but her swallow tattoo kept pulling her here at night. It was almost as if it were trying to tell her something.

But whatever it sought, they never found it.

Arching up toward the dark sky, she saw a shadow moving far below. One that was terrifying and . . .

She saw eyes of steel set in a face that reminded her of warmth.

But as soon as she saw them, they were gone.

Yeah, I've lost my mind now.

And she had.

Time to wake up and see about moving the rest of her things from her home in England to her father's estate. She was still sick from the week she'd been in a coma. And he was too worried about her to leave her alone. Which was fine with her.

Lydia had a feeling that in the coming days, she was going to need someone with her.

She just didn't know why.

Seth felt a presence near him, but he couldn't open his eyes to see if it was Noir or Azura. Not that it mattered. Pain was pain no matter whose hand dealt it.

Was it time to be drained again?

Hadn't they already been here?

He couldn't remember. Each feeding now seemed to hurt more than the one before and they blended together into a never-ending cycle of cruelty.

A hand brushed the hair back from his face. Sick from the agony they caused him, he tried to move away and fight, even though he knew it was futile.

Until he managed to open his eyes enough to see the face of his tormentor.

For a full minute, he couldn't breathe as he saw the last person he'd ever expected to see again . . .

Lydia felt the tears stinging her eyes as she saw what Noir had done to him.

And all because of her.

The bolt was back in place and he'd been beaten so badly that she barely recognized a single feature on his face. He'd been hit so many times that his eyes were swollen out of shape and colored various shades of purple. He could barely open them even a slit.

She bit back a sob before she spoke. "I told you that I would always come for you," she whispered before she placed a gentle kiss on his bleeding cheek. She stepped back so that he could see she wasn't alone.

Ma'at, Maahes, Thorn, and Solin were with her.

Maahes unchained him while Ma'at healed him, and Solin kept an eye out for any of the demons or Noir.

Seth fought against his release, but couldn't speak until Maahes removed the bolt. He choked on his own blood, then refused to leave with them. "I can't go. You won't be safe."

"I'm not leaving you here," Lydia insisted.

Furious at her, he glared at Solin. "Get her out of here before they find her."

Solin snorted. "Believe me, I've tried to talk sense into her. She won't listen."

Seth turned his glare to Thorn. "Why would you bring them here?"

Thorn grinned. "Solin made me an offer I couldn't refuse. Believe me, violating my truce with Noir isn't something I do lightly."

He wanted to kill the bastard for that. But Thorn was every bit the immortal. Plus he had powers even Seth couldn't fathom.

Seth looked back at Lydia. "I have to stay . . . please."

Lydia couldn't believe that he was still willing to stay here for her safety. If she'd had any doubt before about how much he loved her, that cleared it. "All right, fine. If you stay. I stay."

"We all stay," Maahes said.

Ma'at nodded. "Agreed."

Thorn snorted. "You can stay if you want. But

I'm getting the hell out of here. Noir's side smells. I prefer my demons and slime hole to his."

Seth glared at Solin, hating him for his interference. "Why did you tell her? Damn you! She would never have remembered me."

Lydia arched a chiding brow at him. "My father didn't tell me anything and I'm still angry at him for that. But I remembered you. Even though I didn't understand it, I felt you with me constantly. And if that wasn't enough . . ." She took his hand and placed it on her stomach so he could feel the slight swelling there. "You left me with a very special gift."

The news slammed into him harder than one of Noir's blows. She was pregnant?

With his child.

Unimaginable joy ripped through him as he felt the slightest fluttering of his son or daughter moving inside her.

But that only solidified his resolve. "You won't be safe if I leave."

She cupped his now healed face in her hands. "No one ever is, Seth. No matter how hard we try. No matter how much we plan and prepare. There will always be an enemy at the door and a storm trying to knock us down. Life's not about security. It's about picking up the pieces after it's all over and carrying on. We can choose to be cowards who fear letting someone inside us, and do that alone.

Or we can choose to be brave and let someone stand by our side and help us. I'm not a coward. I never have been. And there is nowhere else I plan to be, except beside you. Forever. Be it on earth, or here in this hellhole if that's what it takes. I will always be with you."

In that moment, he realized he didn't need his swallow to fly him away from pain.

All he needed was her.

And she was right. It took much more courage to lay his heart open to someone else than it did to keep it guarded. To let someone else in to that place deep inside where only they could do you harm.

Only Lydia could destroy him.

And yet only she gave him life . . . at least one worth living.

Solin curled his lip at him. "Believe me, I'm not happy about her decision any more than you are, but we are family, and families stay together. So if you don't want to go . . . George will hate you forever. He's extremely fond of his room in Greece and won't be happy about giving up the view. But he'll get used to it. Eventually."

Seth couldn't believe what he was hearing. They were willing to stay here to protect him?

Were they out of their minds?

"What about Verlyn?" Seth asked. Noir would only set him loose again to find him. And now that

Lydia was pregnant, she would be in more danger than ever.

Lydia smiled. "Don't worry. We have a place to take you where you'll be safe from his reach until all of your powers return."

"How can you be so sure?"

It was Ma'at's turn to laugh. "It was what I was working on when you were taken from my temple. I promise you, you'll be safe there. It's the one place neither Noir nor Azura, nor any of their servants can reach you."

Still, he wasn't convinced.

Until he looked into Lydia's eyes. "I won't leave you here alone, Seth." She kissed the cartouche she wore, then pulled it off over her head to hang it around his neck.

At first, he thought it was the one he'd left with her, knowing it would keep her safe once she came out of the spell he'd placed on her to make her appear dead. But as he looked at it, he realized it was different.

She smiled at him. "It's 'I love you' in ancient Egyptian . . . Just so you know. Now, please, come home with me."

He stared at the raised, golden hieroglyphs that spelled out words he hadn't known.

Not until Lydia.

His throat went dry.

Home. He'd never had one of those before either. He wasn't even sure what the word meant.

But when he looked into her eyes, he saw the one thing he couldn't deny.

The only woman he'd die for. So if he was willing to die for her, the least he could do was live for her, too.

"Take me home, Lydia."

EPILOGUE

Lydia lay on the bed, watching as Seth fed their son for the first time. He was still terrified he was going to hurt the babe, even though she'd promised him he wouldn't. He was far too gentle for that.

"What are we going to name him?" she asked.

Seth looked up with the most beautiful smile she'd ever seen. "Ambrose?"

His choice surprised her, but it made total sense. The Malachai had kept his word after all.

Not the elder Malachai, Adarian, who'd made the pact with Seth. It'd been Adarian's son who had honored his father's word and kept them safe in his home in New Orleans until Seth's powers had returned. But for Ambrose, Noir would have found them.

"You don't want to use Nicholas?" It was Ambrose's human name.

Seth shook his head. "It's too common and there's no one else like our son."

That was certainly true. He was a rare, rare breed.

Watching the two of them staring at each other with equal wonder and adoration, she smiled as she remembered what Seth had said when she'd asked him why he made her forget him when he'd left her with her father.

"I couldn't bear living if I knew I'd caused you pain. I'd rather you not know me at all, than to think of me and cry."

He looked up and frowned. "Did I do something wrong?"

Lydia smiled through her tears. No matter how much she tried to explain it, he didn't understand that people could also cry when they were happy. "No, sweetie. I couldn't be happier than I am right now."

Seth swallowed at those words that meant so much to him. He still couldn't believe, after all he'd been through, that he had her in his life, any more than he could believe this tiny little being had come from something like him.

His son was perfect in every way from the top of his bald head that was dusted with auburn hair, to his topaz eyes, to the tiniest toes Seth had ever seen.

And he would never deny him. No more than he could deny Lydia anything she asked of him.

Even the world.

But what scared him was how close he'd come to not having any of this. How many times he'd lain himself down in defeat.

Had he not tried that one last time . . . had he not found the courage he needed when he thought he had none at all . . .

He didn't want to think about that. He couldn't. Because in the end, this one perfect moment was worth every bit of pain he'd been dealt.

For this life, he would gladly sell his soul. And honestly he had.

Lydia owned it and he was ever, eternally, hers.

Do you love fiction with a supernatural twist?

Want the chance to hear news about your favourite
authors (and the chance to win free books)?

Keri Arthur
S. G. Browne
P.C. Cast
Christine Feehan
Jacquelyn Frank
Larissa Ione
Darynda Jones
Sherrilyn Kenyon
Jackie Kessler
Jayne Ann Krentz and Jayne Castle
Martin Millar
Kat Richardson
J.R. Ward
David Wellington
Laura Wright

Then visit the Piatkus website and blog
www.piatkus.co.uk | www.piatkusbooks.net

And follow us on Facebook and Twitter
www.facebook.com/piatkusfiction | www.twitter.com/piatkusbooks

piatkus